"Your

Anna. She wasn't sure she liked the name. She simply didn't feel any affinity for it, any sense of ownership. Her heart started to pound.

"No one seems to know who you are," the doctor said almost conversationally. "You didn't have much ID when they brought you in, just an engraved locket with that name on it."

"How long have I been here?" Even her voice seemed unfamiliar.

"Since late yesterday afternoon."

"What's wrong with me? Why don't I remember anything?" she cried.

"You took quite a bump on the head, and although the tests showed no real damage, temporary memory loss isn't that unusual in this kind of situation. Just relax, and things will probably start coming back to you." The doctor smiled, although he was watching her intently. "The baby doesn't seem to have suffered at all."

"Baby?" she whispered. *What baby? Where?* She looked around her at the sterile, empty room. "I have a baby?"

"You're eight weeks pregnant, Anna." His watchful eyes continued to study her.

Anna. Pregnant. Pregnant Anna.

ABOUT THE AUTHOR

Tara Taylor Quinn says "My husband, Kevin, and our twelve-year-old college-junior daughter, Rachel, are my first loves; my writing is my second."

Father: Unknown is Tara's eighth book for Harlequin Superromance, and she's added another challenge to her life, as well—serving as regional director for the Romance Writers of America.

"Time at home is minimal these days," she says, "much to the chagrin of my four-pound poodle, Quinn (yes, there's significance in that name!). Thankfully, he's too much of a baby to hold a grudge. I'm not always so lucky with our eleven-year-old Sheltie, who's suddenly decided that if I'm not going to use my bed, she will."

Despite Tara's current busy schedule, she's working on a new Superromance novel, which will be published in December of this year. Tara loves to hear from readers. You can reach her at: P.O. Box 15065, Scottsdale, Arizona 85267-5065 or online at http://www.inficad.com/~ttquinn.

Books by Tara Taylor Quinn

HARLEQUIN SUPERROMANCE

Don't miss any of our special offers. Write to us at the following address for information on our newest releases.
Harlequin Reader Service
U.S.: 3010 Walden Ave., P.O. Box 1325, Buffalo, NY 14269
Canadian: P.O. Box 609, Fort Erie, Ont. L2A 5X3

FATHER: UNKNOWN
Tara Taylor Quinn

Harlequin Books

TORONTO • NEW YORK • LONDON
AMSTERDAM • PARIS • SYDNEY • HAMBURG
STOCKHOLM • ATHENS • TOKYO • MILAN
MADRID • WARSAW • BUDAPEST • AUCKLAND

ISBN 0-373-70784-3

FATHER: UNKNOWN

For Scott and Carleen Gumser. July 1, 1997. I was furiously typing the last pages of this book, thinking of a cruise ship in the Virgin Islands, waiting for the phone to ring so I would know "you did." I slept well that night!

For Chum. I hope there are many more memories waiting to be found, and that they're easier ones.

And for Kevin. You are my magic.

CHAPTER ONE

"YOUR NAME IS ANNA."

Anna. She wasn't sure she liked the name. Certainly didn't feel any affinity to it, any sense of ownership. Her heart started to pound.

"No one seems to know who you are," the doctor said almost conversationally. "You didn't have ID on you when they brought you in, just a locket around your neck engraved with that name. We were hoping you could tell us more."

Terror threatening to consume her, she shook her head. "Where am I?" Even her voice was unfamiliar, husky.

She tried not to flinch as he lifted her eyelids and shone his light into her eyes. "You're on the fifth floor of Madison General Hospital in New York City. I'm Dr. Gordon, a neurologist and your attending physician." The tall, thin white-coated man spoke as if reassuring a child.

New York.

"What day is it?"

"Tuesday. The first of July."

July. Summer.

"How long have I been here?"

"Since late yesterday afternoon."

She digested that piece of information slowly, but the cotton wool surrounding her mind remained alarmingly intact. Time meant nothing to her, either, it seemed. "What's wrong with me? Why don't I remember anything?" she cried.

"You took quite a bump on the head, and though the tests show no real damage, temporary memory loss isn't that unusual in this type of situation. If you'll just relax, things will probably start coming back to you almost immediately. In a few days you should be just fine," the doctor said with a smile, although he was watching her intently. "The baby doesn't seem to have suffered at all."

"Baby?" she whispered. *What baby? Where?* She looked around her at the sterile empty room. "I have a baby?"

"You're eight weeks pregnant, Anna," he said, feeling her pulse.

His watchful eyes continued to study her.

Anna. Pregnant. Pregnant Anna.

"None of this sounds familiar?" the doctor asked kindly.

She shook her head, and her fear increased when she saw the disappointment cross his face. Both he and the nurse who'd been in her room when she awoke had been kind to her. She clung to that kindness as Dr. Gordon's words failed to jar any memory from her at all.

"Well, just to be certain that there wasn't more damage than at first appeared, I'm going to write an order for more tests this afternoon. But don't worry,

Anna, traumatic memory loss isn't uncommon. Chances are your memory will return shortly.''

And what if it doesn't?

Dr. Gordon continued to explain her condition, speaking of a subway crash she had no recollection of, the trauma to her brain, the news bulletins being issued statewide in an attempt to reach anyone who knew her. But his words were like background noise, an irritation, nearly drowned out by the voice in her head aimlessly repeating the only words that meant anything to her—and yet meant, frighteningly, nothing at all. *Anna. Pregnant.*

She didn't feel like an Anna. She ran her hand along the flatness of her belly beneath the stark white hospital sheet. And she certainly didn't feel pregnant.

A baby. Surely the doctor was wrong. She'd remember something as important as a baby growing inside of her. She'd remember the man who'd helped put it there. Wouldn't she? Her chest constricted, making it difficult to breathe.

"Am I crazy, Doctor?"

"No! Of course not." He patted her foot beneath the covers. "The mind has its own ways of dealing with shock. Yours is merely doing its job, protecting you to get you through a hellish ordeal. You were one of the lucky ones, coming out of the crash virtually unscathed."

Anna nodded.

"Do you have any more questions?"

Of course she did. A million of them. But only

one that mattered. And apparently one he couldn't answer. *Who am I?*

She shook her head again, harder. And then wished she hadn't as a wave of dizziness washed over her. She did have another question. *What's going to happen to me?* But she didn't ask it. She couldn't. Not yet. She was too afraid of the answer.

"We'll talk later," the doctor said, smiling down at her. "Right now you just need to rest—and eat. You're far too thin."

Was she? Tears flooded Anna's eyes as she realized the doctor knew her body better than she did. Did she have freckles? Birthmarks he knew about and she didn't? Scars she wouldn't know the history of? What color were her eyes? Was there anyone she knew on the subway with her?

"Do you have a mirror?" she asked, hoping he couldn't hear the panic in her voice. How did you live in a stranger's body, in a stranger's mind?

"I'll have a nurse bring one in." Dr. Gordon turned away, almost as if he was finding this incredibly horrible situation as difficult as she was. "You probably have your own obstetrician, but I'm going to send Dr. Amy Litton in to see you later today to talk to you about vitamins and prenatal care. She was called in yesterday when your condition was first discovered. In the meantime try to rest, Anna. There'll be plenty of time for questions tomorrow."

Tomorrow. Anna lay completely still after the doctor left, her heart pounding as his last word brought on another attack of sheer terror. Tomorrow.

How could she face tomorrow when she didn't even recognize today?

Dear God. What's to become of me? Slowly, concentrating, absorbing every sensation, she pulled her hands up the sides of her body and out from under the sheet she'd found tucked around her when she'd first awoken. Her skin was soft, her breasts firm, full. But she was bony, just like the doctor had said. Hadn't she had enough money to eat properly? And what about the baby? If there really was one, had she been taking care of it?

She reached for her hair with trembling fingers. A band at the back of her neck held it in place. So it was long. Long enough for a ponytail. Her fingers explored slowly. The strands weren't silky smooth as she somehow knew they usually were; she needed to wash it. Grabbing her ponytail, she pulled her hair around where she could see it. Blond.

She didn't know what she'd been expecting, but she didn't feel like a blonde any more than she felt like an Anna. Or an expectant mother.

Ceasing her exploration, Anna raised her fist to her mouth, stifling a sob, trying to remember something—anything. And drew a complete blank. What about her baby's father? Had he been on the subway with her? Was he lying in this very hospital, unidentified, as she was? Was he hurt? Or worse? Nausea assailed her.

What if her memory didn't come back as the doctor believed? How was she going to survive? How was she ever going to take care of herself when she didn't even know who she was? When she didn't know what she could do. If she was trained for anything. Where she came from. If she had anyone...or not.

She's pregnant. She has no memory. What's she going to do next? Anna suddenly stepped outside the situation, giving her problems to another woman, an imaginary unthreatening character over whom she had complete control. Something that felt strangely natural. All she had to do was decide what the woman was going to do next.

She's going to handle it. That's what. Somehow.

Deserting the imaginary woman, Anna slid her arms back beneath the sheet and closed her eyes. Her head hurt. A concussion, the doctor had said. A subway crash. She was lucky. Lucky. Trapped in a stranger's body, she didn't feel lucky at all.

WEEKDAY-EVENING newscaster Jason Whitaker choked on his coffee, barely setting the cup down before grabbing the remote control on the table beside him and jamming his thumb down on the rewind button. He'd been watching a clip that was scheduled for the six-o'clock news, reviewing the copy that went along with it. Thirty-seven people injured, two dead, one woman suffering from amnesia. And suddenly Anna's face had been there, transposing itself over the sketch of the woman he was going to be talking about.

Leaning forward in the chair in his dressing room, he watched the screen intently. It couldn't be... He'd just had one too many late nights. He should have gone straight home after the eleven-o'clock show last night, instead of stopping at the piano bar around the corner. He should have gone to bed at a decent hour for once, gotten some sleep—except that he'd known he wouldn't sleep. He'd have lain there in the bed he'd once shared with Anna, albeit in another city, and tear himself up wondering who she was lying with these days. Which was why he'd gone to the bar, instead.

The VCR clicked and Jason jabbed the start button. He was so tired he was seeing Anna everywhere. Even in the poor amnesiac from yesterday's subway crash. The woman shared her first name. Period. He'd better get a grip. Quickly. He hadn't seen Anna in months. It was time to be over her. To move on. To find a woman who wanted him. To find one *he* wanted.

He sat through the first part of the clip again, this time hardly registering the impossibly twisted subway train, the flattened steel of the maintenance vehicle it had collided with, the battered and broken wall that had ended the train's uncontrolled flight. Frightened people poured out of doors that had had to be forced open, some dragging bodies, others trampling over them. Emergency vehicles, police authorities, medical personnel scrambled on the screen. Tearful faces telling of panic, of despair, filled the background.

And then there she was again. Jason froze the frame. The vacant look in her eyes slammed into him, knocking the breath out of his lungs. He shook his head, trying to clear his vision, but she was still there. Not exactly as he remembered her, and yet there was no doubt that the Anna he was supposed to be reporting on was none other than the woman he'd left behind in California three months before—the woman who'd refused his offer of marriage. What was she doing in New York?

His blood pumped feverishly. Had she realized she couldn't live without him, after all? Had she come to her senses? Was she here to beg him to take her back?

The images from the clip suddenly crystallized. The tragic subway crash, the injured, the amnesia victim no one had claimed, the plea for anyone who knew the woman to contact Dr. Thomas Gordon at Madison General.

Oh, my God. The crash. Anna had been in the crash.

Blood running cold, he reached for the phone, dialing the number on the monitor in front of him.

"Dr. Thomas Gordon please." His words were clipped, and the pencil he'd picked up tapped furiously on the table.

"Who's calling, please?"

"Jason Whitaker, Channel Sixteen News." He used his position unabashedly. Anna had obviously suffered some kind of head injury. He had to know how bad it was. What else she'd suffered.

"One moment, sir."

The wait was endless. Jason was tempted to drop the phone and head immediately for Madison General. But with the Friday-afternoon New York City traffic, his chance of getting his answers any more quickly that way were nil.

"This is Tom Gordon."

"Jason Whitaker, Channel Sixteen News, Dr. Gordon. What can you tell me about your amnesia victim?"

"We sent a report to—"

"What's her current condition?" he said, cutting the doctor off. He knew about the report. He'd read and reread it. It didn't tell him what he needed to know.

"Relatively unchanged." The doctor sounded hesitant, and Jason couldn't really blame the man for taking him for an overzealous reporter looking for a scoop.

Throwing the pencil down on the table, taking a deep breath, he stared again at the monitor. "I think I may know her, Doc."

"You think you may? You aren't sure?"

"All right," Jason sighed, still not believing what his eyes insisted was true. "I do know her. Her name's Anna Hayden."

"You know her family? Where she comes from? Where she lives?" Suddenly the doctor was interviewing *him.*

"I know her family, where she comes from. I'm not sure where she's living," Jason said, still studying the vacant eyes of the pencil drawing on the television screen, the blurry photo beside it of the same woman, pale and sleeping. "I haven't seen or heard from her since I moved here three months ago."

"So she's not from New York?" the doctor asked, as if that explained something.

Jason shook his head, thinking of the little beach house Anna had shared with her sisters, those long-ago nights he and she had spent making love under the stars, the sound of the surf drowning out their cries....

"Mr. Whitaker?" The doctor's voice brought him firmly back to the present.

"She was born and raised in Oxnard, California, just north of LA. How bad is she, Doctor?"

"She's a very lucky lady, actually. A concussion, some minor contusions. Nothing that won't quickly heal. If she has someplace to go, I'll probably release her tomorrow."

Thank God. Jason expelled his breath, the knot in his stomach loosening a little.

"And her memory loss?"

"How well do you know Anna, Mr. Whitaker?"

Not nearly as well as I thought. "Very," he said. "And, please, call me Jason."

"Is there someone we can contact? Any family?"

"She has a sister. And parents, though I'm not even sure they're in the States," Jason said, suddenly afraid again. "Why? What's wrong with her, Doc?"

"I'm sorry, but I can only disclose the particulars of her case to a family member."

Frustrated, frightened and strangely hopeful as he considered Anna's presence in New York, Jason dropped the receiver back into the cradle after giving the doctor the information he needed. All he could do now was wait. And pray that Abby would call him.

He'd give her ten minutes, and then he was going to the hospital to get his information from Anna herself if he had to. He'd been in love with her for more than two years. He had a right to know whatever the doctor wasn't telling him.

And if she was alone in New York, she was going to need a friend.

ABIGALE HAYDEN gave a start, her gaze racing to the phone hanging on the wall in the kitchen of her beach cottage, daring to hope, even after two months of silence, that the caller would be Anna.

Hope dropped like lead in her stomach when the caller turned out to be male. How could Anna bear not to call? She had to be suffering the same agony at their separation that Abby was.

"Is this Abby Hayden?"

"Yes." Impatiently Abby waited for the telephone solicitor to recite his spiel so she could tell him she wasn't interested.

"I'm Dr. Thomas Gordon, a neurologist at Madison General Hospital in New York."

No, God. Please. No. She'd only assumed Anna had gone to New York. She could be wrong. She had to be wrong.

"Ms. Hayden? Are you there?"

"Yes."

"I have your sister, Anna, here, Ms. Hayden. She was on the subway that derailed…"

No! She couldn't lose Anna, too. She just couldn't. She still couldn't believe Audrey was gone, still had days when she just plain couldn't cope. If she lost Anna...

"...only minor bruises and contusions—"

"She's okay?" Abby interrupted frantically as the doctor's words started to register again. *God, please. Just let her be okay.*

"All things considered, she's a very lucky woman."

Abby's stomach clenched even more. "All things considered?" she asked, not liking the hesitancy she heard in the doctor's voice.

"Other than the memory loss I just told you about."

"Memory loss." Abby forced herself to pay attention. The doctor must think her an idiot.

"I'm afraid her amnesia is total at this point, Ms. Hayden. She didn't even know her own name."

"It's Anna." Abby blurted inanely, trying to absorb all the ramifications of the doctor's news through a fog of numbness. Anna couldn't remember her? Couldn't remember *them?* Frightened, Abby had never felt so adrift in her life.

The doctor told her more about Anna's condition; the slight concussion she'd suffered, her overall good health, her confusion. He told her about the engraved locket she'd been wearing that had been the only clue to her name.

"We all three have them," Abby said, ridiculously comforted by the fact that Anna was still wearing hers.

"Three?" Dr. Gordon asked.

"My two sisters and I," Abby said with barely a

pause. "Is Anna going to be all right, Doctor? Will her memory return?" It had to return. Abby would sit with Anna every day, work with her around the clock, fill in every memory of every moment they'd ever lived if that was what it took to get her back.

"I expect it to return any time now, or at least portions of it, with the remainder following in bits and pieces. The blow she sustained wasn't particularly severe. I don't foresee any permanent damage."

"Thank God." Abby sank to the floor.

"I'd actually expected her to begin remembering already," the doctor continued, that hesitancy in his voice again. "The fact that she hasn't leads me to wonder if we're dealing with more than just shock here."

"Like what?" The fear was back stronger than ever.

"Ms. Hayden, has your sister suffered any emotional trauma lately? Anything from which she might want to escape?"

Abby almost laughed, except that she suspected the doctor would hear the hysteria in her voice. "Our sister, Audrey, died a little over a year ago."

"I'm sorry."

Abby blinked back tears when she heard the sincerity in Dr. Gordon's voice. "Me, too." She paused, took a deep breath, pushed away memories of that horrible day. "Anna handled it all pretty well, considering," she said. And then had to be honest. "Though Jason would probably know that better than I. He's probably the one you should be talking to.''

''Jason Whitaker?''

''You know him?'' Abby's heart rate sped up. Had she been right, then? Was Jason there with Anna now? Had the two of them managed to undo the damage Abby had done?

''I haven't actually met him. He called in answer to a story we'd put out asking for information.''

''Did he say if he'd seen her recently?'' Abby held her breath.

''To the contrary—he hadn't even known she was in New York. Said he hadn't heard from her in more than three months.''

Oh, God.

''Do you have any idea what she's doing in New York?'' the doctor asked gently. ''Does she have a home here?''

Tears sprang to Abby's eyes once again, and again she forced them back. ''I don't know.'' It was one of the hardest things she'd ever had to admit. ''She called a meeting in my father's office about two months ago to tell us—my parents and me— that she was going away for a year. She said she had to prove to herself that she could get by without us to lean on. She wouldn't tell us where she was headed, and she said she wouldn't be phoning us. She made us promise we wouldn't follow or try to find her.''

''And you haven't heard from her since?''

Not in fifty-nine hellish days. ''No.''

''Do you know if she went alone?''

"No. But I'd hoped she went to Jason."

"Apparently not."

"So what's she doing in New York?" Abby cried, more to herself than to Anna's doctor.

"That seems to be one of many things locked away in your sister's mind at the moment."

"There's more?" Abby asked.

"Anna's about eight weeks pregnant."

The fog swirled around Abby, cloaking her, making it nearly impossible for her to form coherent thoughts. Anna, pregnant? And Abby hadn't known? Hadn't felt...something? There had to be a mistake.

"How?" she asked, slowly getting to her feet.

The doctor coughed. "In the usual way, I suppose."

"Who's the father?"

"I was hoping you could shed some light on that."

Abby shook her head. She could think of no one. Only Jason. It had always been only Jason. And if he hadn't seen Anna...

"...so, I'd like to fax you some information on amnesia, various theories and treatments, if you have someplace you can receive a fax..."

Abby tuned in again in time to rattle off the fax number at the shop. And to inform the doctor, when he asked, that her parents were vacationing abroad, but that she'd leave word immediately for them to call her. Not that she expected much support from them once they learned Anna wasn't in any real danger.

"What happens next?" Abby asked, already looking through a drawer in the kitchen for the number of their travel agent.

"That, in part, depends on Anna. And on you, too." He paused, took a breath. "My recommendation is that you tell Anna nothing, let her remember on her own—particularly because we don't know what aspects of her life she might be trying to escape. But I want you to read the information I'm sending before you make any decisions."

Abby nodded, still looking for the number. "Is Jason with her?" she asked.

"Not yet," Dr. Gordon said. "I wasn't at liberty to apprise him of Anna's particulars without first checking with her family. Especially in a case like this when Anna can't possibly vouch for him herself."

"I'd trust Jason Whitaker with my life, Doctor," Abby answered immediately, almost defensively. "And Anna's, too." He'd been their strength after Audrey died—and so much more. He'd taught them to laugh again.

"Would you like me to call him?" the doctor asked.

"No." Abby stopped rummaging through the drawer. "I'll do it myself." The phone call wouldn't be easy, but she owed it to Jason. She owed him something else, as well, and knew, suddenly, that she'd just been handed a way to right the terrible wrong she'd done Anna and Jason. If she was strong enough.

"Dr. Gordon?" she said quickly, before she lost her courage.

"Yes?"

"As long as Jason's there and I'm not, and assuming he's willing, he's in charge." If Abby hadn't interfered, the right would have been his, anyway. He'd have been Anna's husband by now.

"You're sure?"

She'd never been less sure of anything in her life. "Any choices that have to be made come from him," she said firmly. And then, more for herself than for the doctor, she added, "I'll abide by whatever decisions he makes." With her eyes squeezed tight against escaping tears, she prayed to God that Jason would include her every step of the way.

Though, with her history of unanswered prayers, that didn't seem likely.

NINE AND A HALF MINUTES after he'd hung up from Dr. Gordon, Jason's telephone rang.

He grabbed the receiver. "Abby?"

"Jason?" Anna's sister was distraught, as he'd known she'd be. The amazing thing was she'd called him.

"I can't believe this is happening," she said, hardly a trace of the old Abby in her subdued tone. "Dr. Gordon says you haven't seen her?"

"Only on a piece of footage. I was waiting to hear from you," Jason said, trying to gauge her mood—their relationship. "What else did Dr. Gordon say?"

"He said Anna's fine other than the amnesia,"

she told him. "He needs to know if there are any emotional traumas she might be trying to block." Abby paused. "I told him you would probably know that better than I."

He could hear the hurt in her tone, mingling with her worry. Not that he blamed her. He'd accused her of some pretty nasty things before leaving California. And she *did* have a tendency to control things, always thinking she knew best for everybody, but it hadn't really been her fault that Anna had chosen to stay with her only living triplet, instead of moving across the country with him.

"Did you tell him about Audrey?" Jason asked gently. He loved Abby like a sister. He was sorry he'd hurt her, sorry, too, that Anna's love for him had hurt her.

"Briefly." She paused, then said in a rush, "But then I discovered that I really don't know how Anna dealt with all that. I mean, she never talked to me about it very much." Another pause. "Which is why I told Dr. Gordon he was probably better off speaking with you." Her last words, an admission that had to have cost her plenty, were almost a whisper.

"She never talked to me much about it, either, Abby," he said, feeling compelled to ease her obvious suffering. "You know Anna, she's always been the type who keeps her pain to herself."

A heavy silence hung on the line. Jason would have moved mountains to turn back time, to erase that last scene with Abby. He'd missed her. He'd missed them all.

"Will you talk to him, Jason? Please?" she finally asked.

"Sure. Of course. You know I will."

Another silence and then, tentatively, "So she hasn't been with you these past two months?" It sounded as if she was fighting the tears another person would have cried. Which was so like Abby. Always intent on remaining in control.

"I wish," he said. And then the significance of her question hit him. "You don't know where she's been? She's been away from home for two months?"

"I hoped she was with you." Abby lost her battle with the tears.

"I haven't heard from her since I left California. What's going on, Abby?"

"I don't know," she whispered, sniffing. He could picture her standing in the kitchen of the beach house, scrubbing at her nose with a tissue, her long blond hair falling around her shoulders. "She called a meeting with me and the folks just a few weeks after you left, said she was going away for a year—had to know whether or not she could make it on her own." Abby paused, taking a deep breath, and then continued, "She made us promise not to follow her or contact her until the year was up, at which time she promised to come home—at least for a visit."

His own disappointment was crushing. She'd been gone for two months. She hadn't just left home, just arrived in New York. She'd had two months to contact him. And she hadn't.

"What did I do, Jason? Why won't she talk to me anymore?" Abby cried.

"I don't think it's just you, Abby," he said, glancing again at the vacant stare on the sketch still frozen on his television monitor. "Audrey's death brought home to Anna that the three of you were three separate beings, not one whole as she'd always thought. Maybe she just needs to find out who her part of the threesome really is."

He hoped so. God he hoped so. Because until Anna truly believed she could survive apart from her identical sisters, she'd never be able to live her own life, to love.

"Maybe." Abby didn't sound convinced. And Jason had to admit that his reasoning was probably just wishful thinking.

"How soon are you flying out?" Jason asked, a little surprised she wasn't already on her way. Abby had pulled her sisters through every crisis in their lives.

"I'm going to reserve a flight for tomorrow, but I'll wait to hear from you before I buy the ticket. I won't come if Anna doesn't want me there."

Shocked, Jason said, "It sounds to me like she's not going to know what she wants." What the hell was going on?

"You'll call me as soon as you see her? As soon as you talk to Dr. Gordon?"

"Of course."

"Jason?" her voice was tentative again, but warmer. "You really haven't seen her since you left here?" she asked. "Not even once?"

"No."

"Oh."

"I'll call you later," he said, anxious to get to the hospital, to find out just what he was dealing with.

"Jason?" She hesitated. "I, uh, told Dr. Gordon that you're in charge." Another hesitation when Jason had no idea what to say. "For as long as you want to be," she finished.

Jason had waited too long for Abby to abdicate a single decision in Anna's life to quarrel over the fact that she was doing so three months too late. "Fine."

"You'll be there for her, won't you, Jason? No matter what you find?"

Her query was odd enough to send a fresh wave of apprehension through him. Was Anna's amnesia more serious than he thought? Was it permanent?

"As long as she needs me," he said, wondering if she ever really had. The Hayden sisters had grown up in their own little cocoon, buffered from the world by the unusual bond they shared, a bond made stronger by having been born to two people who were wonderful providers but terrible parents. He'd been a fool to think he could ever penetrate that cocoon, be a part of their world. But then, when it came to relationships, he'd always been something of a fool.

CHAPTER TWO

ANNA WANTED OUT. It was bad enough being mentally trapped, but to be stuck in a hospital room, too, was driving her insane. After another nap, a huge lunch and a visit from Dr. Litton, she was ready to get on with things. Whatever they were.

As she lay in bed, her restlessness grew. She needed to take a long walk, to smell the breeze. To do something.

But fear kept her paralyzed. What would she do? Where would she go? What clothes was she going to wear to get there? She could hardly wander around New York City dressed in a hospital gown. Her nurse had told her not to worry, that the city was assuming full liability; she'd have money for new clothes, might even end up a rich woman when all was said and done. Her nurse didn't seem to understand that money was the least of Anna's worries at the moment.

She'd had the second set of tests Dr. Gordon ordered, but she hadn't seen him again since she'd awoken that morning. Was it a bad sign that so many hours had passed and she still hadn't remembered a single thing? She was trying to relax like he'd said, but was beginning to suspect it was time to panic.

What happened to people like her? Were they institutionalized? Locked away until their only reality was the walls around them? If so, she'd rather have died in the subway crash.

Her gaze darted desperately about the small room—and alighted on the pamphlets Dr. Litton had left for her to read. The authorities couldn't put her away. At least not anytime soon. She was going to have a baby.

Picking up one of the pamphlets, Anna's panic eased just a bit. She liked Dr. Litton. Whether or not she ever remembered seeing another obstetrician, she wanted Dr. Litton to help her bring this baby into the world.

Baby. She was going to have a baby. Sometime around the middle of January.

As crazy as it seemed, Anna was glad.

DR. GORDON HAD a gentle bearing that bespoke calm, as well as confidence. Jason liked the middle-aged man immediately. Sitting in the doctor's office at Madison General, he listened intently while Dr. Gordon described Anna's condition.

"Her amnesia is a direct result of a blow to the lower left portion of her cranium. As the brain doesn't appear to be anything more than superficially bruised, I must wonder if perhaps her subconscious has used the impact as an opportunity to escape something that came before the crash," he said, joining Jason on the couch opposite his desk.

"You mean, something she saw just before the accident, something like that?" Jason asked.

"Possibly." The doctor's clasped hands lay across his stomach. "But I would expect the memory loss to cover just those few minutes if that were the case."

"Are you saying there's more to her condition than just the crash?"

"I believe she might be suffering from a posttraumatic stress form of amnesia, sometimes called hysterical amnesia."

Jason's blood ran cold. Was the doctor trying to tell him Anna's condition was permanent? That she was mentally ill?

"Which means what?" he asked. They'd handle it. Whatever it was, they'd handle it together. His right leg started to move up and down rapidly, the motion barely discernible, keeping time with his thoughts.

"Simply that she was suffering from an emotional crisis that was more than she believed she could bear. When she hit her head, lost consciousness, her subconscious grabbed the opportunity to escape."

"Permanently?"

"Most likely not," Dr. Gordon said. "When her subconscious believes she can handle whatever it is she's trying to escape from, her memory will return. Though probably not all at once."

Jason stared silently at the doctor, trying desperately to grasp the big picture. He had so many questions vying for attention, he couldn't settle on a single one of them.

"This reaction is really quite healthy in one sense," Dr. Gordon said, as if he knew Jason needed a little time to arrange his thoughts. "Rather than having a breakdown or falling prey to various other stress-induced mental and physical disorders, Anna is simply taking a vacation, gaining herself a little time to shore up the defenses necessary to handle whatever it is that's bothering her."

Jason's heart faltered as he realized the extent of the pain Anna must have been in to react like this. "How long do you think it's going to take?"

Shrugging, Dr. Gordon sat forward, steepling his fingers in front of him. "That's entirely up to Anna." He looked directly at Jason, his expression serious. "Her sister tells me you might be able to shed some light on whatever it is Anna's running from."

"Abby told you about Audrey?"

"Only that she died last year."

"Did she tell you the three of them were identical triplets?"

"No!" The doctor frowned. "But that explains a lot. The premature death of a sibling—only twenty-seven, Abby told me—is hard enough to cope with, but the loss of an identical sibling..."

Jason thought of that time, the horror. Hell, he'd been practically living at the beach house, ready to ask Anna to marry him, when their world had exploded around them.

"Audrey didn't just die, Doctor, she was murdered," he said, his throat dry. An entire year had passed—and the pain was still as fresh as if the murder had happened yesterday.

The doctor moved to the seat behind his desk, grabbing a pad of paper. "What happened?"

Jason shrugged. "No one knows for sure. After months of investigation the police determined that the whole thing was the result of an attempted assault that Audrey resisted."

"You say that as if you don't agree." Dr. Gordon looked up.

"I have no reason to doubt them, except that Audrey wasn't the type to resist…anything. She was the baby of the threesome and always seemed to take the easiest route."

"Did Anna accept the police explanation?"

Again Jason shrugged. "Let's just say she never expressed any disagreement with it. But then Anna has always kept her thoughts to herself. Comes from being the middle triplet I guess." His leg continued to vibrate, marking time.

"What about the girls' parents? Abby said this afternoon that they're in Italy. Do they travel a lot or were they around at the time of Audrey's murder?"

"They were around, as much as they ever are. The Haydens love their daughters, but they make much better entrepreneurs than they do—or ever did—parents." Jason thought of the handsome older couple, of how little he knew them, considering all the time he'd spent at their daughters' beach house the past couple of years. "The triplets weren't planned," he told the doctor. "I've pretty much figured out that practically from the stage they were in diapers, Abby stepped in to fill the void their parents' frequent absences left in the girls' lives. She's always watched out for them, made their business her business, bossed them around.'' He studied the diamond pattern in Dr. Gordon's tie. ''But she's also, in all the years I've known them, put their needs before her own.''

Dr. Gordon stopped writing and laid down his pen. ''And yet Abby tells me that she hasn't seen or heard from her sister in over two months. From what you describe, this in itself is highly unusual.''

''It is. I can hardly believe it.'' Standing, Jason paced slowly around the couch. ''In all the time I've known Anna, she's never made a move without discussing it with Abby first.'' He shook his head. ''I actually thought Anna's leaving was a good sign when Abby told me about it,'' he admitted. ''I hoped it meant that Anna was finally beginning to believe she's a person in her own right, not just a third of a whole.''

''Seems logical.'' The doctor nodded. ''Or at least that Anna was ready to find out one way or the other. According to her sister, Anna said she was leaving to prove to herself that she could handle life on her own—apart from her family.''

Jason stopped pacing and placed his hands on the back of the couch. ''Do you think this could be what's behind her amnesia? Is she maybe allowing herself a respite from the compulsion to return to California, time to find out who she is apart from Abby?''

"I suppose it's possible," Dr. Gordon said, frowning again. "She might even have been at war with herself—unable to make it on her own, unable to cope with *not* being able to make it alone."

"You don't sound convinced."

The doctor fixed Jason with an intent look and asked, "Just what is your relationship with Anna?"

Jason resumed his pacing. With the past three months uppermost in his mind—that last terrible scene with Anna still haunting him—he wasn't sure how to answer.

"We're friends," he said finally, stopping once again behind the couch and clutching the frame.

"You said when you called earlier that you haven't seen her since you left California, that you didn't know she was in New York?" Dr. Gordon continued to probe.

"That's correct," Jason admitted.

"Did her sister say anything to you about anyone else in Anna's life? Someone she may have been seeing? Either before she left home or just after?"

Jason shook his head. "No one's heard from her in two months. Why?" he asked, although judging by the concern in the doctor's face, he was pretty sure he didn't want to know. Had Anna said someone's name in her sleep? Someone none of them knew?

"She's pregnant."

Jason's knuckles turned white as he gripped the back of the couch. He'd heard wrong. He thought the doctor had said Anna was pregnant.

"Under the circumstances I can't help but wonder..." Dr. Gordon's words were muted by the roaring in Jason's ears. "...perhaps Anna's pregnancy is what she's hiding from. At no more than two months, she can't have known very long herself..."

Two months pregnant. God. No.

"...entirely possible she's not ready to handle the circumstances behind the child's conception."

Conception. I haven't slept with her in over three months. Oh, God. No!

"You think she was raped?" Jason's voice was a rasp. *Please, God, not my precious Anna. Anything but that.*

"It's possible." Dr. Gordon shrugged. "But I don't think so. The amnesia appears to have affected only the personal portion of her memory, not the memory that controls basic needs. If she'd been raped, I would expect to see signs of fear for her physical self, even if she didn't understand why she felt those fears."

The back of Jason's neck ached. "So, what..." his words trailed away. He couldn't believe it. Anna was pregnant. With another man's child. The world had tilted on its axis and he had a feeling it wasn't ever going to right itself again.

Dr. Gordon stood up, coming around to lean one hip on the corner of his desk. "It's my belief that Anna's amnesia is emotionally based," he said. "That she's running from something. Perhaps she doesn't want the baby." He lifted a hand and let it drop back to his thigh. "Maybe the father is married, or maybe it's someone her family wouldn't approve of, or even someone who didn't want her."

None of which applied to Jason. He continued to grip the back of the couch, using it to hold himself upright. He thought he was going to puke. If, by some miracle, Anna's baby had been his, she'd have known she could come to him. She *would* have come to him simply because she would never have kept something like this from him.

The phone rang and Dr. Gordon excused himself, turning his back as he picked up the receiver and spoke quietly.

Jason continued to stand, still as a statue, his thoughts torturing him. Anna's family, her sister, would have been supportive if Anna was pregnant with his child. He'd been a part of them for so long he'd forgotten they weren't actually his family—until the day Anna had told him she wouldn't marry him, wouldn't move to New York with him. The day Anna had chosen Abby. Two days later Jason had hunted Abby down, hurling all his anguish, his pain at her.

But even that had been more like a brother furious with his sister than anything else.

Left to his thoughts as the doctor continued his low-voiced conversation, Jason faced the truth. Anna was no more than two months pregnant. He hadn't slept with her in more than three. Anna had been with someone else. Her baby wasn't his.

So what was wrong with the bastard? Why wasn't he here now, claiming her, claiming his child? Was he someone who, as Dr. Gordon suggested, would shock her family? Family was the one thing that mattered most to Anna—or at least Abby was. Anna truly didn't believe she could exist without Abby. He'd learned that the hard way. Had this other guy, too? Had Anna loved him and then sent him out of her life?

"Sorry about that," Dr. Gordon said, hanging up the phone. "My wife's pregnant with our first child at forty-one, and she's a nervous wreck." He shook his head. "We were all set to adopt, and my wife suddenly turns up pregnant. After more than ten years of trying."

Jason appreciated the doctor's attempt to lighten the moment, but he could barely manage a smile. He needed to throw something.

"You know, there's a remote possibility that Anna knew she was pregnant before she left home," Dr. Gordon said.

Jason remained silent, a raised eyebrow the only acknowledgment that he'd heard the other man.

"She could have left home to have the child in secret," the doctor continued. "She may have been planning to give the baby up for adoption without anyone ever knowing she'd had it. Hence her request for a year with no contact."

She'd left home only four weeks after he'd last seen her. Could the baby possibly be his, after all? Jason wondered. Had she taken their breakup to mean he wouldn't expect to know if he'd fathered a child? The thought wasn't pleasant.

"You said she's two months along. Could she be more? Say thirteen, fourteen weeks?"

Dr. Gordon shook his head. "I seriously doubt it. Judging by the baby's measurements from yesterday's ultrasound, eight weeks is just about max. Could be closer, in fact, to six or seven.''

''But you just said she may have known about the pregnancy before she left.''

The doctor shrugged. ''With early detection, women can sometimes know within days after conception,'' he said. ''Then again, she may have known only that she'd had unprotected intercourse at her fertile time.''

In that instant the vulnerable part of Jason that had somehow survived his childhood died. While he'd been making himself crazy with wanting Anna, she'd been making a baby with someone else. Hell, maybe there'd been someone else all along. Maybe that was why she wouldn't marry him. Maybe the unusual bond between Anna and Abby wasn't the problem at all—but rather, an excuse.

No. That didn't ring true. He knew that Anna would never have made love with another man while still sleeping with him. He knew, too, that her bond with Abby *had* been the biggest rift between them. Still, Jason couldn't escape one undeniable fact. Anna was pregnant and he wasn't the father.

She must have fallen head over heels in love with someone the second he left town. And if that was the case, he really had no one to blame but himself. He'd given her an ultimatum. And then he'd walked out on her.

Which was just what he wanted to do again.

Dr. Gordon's name suddenly came over the loudspeaker. ''I'm going to have to go,'' he said. ''If you don't mind, I'd like you to wait to visit Anna until I can go with you," he added, putting Anna's file back together.

Jason nodded, grateful for the reprieve.

"Can you meet me here this evening, say, around eight?"

Eight o'clock was right between shows. He could make it back. But he knew he'd have been there even if it wasn't convenient. "You think she might remember something when she sees me?" he asked, following the doctor out into the hall.

"It's possible," Tom Gordon said. "I think we need to be prepared for that eventuality. See you at eight," he called as he rounded the corner and was gone from sight.

Jason strode from the chilly hospital into the warm July sun, as if by leaving the building he could leave behind everything that waited for him there. Except that Anna was still in his heart, and he had to take that with him.

ABBY WAITED for his call. She had errands to run, some fabric to pick up for the shop, an order to deliver to the new kids' shop out by Beverly Center, but it all had to wait. When Jason heard what Dr. Gordon had to tell him, he was going to need to talk. Abby would have told him herself except she hadn't had that much courage. Hadn't been able to bring herself to hurt him again.

They hadn't parted well. And because of that last horrible scene, they'd both been awkward on the phone earlier. But he was family. By virtue of his love for her sister, his unending support to all of them when Audrey was killed the year before, he was family. Besides, as much as she hated the things he'd said to her that last day, the brutal accusations, she was grateful to him, too. If not for him, she probably never would have seen that she was ruining her sister's life with her controlling ways. When her sister had come to her telling her she was leaving, she'd have talked her into staying. Because she'd have been so sure that staying would have been best for Anna.

She wasn't sure about anything anymore. Except that Jason would call. Because of the baby. And she owed it to him to be there when he did. He was going to be devastated.

He'd been on her conscience for three long months. She'd never seen anyone as hurt, as bitter, as he'd been the day he'd stormed into the back of the shop. And he'd been right to accuse her of creating a rift between Anna and him.

She'd ruined his life. And probably Anna's, too. She'd never seen two people more in love, more suited to each other than Anna and Jason. And she'd been too selfish to free her only living triplet from *their* bond, to let Anna share an even closer bond with the man she loved. She'd been too blissfully blind to see that she had the power to hold Anna—or to let her go. She'd been so sure she and Anna were meant to live out their lives together, neither one making a decision without the other—almost as if she, Abby, had one part of their brain and Anna another. Audrey had had the third.

It had always been that way. The three of them

together, through thick and thin, grades and boy-friends, lost friends and forgotten birthdays. No one had ever told them it would ever be any different. They were a package deal, their fate sealed in their mother's womb.

The phone rang, and Abby jumped, knocking over a stool as she grabbed for the telephone hanging on the wall.

It was Jason. And doing worse than she'd feared.

"You've heard," Abby said. She was having trouble comprehending that Anna was pregnant without her knowing, without her sharing in Anna's elation, her excitement, her fears. Jason had to be feeling ten times worse.

"Who is he?"

Tears sprang to her eyes at the raw emotion in his voice. "I don't know. I was praying it was you."

"No chance."

"Oh, God."

Silence fell heavily on the line. Abby felt as if she was coming unglued. She could hardly concentrate, couldn't make sense out of the past six hours at all. Her sister had been a victim in a serious accident, had amnesia and was pregnant, and she'd known nothing about any of it. Shouldn't she have sensed Anna's need? *Shouldn't Anna have reached out to her?*

"Have you seen her?" she asked, unable to stand the silence any longer.

"No." The single syllable was racked with pain.

Abby was almost afraid to ask. "Are you going to see her?" Anna would be all right if Jason was there. She didn't know why she was so sure of that, but she was.

"Of course," he said, and Abby heaved a sigh of relief. "Dr. Gordon was called away in the middle of our meeting," Jason continued, "but he asked me to wait to see her until he can go with me."

He didn't sound like he objected to the delay all that much. "Does he expect something to happen when she sees you?"

"I don't think he knows what to expect," Jason said on a sigh. "This is Anna's show all the way."

"She loved you, Jason, with all her heart," Abby felt compelled to tell him.

"Right." His sarcastic tone cracked across the wire.

"Those weeks after you left were awful." Abby insisted. "I've never seen Anna like that, not even after Audrey died."

"Yeah, well, apparently she recovered."

Abby had to find a way to make this all better. There was no one in the world she loved more than Anna—but Jason came in a close second. She'd always wanted a big brother, had often fantasized as a child about having someone older and stronger to look after them.

"Maybe he was just a one-night stand," Abby said in a rush. "You know, someone she turned to in a fit of loneliness, pretending he was you."

"Maybe."

He wasn't buying it and she couldn't blame him. But neither could she imagine, in any way, shape or form, that Anna had fallen in love with another man.

Her sister was too besotted with Jason even to look at anyone else. Anna was the most steadfast person she'd ever known, and she'd given her heart completely to one man. She just wasn't the type to give it to another, not if she lived to be a hundred and never saw Jason again in her life. That was Anna. Though even Abby hadn't understood the depth of Anna's commitment—not until she'd seen what having to choose between conflicting commitments had done to her sister.

"What are you going to tell her?" Abby asked. She was almost afraid to hear the answer. Would Anna hate her when she heard about the part Abby had played in her life? If Anna had no memory of her love for her sister, Abby could well believe it.

"I don't know, yet," Jason said. "I suspect that's one of the things Dr. Gordon will go over before we see her."

He sounded tired and Abby's guilt grew.

"Call me, okay?"

"Yeah. You coming out?" he asked.

Abby shook her head, her tears finally brimming and falling down her face. "I don't know," she said. She wanted to—more than anything. But only if Anna and Jason both wanted her there. "I'll wait and see what happens tonight."

And she would. Wait right by the phone. She simply didn't know what else to do. Her entire life had consisted of taking care of her sisters, getting them out of scraps, Audrey mostly, guiding them, loving them when their parents weren't around to do it. But Audrey was dead. And Anna no longer remembered her. So what was left?

CHAPTER THREE

HE DID THE NEWS BROADCAST. He even gave the report on Anna. For all he knew, the father of her child was in the city somewhere, willing to claim her. Jason almost hoped another man *would* come forward—then he, Jason, would be free to walk away. But somehow, as he took a cab back to the hospital shortly before eight, he had a feeling that no matter what transpired, he wasn't going to be free from Anna Hayden for a very long time. Possibly never.

And in the meantime no one had reported her missing. She was all alone—and pregnant—in a strange city, thousands of miles from home. He couldn't walk away. He couldn't leave her lying there. But neither could he help wishing that the child she was carrying was his, that by some fluke her baby could really have been conceived fourteen weeks ago, instead of eight. That he actually had a right to be the one to care for her, to claim her.

The sick feeling increased as soon as he walked in the door of Dr. Gordon's office. There was nothing wrong with the room. Standard desk littered with charts, bland blue couch and matching armchairs, carpet, diplomas on the wall, and books. Lots of books. But Jason hated the room; he hated being there.

Hanging up the phone as Jason walked in, Dr. Gordon frowned. "That was the police," he said. "No one's come forward, yet."

Jason nodded, truly undecided whether this was good news or bad.

"Do you think she'll know me?" Jason asked the question that was uppermost in his mind. This wasn't how he'd pictured his reunion with Anna. In every single one of his fantasies, she not only knew who he was, but insisted she couldn't live without him.

The doctor leaned his hip on the corner of his desk. "It's possible she'll recognize you," he said. "But don't be surprised if she doesn't."

"Is she, you know, normal? Other than her memory, that is?" he asked quickly.

"Her intelligence hasn't been affected, if that's what you've been imagining," Dr. Gordon said, smiling. "Information is stored in many different areas of the brain. General learned information is separate from personal or emotional memories, for example. Apparently the only area in Anna's brain that's been affected is this last one," he said. "Which is, again, why I feel certain that she's suffering from hysterical amnesia."

At least somewhat relieved by the doctor's words, Jason asked, "So do we tell her who I am?"

The doctor gave Jason an assessing stare. "How recent is your personal history with her?"

"I'm that obvious?" Jason asked. It was impossible to feel embarrassed with this man.

"Not really," the doctor said. "But her pregnancy hit you hard."

Jason nodded. "I asked her to marry me a little over three months ago," he admitted. "She refused."

Dr. Gordon watched him for another moment and then got up to go sit behind his desk. "I'm sure there's more there, but I've heard enough to know that if she doesn't recognize you, we're going to have to proceed with caution." He pulled some printed material from a folder on top of his desk and handed it to Jason.

"I ran this off for you earlier," he said. "You're going to find that amnesia isn't treated like other mental illnesses. Some doctors are skeptical about its even being a valid diagnosis."

"They'd think Anna's faking it?" Jason asked.

The doctor shrugged.

"Do you think she is?"

"I'm certain she's not," Dr. Gordon said, leaning back in his chair. "But as you read, you'll find that even among the medical professionals who do recognize amnesia as a legitimate condition, there's a vast difference in beliefs when it comes to treatment."

Jason looked down at the pages the doctor had given him, and then back at Dr. Gordon. The man had instilled trust from the moment Jason had met him.

"Go on," he said.

"All right, I will give you my recommendations, but with the understanding that after you've done some reading, you call in other opinions if you feel the need."

"I'll fax the stuff to Abby tonight."

The doctor shook his head. "No need," he said. "I've already done it. I spoke to her again a little over an hour ago."

"And?"

"She agrees, though not enthusiastically, with my recommendation, but will abide by whatever you and Anna decide."

She'd said the same to Jason earlier, but until that minute he hadn't really believed she'd follow through on it. Abdicating decision making was so un-Abby-like Jason felt his world tilt just a little bit more. Maybe this was all just one hell of an alcohol-induced nightmare.

But he knew it wasn't. Anna lay in a hospital bed just floors away from him, their love not even a memory.

Jason set the papers down beside him. "So what do you recommend?"

"Assuming she doesn't recognize you, I'd say as little as possible. Because as certain as I am that this is temporary, I have to warn you that if you try to force Anna to listen to what her mind's not ready to deal with, you could very well send her into a permanent state of memory loss. If we knew for certain what she's trying to escape, we could just avoid those areas, but since we don't, the less said the better."

Recognizing the sense in the doctor's words, Jason nodded, but he didn't like what he was hearing. How could he see Anna, possibly spend time with her and act as though he hadn't spent the best two years of his life with her? "Can I tell her I know her at all?" he asked.

"Certainly," Dr. Gordon replied, steepling his fingers under his chin as he watched Jason. "Tell her you're an old friend of the family. Tell her she *has* family. Even tell her that, according to her sister, she's in New York on a sort of year's sabbatical from her life. She should know that she demanded her family leave her alone for a year. Anything to give her confidence in her own mental strength.

"What I wouldn't do," he continued, "is tell her anything emotionally threatening. I wouldn't tell her that she's one of a set of triplets, for instance, which means that it might very well be best to keep Anna and Abby apart for the time being. You said they're identical?"

"Completely," Jason said, nodding. Though *he'd* never had trouble telling them apart. By the time he'd met her sisters, he'd already been half in love with Anna. Their resemblance to each other had taken some getting used to, though; three gorgeous, blond-haired, brown-eyed beauties. But he'd never confused them. They were such different people, in spite of their physical sameness.

"Which means it would be impossible to keep Anna's multiple-birth status a secret if the two women met, and since being one of triplets is one of the things we suspect she's running from..."

Jason nodded, following the doctor's train of thought as the older man's words trailed off.

"I also wouldn't mention Audrey's murder or your own recent breakup," Dr. Gordon continued. "All these things combined are very likely a large part of what's paralyzing her."

"But there could be more," Jason said, thinking about what the doctor had already told him. "Something that happened in the past two months that we know nothing about. Something to do with the baby."

What hurt most of all was knowing Anna had been in New York, in trouble, and she hadn't called him. That, more than anything else, killed the hope he'd been harboring that she would one day come back to him.

"I suspect that Anna's suffering from not one huge trauma, but rather a combination of traumas—put together, they became too much for her. I'd say most definitely something in the past two months has contributed to her current condition."

Jason nodded numbly as he accepted the need to ride this thing out. To let Anna remember her life in her own time. "How soon can she leave here?" he asked.

"Tomorrow if she has a place to go. Physically there's no reason for her to stay in the hospital."

"She has a place." It didn't matter how stupid he knew it was, he couldn't have walked away from Anna if his life had depended on it.

Dr. Gordon stood up, accepting Jason's claim

without further question, as if he'd been expecting the response. "Are you ready to see her?"

As ready as he was going to get, Jason thought. But still... "There's no chance she's three months pregnant?" He felt compelled to try one more time.

Dr. Gordon shrugged, heading for the door. "Anything is possible," he said—but he didn't sound like he believed it. "Anna's underweight, which could make her baby small."

The doctor stopped, looking at Jason, one male to another. "You want my professional opinion?"

Jason looked away from the pity reflected in the other man's eyes. He was done fooling himself with false hopes, with dreams.

"Of course."

"She's eight weeks along."

Filled with apprehension, his stomach tied in knots, he followed the doctor from the room. After three months of being haunted by images of this moment, none of which were even remotely accurate, he was finally about to see the woman he loved again.

STROLLING DOWN the hallway for what seemed like the hundredth time, Anna studied everything around her. Surely something would spark a memory. A color, an emblem, a hairdo. Something must be familiar to her.

But nothing was. Except for the nurse who'd been caring for her most of the day. Anna smiled as the woman hurried past. Eileen. One of the three people Anna knew by name in the whole world. The other two were the doctors who'd visited her that day. Ready to climb the walls, instead of walking calmly beside them, she returned to her room and slipped back into bed, deciding it was more comfortable than the chair by the window. She knew, because she'd spent more time than she cared to think about in the chair that afternoon staring out into the summer sunshine, hoping to see someone or something she recognized, and then she'd remember.

There was no reason for her to remain in the hospital taking up a bed someone else might need. Physically she felt fine. Amazingly unaffected by the crash, considering the fact that she was two months pregnant.

But if she left the hospital, where would she go? How would she get there? What would she do once she arrived? Where would she get the money to survive? Especially if the city hadn't settled with the accident victims yet?

She started to shake when she came up with no answers. Because she had to do something. She could hardly raise her baby in a hospital room.

Nervously she reached for the chain around her neck, pulling the locket out from beneath her hospital gown. She'd kept the locket on all day because it had her name on the inside, but she didn't like wearing it. Though it appeared to be good quality gold, it had a very odd shape. Reaching up, she unclasped the chain, pulling it from around her neck, and suddenly felt better than she had in hours. Freer. She could no more explain the odd sensation than she could say who'd fathered her child, but she decided to leave the chain off.

She lay back against the mound of pillows, the locket clutched in her fist. She was going to have to find someplace safe to keep it. As much as she didn't want to wear it, she couldn't bear the thought of losing it.

Men's voices could be heard just down the hall, and Anna sat up straighter in anticipation. *Dr. Gordon.* When you only knew three people in the world, it was an event to see one of them. And if anyone could make this feeling of panic go away, Dr. Gordon could.

They came into the room together, Dr. Gordon and an incredibly handsome man. He was tall, well over six feet, with thick blond hair and blue, blue eyes. She could tell because they were trained right on her. As Dr. Gordon came forward, the stranger's eyes never left Anna, never even glanced around the room. A part of her was aware that she should be uncomfortable, maybe even offended by that piercing stare, but instead, all she wanted to do was stare right back. Her heart sped up in excitement.

"Anna, I've brought someone to meet you," Dr. Gordon said, ushering the stranger forward. "This is Jason Whitaker, a longtime friend of your family."

Her heart continued its rapid beat, but now it was in fear. *She didn't recognize him at all.* Her gaze flew to Dr. Gordon as her mind tumbled over itself, searching frantically for something that just wasn't there. Even faced with proof of her former existence, she couldn't recall any of it. Was this it, then? Was she trapped in this terrifying void forever?

"Hello, Anna." Her head jerked toward the stranger as he spoke. He had a wonderful voice. Just not one she'd ever heard before.

"Hello." She tried to act normally, but she could hear the panic in her voice.

"Anna—" Dr. Gordon started.

"It's okay, Anna," the man called Jason Whitaker interrupted. "Just try to relax."

And strangely, although he didn't sound the least bit relaxed himself, his words had some effect. The bands around her chest loosened enough for her to speak.

"But I don't know you," she said, staring at him, at his face, at his broad-shouldered physique. She'd never seen the man before in her life.

Her words hit him hard. Not only did he flinch, but she saw the quick flash of anguish in his eyes before he quickly recovered. "It's okay, honey," he said. "Dr. Gordon warned us this might happen."

He smiled at her and there was no doubt that that, at least, was genuine.

Suddenly the ramifications of the man's presence hit her and she sat straight up. "Us?" she asked. Dr. Gordon had introduced him as a friend of the family. Which meant she *had* a family. She clutched that one small piece of information for all she was worth.

"Who am I? Where are they?" she cried, looking around.

Jason glanced at the doctor and Anna's gaze followed. Filled with a sense of foreboding, she watched as the men came forward and flanked her bed. Jason reached for her hand, but pulled back before he made contact. She couldn't believe how much she'd wanted him to touch her.

"What is it? What's wrong?" she asked. Was her family dead? Had they been in the crash with her?

"You have a sister and parents living in Oxnard, California," Dr. Gordon finally said slowly.

A sister. Parents. The relief was so great it left her light-headed. She wasn't alone.

"Do they know...about me?" she asked. Were they on their way to see her? Take her home?

The doctor nodded. "Your sister does," he said. "Your parents are traveling in Europe and your sister's still trying to reach them."

A sister. Anna smiled. She was really glad to have a sister, someone she assumed would know her like no one else in the world could. Someone she could trust.

"What's her name?" she asked, looking from one man to the other.

"Abby." Jason's voice was odd, but Anna was too overwhelmed to do more than notice.

"Abby," she said, testing the name, liking it. The usual lack of familiarity didn't scare her as much now.

"Is she coming here to get me?" she asked, somehow knowing that if this Abby were there, everything else would be okay.

"That's up to you, Anna," Dr. Gordon told her, his face, as usual, a study in kindness.

Anna frowned. "Of course I want her here." Her sister would be able to fill in all the gaps in her life, wouldn't she? Abby could simply tell her everything she couldn't remember, until her mind was as full as if she'd never lost her memory.

Abby would know who'd fathered her child.

The two men looked at each other, and watching the silent exchange, Anna could see exactly when Jason Whitaker abdicated to Dr. Gordon, leaving the doctor to explain whatever they were hiding from her. What was going on here?

And then it hit her. Horrifyingly, embarrassingly. Was Jason Whitaker the father of her child? Was that why he was here?

"Did I sleep with you two months ago?" Anna blurted, in spite of the blush she could feel creeping up her throat and face. She was beyond manners. If Dr. Gordon and Jason knew something about her, she had to know, too.

Still suffering from acute embarrassment, still hardly comprehending what it might mean to have Jason Whitaker so intimately entangled in her life, crushing disappointment tore through her as he shook his head.

"I haven't seen you since I moved to New York three months ago," he said. He sounded sad, and she hated that he must pity her.

"I didn't even know you were in New York." He twisted the knife further.

Anna nodded. Her limited experience left her no clue what to say. How to handle such awkwardness was beyond her.

"You're in New York on a self-imposed sabbatical, Anna." Dr. Gordon freed her from the horrible moment.

"According to your sister," he continued, "you left home two months ago saying that you wanted to have a year apart from your family, that you needed to prove you could make it on your own. You demanded your family promise not to contact you for any reason during that year."

"Two months ago?" Anna asked. Right about the time she got pregnant—or right before.

Both men nodded. "No one's heard from you since," Jason said.

"Did you tell my sister, uh, Abby, about my baby?" Her eyes were pinned firmly on the doctor as she asked the question. She couldn't even look at Jason Whitaker.

The doctor nodded again. "I did."

"Does she know who the father is?" Anna whispered. She had to know whose baby was growing inside her. She had to see the man, find out what part he was going to play in her life, in his child's life.

Tears flooded her eyes when the doctor shook his head. She was falling apart and she couldn't help it. A victim of the confusing and volatile emotions swarming around inside her, she had no memory of how to cope with them. She was losing it.

The touch of Jason Whitaker's hand distracted her. "We wouldn't tell you, Anna, even if we knew," he said, his gaze full of something warm and powerful that she didn't understand, but that made her want to trust him.

"Do *you* know?" she asked, tears running slowly down her face. The irony of her situation hadn't escaped her. She'd left home to find herself and, instead, had lost all recollection of herself completely.

"No."

"I've told both Jason and Abby that I believe it would be harmful to fill you in on your past, Anna." Dr. Gordon broke the silence that had fallen. "Your mind is hiding from something, and until your subconscious feels you're ready to cope with it, any attempt to force you to shoulder it could result in permanent memory loss."

"Oh." She wiped her tears with her free hand. Her head was hurting again.

"Amnesia is a gray area, Anna. Each case is different. And while some doctors would probably tell you that to be informed of your past might be for the best, I believe such a move is potentially dangerous."

"Dangerous," she repeated, and felt Jason squeeze her hand more tightly.

Dr. Gordon nodded and continued to gaze kindly down at her. "But I also believe, as do the associates I've conferred with, that when you're ready, you'll remember everything."

"But how long will that take?" she cried. Couldn't they understand she didn't have the time to just sit around and wait? She had to get on with her life—whatever it was.

The doctor shrugged. "That's entirely up to you, Anna."

"And what if I say I want to be told, anyway? In spite of the risk?"

"Then we'll tell you," Jason said immediately. "But according to Dr. Gordon, even if the information doesn't cause permanent memory loss, you won't know later if you're remembering things because you truly recall them, or only because you're remembering what we've told you."

"Keep in mind," Dr. Gordon added, "that neither your family nor Jason know anything about the occurrences of the past two months of your life."

Anna's gaze moved sharply between the two men, although she continued to cling to Jason's hand. "You think what my mind can't cope with is something that happened since I left home?"

"Possibly," the doctor answered. "It's more likely a combination of things."

Anna thought she'd experienced every kind of fear imaginable over the past hours, but nothing compared to the dread freezing her now as she contemplated doing anything that could impair her complete recovery. Nor was she honestly sure she wanted to know—at least not yet—what possible horrors had led her to this place, this time. And perhaps this pregnancy?

Pulling her hand from Jason's, she asked the doctor, "Do you think I was raped?"

She almost started to cry again, with relief this time, when he shook his head. "Apart from the bruises you suffered in the crash, there's no physical or psychological evidence of abuse," he said. "No old contusions, no neurotic fears when people get close to you, touch you."

"But if I don't remember anything, why would I act afraid?"

"You don't remember experiences, Anna, but fear for your physical safety is a conditioned response. In cases like yours, that's usually not something the patient loses."

"Okay." She needed to believe the doctor, to trust him, to trust someone. "Say we do it your way—no one tells me anything. What happens next?"

His brows raised, the doctor looked at Jason, who nodded. "Your sister has put Jason in charge of that," Dr. Gordon said. "And I'll be back to see you in the morning. If you're satisfied with what Jason has to offer, I'll release you then."

"Thank you," Anna murmured, watching as the doctor turned and left the room. She continued to stare at the empty doorway until she'd worked up the courage to look at the man still looming over one side of the bed.

He wasn't watching the door. He was staring straight at her, and the longing she thought she glimpsed in his eyes before he quickly shadowed them made her feel incredibly sad, though she had no idea why.

"You're sure you're just a friend of the family?" she whispered, frustrated to the point of despair that she couldn't remember, that she had nothing to call upon to tell her the reason for his lost look—or her reaction to it.

"Positive," he said.

"And you really didn't sleep with me two months ago?"

He shook his head. "I wish I could tell you I had, Anna," he said with such finality she knew he spoke the truth.

Knew, too, inexplicably, that she wished his answer was different.

CHAPTER FOUR

"YOU WANT ME to come live with you?" Though Jason still stood beside her bed, Anna couldn't look at him, couldn't meet his eyes. Not because she was embarrassed by what he had in mind. She'd be an idiot to think that this gorgeous man could possibly have any sexual interest in a pregnant, currently demented family friend. He was taking pity on her, nothing more. No, what embarrassed her was her own reaction to his offer.

She *wanted* to go with him. She suddenly felt exposed, naked, vulnerable. She, who hated being a burden, who went out of her way not to bother anyone, wanted to saddle this man with an unexpected and very troubled houseguest.

"Oh!" she said suddenly, frantically retracing the pattern of her thoughts.

"What?" Jason leaned down. "What is it? Does your head hurt?" His worried gaze traveled over her. "Or...?"

"No! I..." How could she explain without sounding completely stupid? But looking into his eyes, how could she not? "I just had a thought, that's all. I knew something about myself. Really knew."

"You remembered something?"

She shrugged. Thinking back, she couldn't be sure how solid the feeling had been, was afraid to analyze it, afraid to dig too deeply, afraid she'd lose that little glimpse that was all she knew about herself. She was also afraid to test his reaction to her discovery. How well did he know her? Well enough to know she *hadn't* been overly concerned with being a bother in her other life? That these feelings were new, brought on by this horrendous situation? Not a part of her lost self at all?

"Whatever it was, it's gone," she said disappointedly, already convinced that her great self-discovery had been no discovery at all, but merely a reaction to her current circumstances. How could she possibly know whether or not she'd been a burden in someone's life when she didn't even know if she'd *been* in someone's life?

"It's okay, Anna." Jason sounded encouraging. "It's still a good sign. The doctor said things will probably come back only a little at a time."

She nodded, but it wasn't okay at all. He was suddenly too large, cramping her with his size, his broad determined shoulders blocking the door from her view, his optimism hanging over the room, pressing down on her, until her chest felt so tight it hurt to breathe. It took everything she had just to hold herself together. Optimism was beyond her.

Was this how it was to be? Was she to go through life looking for things that didn't exist, reading more into every situation because she so desperately wanted more to be there?

"My place is in Chelsea. It's fairly large for being

in the city," Jason continued as though the last moments had never happened. "There's a loft bedroom, and a bedroom downstairs, as well."

Anna's gaze followed his back as he moved to the window and gazed out into the night. There must be a woman someplace who wouldn't like a stranger moving into his home. No one as charming, as handsome as he was, would be living his life alone.

"You're welcome to stay as long as you like," he added.

He was being so nice. And without a dime to her name at the moment or anything else, for that matter, she had almost no immediate options. Still, she wasn't sure she could take him up on his offer, mostly because she wanted to so badly.

"You live alone?"

His shoulders stiffened, not markedly, but knowing nothing about him, about herself, her senses were acute to every nuance in her small world.

"Yes," he said, his voice as captivating as ever, no sign of the tension she'd witnessed—or thought she'd witnessed. "But you'll be perfectly safe. Your sister can vouch for me."

Funny, she'd never even considered her safety, although she supposed she should have. She was contemplating putting herself into this man's hands. Did she trust him so instinctively? Or had she just lost her common sense, along with her memories?

And what about her sister? Wouldn't *she* take her in? Would it really hurt to go back home to heal?

"Tell me something about Abby," Anna pleaded. "Anything." She'd agreed not to probe, but the blankness was more frightening than she could stand.

Jason spun around. "You've changed your mind, then? You want to go against the doctor's advice?" There was no condemnation in his voice, but there was urgency.

Anna shook her head. "I just need something a little more tangible than a name. Something to hold on to." She felt ridiculous pouring her guts out to a perfect stranger, and yet she couldn't stop herself. Because he was easy to talk to, or because she was just so damn needy, she didn't know.

Shoving his hands into his pockets, he watched her silently. Anna could almost see the thoughts running through his mind, see him discarding one after another. She waited for him to find something he could share until she was ready to scream. Every thought he was discarding was something she desperately wanted to know.

"Is she close to me in age?" she finally blurted. Or was this phantom sister a mere baby? Someone too far removed from her in years to be truly close.

He deliberated for a couple of seconds. "Yes."

"Older or younger?"

Another hesitation. And then, "Older."

Anna laid her head back against the raised mattress behind her. She was glad she had an older sister. The thought was comforting.

"Do you really believe that whatever I'm running from—" she flipped her hand up toward her recalcitrant brain "—is back in California? That to go back, to possibly force memories I'm apparently not ready to face, could do permanent damage?''

''I do.''

And he knew things she didn't know. Suddenly the thought of California frightened her—and yet, at the same time, called out to her.

''Would you like to speak to Abby?'' Jason asked, indicating the phone on the nightstand beside her bed. ''We can call her.''

Turning, Anna glanced at the phone. Willing it to tell her what she should do.

''Is she home?'' she whispered. Never had she been so tempted—at least, she didn't think she had. Just to hear her sister would be bliss. To have a voice on the other end of the line belong to her. Still, she couldn't forget the sabbatical she'd apparently taken from her family. Couldn't help but wonder why.

''She's home,'' Jason said, maintaining his position by the window. ''Waiting to hear how you are.''

Anna wondered what he thought she ought to do, but was reluctant to ask. He was leaving this completely up to her. Just as he should. So, had she and Abby had a fight? Was there a rift in their family? Had she, Anna, caused it? She didn't feel like the kind of person who would throw a tantrum or leave town in a huff, but then, she could hardly claim to know herself.

''She's waiting for me to call?'' she asked.

''Or me.''

Anna studied his face, looking for a sign, anything that would help her. His expression remained blank. Kind, but impassive.

"Do you think there was a valid reason for my going away?" How could she possibly know what to do when she had nothing to base a decision on?

"You weren't irresponsible, Anna," he said slowly, as though choosing his words carefully. "I fully believe that you thought things through and felt you had to leave."

"Do you know the reason?" She was being unfair, asking him for information that, were he to give it, could very well harm her permanently, but she couldn't help herself.

"Do you really want me to answer that?"

Yes. No! She wanted to get well.

"I'm not asking you to tell me the reason, Jason," she said, her voice stronger than it had been all day. "But give me a break here. I have no idea whether I'm apt to dream things up or to see clearly. Was my reasoning generally sound, or was it cockeyed?"

"Your reasoning was always sound."

His words were reassuring, but it was the steady look in his eyes, the way he spoke to her without words, that calmed the panic rising inside her.

She nodded, holding that gaze for another couple of seconds.

"Then I'm just going to have to trust myself, huh?" she finally said, trying for a grin and missing. "Until I know why I demanded no contact with my family, I'm going to abide by my wishes."

Jason nodded, saying nothing, but Anna could tell

he was pleased. Satisfied she'd crossed one small hurdle successfully, she turned her thoughts to more immediate decisions. Like where did she go when the doctor released her tomorrow? With nothing to her name, not even a shirt on her back, her options were nil.

"I must have a place somewhere." She hadn't meant to voice the thought.

"If you do, we'll find it," Jason said. "I have most mornings free, and a bit of investigative skill left over from my reporter days. Finding your place'll be a piece of cake."

"And a job. Surely I was working."

"As soon as we find out where you were living, we'll be able to ask your landlord where you work. Or your neighbors. You may even have a check stub lying around somewhere."

There was that damned optimism again. But this time she welcomed it. She needed his encouragement. And he said he had investigative skills, too.

"What do you do?" she asked, suddenly realizing how little she knew about him.

He blinked, opened his mouth to speak and then closed it again. "I'm a newscaster," he finally said, still holding guard at the window.

"I knew that, didn't I?"

He nodded. And it hit her then how hard this had to be for him. How awkward and uncomfortable she must be making him feel. To be looking at a friend and yet speaking with a stranger. A stranger he was determined to help whether she agreed to his plan or not. And he was acting as though there was nothing to it, as if she hadn't already taken up more of his time than she had any right to, as if he, a busy newscaster, didn't have a million other things he could be doing. Would rather be doing. She made up her mind then and there to make this whole ordeal as easy on her benefactor as she could.

"This is really what you want—for me to come home with you?"

He crossed his arms over his chest. "Yes."

"And you honestly don't mind me camping out at your place until I find my own?"

"Nope." He stood still as a statue, waiting.

She wanted to ask once more if he was sure she wasn't going to be any trouble, but she didn't. Of course she was going to be trouble. She was going to be a complete nuisance for a day or two. She'd just have to make sure that it *was* only a day or two. Forty-eight hours to find her life. It would have to be enough.

"Then, thank you. I accept."

Jason glanced at his watch. "Okay, then, I've got to go," he said, moving toward the door almost as if, now that he had her acquiescence, he suddenly couldn't get away fast enough. "I'm on the air in half an hour. But I'll be back around ten in the morning."

Struck with sudden irrational fear as he departed, Anna lay perfectly still and closed her eyes. She might not remember anything, but at least she knew who she was now. And she wasn't all alone. She opened her eyes to stare at the telephone. She could always call the sister she'd left behind if she had to.

"Anna?" Jason's blond head appeared again around her open door.

With her stomach flip-flopping at the sound of his voice after she'd thought him gone, she met his gaze.

He pulled a card out of his jacket pocket and walked over to drop it on the nightstand. "That's my number," he said, backing slowly toward the door again. "If you need anything, call." A couple of more steps and he'd be history. "Anytime. I'm a light sleeper."

Her throat felt thick. "Thanks," she said, trying to smile without letting the tears fall.

Now he was at the door, standing there poised to leave, and yet, still there. She withstood his perusal, holding his gaze.

"It's good to see you again," he said finally. And then he was gone.

Her taut body relaxed back against the mattress, a tiny smile contrasting with the tears that dripped down her face as she reached for the television remote control. She just had to wait thirty minutes and he'd be there on her screen.

HE MADE IT to the station in time to change into his jacket. Barely. And he made it through the show, as well. Though not with his usual style. The natural repartee for which he'd become known wasn't flowing, his mind not on what he was saying but on the woman lying alone and frightened in a hospital bed across town.

"You feeling okay?" his co-anchor, Sunny Lawson, asked as soon as the On the Air light clicked off.

"Fine," he lied. He didn't need her attentions tonight.

She pouted her lovely lips at his curtness, her flirtatiousness as natural as her beauty. "What's wrong?"

"Nothing." Clearing his papers, Jason stood up, hoping to leave the set without hurting Sunny's feelings. She'd been a good friend during the months he'd been in town. He just wasn't fit company tonight.

Walking beside him, her heels clicking on the cement floor in front of their set, she suggested, "How 'bout a drink?" She linked her arm through his. "You can tell me all about it."

The offer was nothing new. He and Sunny often had a bite between shows or a drink afterward. "Not tonight," he said impatiently, realizing he should have suggested a rain check.

"Jason?" She stopped, hauling him to a standstill beside her. "You mad at me or the world in general?" she asked, frowning.

He opened his mouth to tell her about Anna. But the words didn't come. He didn't want to talk about Anna. Not yet. Not while he still felt so raw.

Leaning over, he planted a friendly kiss on Sunny's full lips. "I'm not angry. Just tired," he said, feeling a twinge of guilt as he kissed her again just to shut her up.

His guilt increased as the kiss worked. She smiled

at him. "You should have left when I did last night, instead of staying for one more," she said.

"I know," he acknowledged. "Which is why I'm leaving tonight. Right now."

"Well, get some sleep, friend," she said, chuckling. "Your disposition could use some improvement."

"I'll be asleep the second I get home," he assured her, leaving her at her dressing-room door, feelings intact.

HE CALLED ABBY the second he got in. It was after midnight in New York, but only nine-thirty at the beach house in California.

"How is she?" Abby said in lieu of hello.

"Fine." He shrugged out of his sport coat and tossed it on the back of a kitchen chair. "Good. Really," he added as Abby's silence hung on the line. "Considering."

"You've seen her?"

Abby was crying and trying to hide it. He ached for her. For all of them.

"Yeah. She looked good, Ab, really."

"She looked the same?" Abby asked.

"Her hair was pulled back in a ponytail, but she was as beautiful as ever." Which was an understatement. To his starved eyes she'd been a vision, stealing the breath from his lungs.

"So what'd she say? Was—" Abby took a shaky breath "—was she crying?" Then Abby lost her own battle with tears completely.

Jason swallowed, hating the helplessness he felt,

his inability to make everything right for them.

"She cried a little." He rubbed the back of his neck. "She's confused, Ab, frightened," he admitted. "But she's strong, too. In a way I've never really seen before." He took a breath and plunged ahead. "She's coming home with me tomorrow. She's going to stay at my place until we can find out where she lives, where she works."

Abby digested that in silence, and Jason knew she was drawing the right conclusions—just as he'd meant her to. Anna had decided not to go home.

"I didn't think she'd stay in New York."

"I know." Jason hadn't been sure, either, that Anna would be strong enough to fight the temptation to run to Abby. Whether she remembered home or not, some habits were just too ingrained to break. He'd seen Anna looking at the telephone, had felt her teetering with indecision. But she'd refused to call. That was when he'd known he was in for the long haul.

Silence once again stood between Abby and him. Silent accusation, silent concession, silent relief.

"You told her about me?" Abby finally asked.

"Of course." It bothered him she even had to ask, that things had become so strained between them she'd wonder such a thing. "Although Dr. Gordon advised against telling her you're triplets."

"I know." She sighed. "And as much as I hate it, I think he's right."

"I think so, too, Ab," he told her. "And who knows, it might only be for a few days. The doctor said her memory could start coming back anytime."

He didn't tell Abby about the brief flash Anna had had earlier that evening; he didn't want to get her hopes up, having her waiting for breakthroughs by the hour. Especially since this one had gone as quickly as it had come.

"I got hold of Mom and Dad." The words were too casual. "They're in France now."

"And?"

"They were horrified of course, but calmed right down when I told them you were with her."

"Are they coming home?"

"Not just yet." The words were almost defensive. "They're thinking about investing in some perfume company, already have meetings scheduled for next week," she explained in a rush. "I told them there wasn't any real danger. And it's not like we can see her."

No. But they could have come home for Abby's sake. Their eldest daughter was all alone, confused, hurting.

"Did you tell them about the pregnancy?"

"No."

Some things never changed. The elder Haydens sailed through life focused only on themselves and left Abby to bear the burdens.

"Anna was thrilled to know she had a sister," he said when Abby was silent for too long. "And though she'd already made the decision to abide by Dr. Gordon's advice, you should have heard her pumping me for information about you."

Abby chuckled through her tears. "She was always the smartest one of us."

From his tenth-floor window Jason looked out over the flickering lights of New York, wondering if one of the lights was Anna's, if she was sleeping. "Don't sell yourself short, Abby," he said. "You did a damn fine job holding the three of you together all these years." There. It was three months overdue, but it needed to be said.

"Yeah, right," she snorted. "Damn fine. That's why we're all living happily ever after."

The bitterness in her voice worried him. "You can't control fate, Ab," he told her sternly.

"That's not what you said three months ago," she reminded him. "I remember quite clearly you telling me I control everything."

He hadn't put it so nicely. "I'm sorry, Abby."

"I know," she said, her voice softer, more like the Abby he knew. "Me, too."

There was more Jason needed to say, but he'd be damned if he could come up with any words. Glib, smooth-tongued, always-know-what-to-say Whitaker was fresh out.

"The doctor said Anna came in with no ID on her except her locket," Abby said, rescuing him.

"Apparently her purse and whatever else she had with her was either destroyed in the crash or stolen during the mayhem that followed."

"That means she won't have her health-insurance card."

Right. Good. Something practical to think about. Jason grabbed a pencil, repeating the information Abby was reading to him from the health-insurance policy the triplets had through their shop.

"She's probably not going to need this," he said, the phone held to his ear with his shoulder as he wrote. "The city's liability insurance will cover all her medical expenses—and probably a lot more. The accident was so clearly the fault of a system's engineer—he was in the wrong place at the wrong time—that there's already talk of settlements."

And then another thought struck him. "What about her pregnancy?" he asked. He was doing his damnedest not to think about that part of Anna's life at all. But she'd need to know. "Will the shop's insurance cover that?"

"Yes." And that quickly, the tension was back. "So...how are you doing?" Abby's voice was soft.

"Fine," Jason lied. His insides felt ripped apart, but that was his own business.

"You'll keep in touch?"

"Of course." He should really turn on some lights. Except that he preferred the darkness.

"Jason?"

"Yeah?"

"Thanks."

Grunting a reply, he rang off, stripped to his briefs and dropped to the hardwood floor, doing as many pushups as his tired body would allow. Forty-nine. Fifty. Getting involved with Anna again was sheer stupidity. One hundred. It was nothing short of lunacy. One hundred fifty. It was masochism. Two hundred. Suicide.

But he'd loved her once. Had actually, for the first time in his life, believed himself loved. And love meant you cared even when it hurt. It meant putting someone else's needs above your own. It meant loyalty and reliability. It meant all the things he'd always wanted but never known. It meant everything that was most important to him.

Rolling over, he lifted his legs an inch off the ground and crunched forward, pressing his lower back into the floor. One, two, three…fifty-one, fifty-two, fifty-three… Though he wouldn't have thought it possible, he'd underestimated how much he'd missed her. He'd also thought he'd suffered as hellishly as any one person could and still function, until she'd turned those big brown eyes on him—and hadn't known him from Adam.

One hundred twenty-one, one hundred twenty-two. She didn't know she'd sent him out of her life.

Jason spent the next hour moving his things to the downstairs bedroom. Whether she remembered growing up by the ocean or not, Anna would crave the openness of the loft just as he did, and he wanted her as comfortable as he could make her. Besides, he'd sleep better knowing she couldn't slip out without him knowing. His bedroom door was right at the bottom of the stairs.

Not that he thought for a second that Anna would run out on him. Or that she wouldn't be leaving just as soon as she was able. But old habits died hard. He couldn't stop people from leaving him. It was a fact of life—at least of *his* life. But he was damn well going to watch them go. He'd learned a long time ago that goodbye didn't hurt quite so badly when he knew it was coming.

It was when he cleared the last load of his clothes

out of the closet that he saw the box he'd known was waiting there. Still taped up from the move from California, the small cardboard carton had one word scrawled across the top in black magic marker. *Anna.* Jason ripped it open.

He'd found a few of her things at his condo when he'd packed up so hurriedly to leave for New York. He hadn't been in any kind of mood to return them to her, to see her again. But he hadn't been able to toss them away, either. So like a fool, he'd thrown them in a box and carted them across the country with him.

A couple of pairs of silky bikini underwear. His body hardened immediately as he pictured her roaming around his condo back in California in them— and nothing else. Making them both breakfast or a midnight snack. Always fresh from lovemaking.

A long black spaghetti-strap nightgown he'd bought for her, but she'd never worn. Not because she hadn't liked it, but because once he got her to his place, he never gave her time to put it on.

And a couple of the loose-fitting, earth-toned dresses she wore almost every day of her life. Garments that would have looked drab on most women, but flowed lovingly around Anna's curves, giving her an air of womanly grace.

Jason smiled, remembering the first time he'd seen Anna standing on the street outside her shop in Oxnard, the wind whipping a dress just like one of these up around her hips while she'd laughingly tried to preserve some dignity. He hadn't had a hope in hell of escaping her allure. He'd been turned on then, as he pretended not to notice her gorgeous thighs, and ever since. Of course later, when he'd known she wore nothing under her dresses but silky bikini briefs, the damn garments had driven him crazy.

He was going to have to iron at least one of them. Three months in a box hadn't done them any favors. Both dresses had tints of mauve in them as did most of Anna's things. She'd told him once that she loved the shade because of its softness, its ability to meld with other colors without causing a stir. Only Jason had seen the fire hidden in her favorite hue.

After ironing and then showering, he finally lay down in his newly made bed sometime around three. And although he'd been up more than fifteen hours and was both mentally and physically exhausted, he still didn't sleep. In less than eight hours Anna was going to be here. In his home. With him. Just where he'd refused to allow himself to picture her for three torturous months.

And then she'd be leaving. Because while he'd been spending his nights trying not to remember her in his bed, she'd been in bed with someone else.

He'd deal with it. Anna wasn't his anymore. It was over. She'd told him so more than three months ago. He was a little slow, but he was getting it. Finally. She was just an old friend in need. He could handle this. No problem.

No problem to give her this chance to find out for herself who she really was. Anna Hayden. One person. Not Audrey, Anna and Abby.

All of this would be worth the effort if Anna discovered she could be Anna alone, not Anna, one-third of a whole—working a job she didn't love for a sister she did. Living a life that was content, but couldn't include the frightening, exhilarating experience of being completely, totally, in love. Couldn't include commitment to anyone but the other two-thirds. Anna, one-third of a whole, believing in her sister's opinion as much or more than she believed in her own. Believing that her strength and Abby's was to be found only in their togetherness.

Anna, one-third of a whole, and never really happy.

CHAPTER FIVE

SHE WAS GOING TO BE horribly embarrassed. She'd called the nurse, a new one since yesterday, and that harried woman had assured Anna that she'd see about getting her something to wear. But it was almost ten o'clock. Jason Whitaker was due to arrive momentarily, and Anna still had nothing on but a very short, very thin hospital gown with a slit all the way down the back. And her hair was still dirty. The hospital had been without hot water for most of the morning.

She considered calling the nurse one more time, but hated to be a bother. The woman was obviously busy taking care of people who really needed her. Sick people who were suffering. People who couldn't care for themselves. Anna felt like a fraud for even considering taking up the woman's time.

Of course the alternatives weren't much better. Either leave the hospital wrapped in a robe, assuming they'd let her borrow one, or ask Jason to go out and buy her some clothes with money she didn't have, and then come back and get her.

Or she could ask the doctor to delay her release for one more day, call her sister and have Abby wire her some money. Better yet, have Abby send her a plane ticket home.

Home. She closed her eyes, willing something, anything, to appear in the blankness—a picture, a feeling. A memory. But try as she might, she couldn't raise a single image of the place where she'd grown up, or the people she'd known. Knew only that she didn't want to go there now. Not until she remembered why she'd left.

What she wanted to do was see Jason Whitaker. She wanted him to help her find her life. She wanted to get to know him again, this family friend who'd come to rescue her. Though she'd awoken this morning with the now familiar emptiness, the horror of living with a mind that had let her down, she'd also felt a flicker of anticipation. Simply because she was going to see Jason Whitaker again.

And therein lay her biggest fear of all.

Because she was scared to death he wasn't going to come get her. Surely, with time to consider the commitment he'd made, he'd change his mind. Any sensible person would. She could hardly blame him for not wanting to saddle himself with a crazy woman who also happened to be homeless, temporarily penniless, pregnant and who had absolutely no recollection of the father of her baby.

Jason had no way of knowing that his presence was the only thing that had made her feel safe since she'd opened her eyes the day before to a waking nightmare. That she was holding on to his offer to help her with every fiber of her being. That he made her believe she really could get her life back together, that somehow she'd find a way to be a mother to the child she knew she carried, but had yet to feel.

He owed her nothing. She hadn't even done him the courtesy of remembering him. Had no idea how close a family friend he was. He'd be a fool to come back. And if he didn't...

She'd been fighting her fears all morning, trying to concentrate on the mundane tasks necessary to prepare herself to go out in public, tracking down a toothbrush, washing her face, contemplating her nonexistent wardrobe. But as ten o'clock drew nearer, she could no longer keep her panic at bay.

He wasn't going to come. How could she possibly expect him to come? The walls started to close in on her. She was going to have to go back to California—without any idea what kind of a minefield she'd be walking into. Or maybe, worse yet, everyone would keep her reason for leaving a secret forever, treat her like some kind of invalid. What if they coddled her so much she'd never again have a life of her own, never be able to take care of herself, let alone be a good mother to her baby? She'd rather die first.

"Hey, sunshine, you ready to blow this joint?" Jason's cheerful voice put an end to her frantic soul searching.

Tongue-tied, Anna stared at him as he came through her door. He'd come back. And this morning, in form-fitting faded jeans and a polo shirt, he looked so classically gorgeously male he took her breath away.

When she didn't speak, he frowned, coming closer. "What's wrong?" he asked. He set a bag she hadn't even noticed he'd been carrying on the end of her bed.

"Nothing," she said, hot color spreading up her neck. How could she possibly ask this man to go buy her some underwear? She pulled the sheet up to her chin. "I, uh, have a small problem."

"Something we can fix, I hope?"

His warm blue eyes met her gaze directly, full of friendliness—and something more. Something she couldn't define or understand.

She couldn't do it. She just couldn't ask him for panties.

He picked up the paper bag he'd dropped on the end of the bed and tossed it onto her lap. "Tell you what," he said, backing toward the door. "I'll go get some coffee from the machine I saw down the hall while you get ready, and then we'll talk. Okay?"

He smiled, sending shivers all the way down to her toes, and she merely nodded. If there weren't clothes in this bag, she was going to crawl under the covers and never come out. And if there were, then he was the most amazing... He was a good friend. That was what he was. All he could ever be. Period. And she needed to get that straight right now. No matter how attractive she may find him, no matter how thoughtful and warm and kind, no matter how attached to him she was growing already, she was pregnant with another man's baby.

As soon as he was out the door, she ripped into

the bag. Clothes. Thank God! Pulling them out of
the bag as she climbed from the bed, she hurried
into the bathroom. She was at least going to have
the armor of decent covering the next time she came
face-to-face with Jason Whitaker.

She liked his taste in clothes. The dress was loose
and flowing, and the soft cotton felt good against
her skin. As did the silky panties she found folded
up inside the dress.

Blushing from head to toe, she slipped them on
beneath the dress, chastising herself for thinking of
the man who'd brought them as she slid them up
her thighs. She might as well commit herself to the
loony bin if she was going to start having romantic
thoughts about her benefactor. Not only would it be
sheer stupidity to think that Jason could ever be attracted to her, lunacy to read anything personal into
his friendly gestures, it was also impossible to in-
volve herself with anyone at this point in her life.

Somewhere in the world there lived a man with
whom she'd quite recently been intimate. A man she
hoped to God she loved, since she had his baby
growing in her womb. A man who, if she saw him,
may just attract her more than Jason Whitaker did.
It was this crazy situation, that was all. Jason was
the knight saving the damsel in distress. And he was
the only attractive man she could ever remember
seeing. Her strong reaction to him was because of
the situation. It had to be.

And then it hit her. There'd been no tags on the
clothes she was wearing. The underwear, in fact,
while fresh and clean, was faded. She couldn't help

wondering whom they belonged to or how well Jason knew the woman. And couldn't seem to help the sick jealousy that attacked her as she answered her own question.

Swearing at herself, she yanked the band from her hair, resecuring the ponytail with more force than necessary. One thing she knew for sure, she needed to find her own place—damn quickly. Had to get out into the world, meet so many people that rather than being the sole individual in her life, Jason Whitaker was merely one of a crowd. A huge crowd.

She was starting to obsess about him and was at least rational enough to recognize the very real danger in allowing herself to need him too much. He was making it so easy for her to rely on him for everything. But he was going to be gone from her life in just a day or two, back to his own life, his own woman, and she had to be able to stand by herself when he left. For her baby's sake and for her own. She couldn't afford another problem.

Her resolution to get away from him lasted right up until he came walking back into her room five minutes later. He smiled at her. And all she could do was smile back.

"You look good. Just like your old self."

His words gave her pause. It was so hard for her to accept that while she was getting to know a stranger, he was seeing an old friend. "I like the dress," she said. "Thanks."

He opened his mouth, closed it then opened it again to say simply, "You're welcome."

Anna had a burning urge to know what he'd almost said, but she didn't ask. She also didn't ask whose dress she was wearing. She wasn't ready to hear about another woman in his life.

"You ready to go?" he asked, looking the room over as if she might be forgetting something, as if she had something of her own to take with her. She followed his gaze around the stark room, struck again by the total emptiness that was her life.

"I don't know what I'm supposed to do about the bill," she admitted, something else that had been on her mind that morning. "I don't even know if I have health insurance."

"You do." Jason handed her a slip of paper. "That'll see you through until you can get a new card, but you won't need it today," he said. "The city is covering all your medical expenses. There'll probably be a settlement shortly, as well."

Anna stared at his forceful handwriting, wondering how many other things he knew about her that she didn't. She hated the way her condition made her so helplessly vulnerable, hated Jason seeing her like this. She swore to herself that she wouldn't rest until she'd taken back control of her life—and that once she had, she'd never let it go again. The insurance card was a good start. She no longer had to worry about financing her pregnancy. Now she just had to figure out how she supported herself.

"What kind of settlement?" she asked, sitting down in the wheelchair she had to be wheeled out of the hospital in.

Jason shrugged. "I don't know yet, but the city

has already admitted liability. It's just up to their lawyers to determine amounts.''

She turned to look at him as he pushed her from the room. "Do I need a lawyer?"

"I don't think so, honey. Only if you're not satisfied with whatever amount they offer."

"It was an accident, Jason," she said, crossing her arms over her chest. "They don't owe me anything."

"*They* seem to think they owe you something," he said, stopping at the nurses' station. "So I'd take what they offer—just to see you through until you're back on your feet."

Understanding that she would be less of a burden to him with money of her own, Anna just nodded and proceeded to sign the papers the nurse handed her. The sooner she was back in her own place the better. She had to believe that.

JASON THOUGHT it best to put off their investigating until the next day. "You're probably going to tire a little more easily than you're used to," he'd said.

And because she'd read his words to mean that he had something else to do, she'd agreed with him. But after a brief shopping trip for some toiletries, another dress, purchased with money he'd lent her, and moving her few things into the beautiful loft bedroom in his apartment, she wished she hadn't agreed so readily. He wasn't going anywhere. And surely a possible bout of fatigue, heck, even passing out at his feet, was better than sitting intimately on his couch in the quiet of his apartment. She had nothing to say, no repertoire of small talk, of reminisces to draw upon. And the way he was looking at her, his eyes brimming with things she couldn't decipher, was making it hard for her to remember the reasons she couldn't allow him to mean anything to her.

"How well do I know you?" she asked suddenly. He had all the advantages and she had none. Had she been fond of him before? Was that why she was so instantly drawn to someone who, for all intents and purposes, was a complete stranger?

He shrugged, looking away. "I've known your family for several years."

"Well? Or just acquaintances?"

"Well."

"Did we see each other often?" she asked. She couldn't see how, if they were at all close, she hadn't been head over heels in love with him.

"We saw each other fairly often," he finally said.

"Why?" She couldn't have been in love with him. Loving Jason wasn't something she would ever forget. Not in a million years, or after a million bumps to her head. But even more, being her lover wasn't something he'd keep quiet about. Especially not now—not with her pregnant.

"You have a nice family, Anna. I enjoyed being with you all."

"Were you a friend of my parents?"

His right heel started to bounce, almost imperceptibly, his leg up and down. "Not until you introduced me to them."

"*I* introduced you?"

His leg was still. "You and Abby."

"Do you have a nice family, too?" Her bluntness made her uncomfortable, but the void where there should have been memories drove her on.

He shrugged. "They're nice people. I just don't see them much."

"They live faraway?"

His leg started to move again. "No."

She was treading on sensitive territory, and yet she wasn't getting any signals from him to stop. "Did you have a falling-out with them?"

He stretched his arm along the back of the couch, the tips of his fingers almost touching her shoulder. "My parents divorced when I was five," he said. "I grew up spending three days a week at one house and four at the other."

"Almost like a visitor," she said, frowning. "That must have been hard. Did you have a room in each house? Where'd you keep your toys?" She couldn't imagine anyone agreeing to raise a child that way.

He smiled sadly and she had a feeling she was seeing a part of Jason not many people saw, and wondered if he was telling her things he'd told her before. Or if, perhaps, the fact that he was to all intents and purposes a stranger to her made it easier for him to speak of things he usually kept to himself.

"For a while I had a room in both places," he said. "Until my father moved closer to work and my mother remarried."

"What a tough way to grow up." She wondered if she'd ever met his parents. And if she had, if she'd been able to be civil to them. "I can't believe the courts allowed it."

"It was pretty unheard-of back then," he said. "It's not so unusual now. That way the child is still raised by both parents, has the benefit of a close relationship with both parents." His leg continued to bounce.

"Was that how it was with you?" she asked, filled with a need to understand everything she could about him.

"My father had his career." He shrugged. "Mom, her husband and new baby daughter. I always knew they cared—I just wasn't their first priority." He said the words easily, but Anna didn't believe for a second that his feelings were that uncomplicated.

And as he talked to her, as she caught a glimpse of the sensitive boy he'd been—sensitive to hurt, but sensitive to his parents' needs, as well—Anna wondered again why she hadn't been in love with him.

Had she already been in love with someone else? Someone who affected her even more deeply than he did?

"Were you ever in love?" she blurted. *Was I?*

He stiffened. "I thought I was."

It had to be difficult for him, hearing her ask things she should already know, but as long as he was willing to answer, she had to ask. And he'd just cleared up one mystery. There'd never been anything more than friendship between them because he'd been involved with someone else.

"What happened?" She curled her legs up beneath her.

"She chose someone else." And he was still hurting.

Anna couldn't imagine any woman turning Jason Whitaker away. Quite the opposite, in fact. She'd been picturing a string of broken hearts leading straight to his door. Maybe her own included. Maybe she'd loved him—and he'd loved someone else.

"I'm sorry."

He glanced over at her, a sardonic grin on his lips. "Don't be," he said. "It doesn't matter anymore." But somehow she knew it did.

"Did I know her?"

"Yes."

Anna wondered if she'd ever been as jealous of this unknown woman as she was of the woman whose dress she now wore. "Did I like her?"

He looked at her, his assessing gaze making her uncomfortable. "You never told me you didn't."

His fingers moved absently along the back of the couch, and Anna could feel every imaginary brush through the thin material of her dress, aware of him in a way that could only embarrass him, stir his pity. She was crazy. And pregnant. And the man was probably still in love with someone else.

"How long ago was this?" she asked.

"A few months." He looked away and then back again, his leg still. "Just before I came out to New York."

This woman was in California, then, Anna

thought, worried by her sudden sense of relief. But worried even more by how deeply she felt the pain he was denying. In any way that mattered, she'd just met this man. "She was a fool," she said aloud.

He shrugged. "It's history."

She wasn't sure she believed him.

IT WAS A RELIEF to leave for work. Though he felt guilty about leaving Anna alone sooner than he had to, Jason gave himself enough time to walk part of the way to the station that balmy New York evening, catching a cab at Madison Square. People had been complaining about the summer humidity, but having grown up on the coast, Jason found New York's humidity no problem. And as much as he missed the ocean, he loved New York. He loved the rush, the life that surged around him every time he stepped outside his door. Everywhere were people with goals to achieve, important things to do, destinations to reach. He needed to get caught up again in the activity, the enthusiasm, remember who he was, the person he'd become since leaving California. He also needed to lose some of the tension that was building to an exploding point within him.

He needed a break from Anna.

She'd been in his home one afternoon and he was falling in love with her all over again. She was another man's woman now. A woman who was sitting in his apartment in the dress he'd stripped off her the last time she'd worn it, and she was carrying another man's child.

He'd had to leave before the anger building inside

him spewed out and scalded them both. How could she have allowed another man to touch her, to know her, to leave his seed in her? And why wasn't she different because of it? Why was she still, even minus her memory, so much the Anna he'd known and loved more than anyone else, ever?

He'd have given his life for the woman. And she was giving life to another man's baby.

While he, like some kind of sick fool, still burned with desire for her. Her scent, her soft husky voice, the way she glided when she moved—all had driven him to the point of insanity that afternoon.

He understood how her separation from Abby had been more than Anna could bear. Understood that she badly needed this chance to emerge from the cocoon of her family to become a separate and complete individual. Accepted the fact that her mind was ensuring she got that chance.

But as the afternoon dragged on, even stronger than his need to take her to bed, stronger than his anger, was the hurt he'd thought he'd buried forever, rising closer and closer to the surface. He was having a hard time accepting, forgiving, that she'd forgotten *him.*

"Sleep improved your tongue, but it didn't seem to do much for your disposition," Sunny said as they left the set after the six-o'clock news.

She hadn't appreciated his curt acquiescence when she'd asked him out to dinner. But at least he'd been at his best on the air. His thoughts had flowed as freely as the cue cards, allowing him to add his own slant to the news he imparted the way his loyal viewers had come to expect. And if his grand performance had had anything to do with the fact that he knew Anna was watching him, he damn sure didn't want to know about it.

"Let me make a phone call and we can go to dinner," he said, tossing his station jacket on a chair just inside the door of his dressing room. "But I'm buying."

For once she didn't argue with him.

Sunny drove a fire-engine red Mercedes convertible, and Jason envied her only for having a garage close enough to home to drive her car to work almost daily. The Jaguar he'd brought with him from California was every bit the vehicle her Mercedes was, but it was a twenty-minute cab ride away, parked in a garage that cost him nearly as much as his apartment did each month.

Still, he appreciated a powerful car, and Sunny was a good driver. Settling back in the passenger seat, he enjoyed the view, the warm breeze in his hair, as she maneuvered through midtown Manhattan toward the seafood restaurant she currently favored on the Upper East Side. Anna had already eaten, she'd assured him when he'd called her from his dressing room. She'd found the stash of TV dinners in his freezer and had eaten one while watching his show. She was understandably exhausted and was planning to shower and be in bed by nine o'clock. He was planning not to think about her in that spaghetti-strap nightgown.

"So what's got you so uptight?" Sunny asked as

soon as they had their predinner drinks in front of them.

"You remember that amnesia victim?" he asked her, studying the ice in his glass. It was going to take a lot more than a glass of scotch to put him to sleep tonight.

"The one from the subway crash? Anna, didn't they say?"

"Anna Hayden," he said. "I knew her in California."

"And?" she said when he paused. She'd stopped swishing her straw in her drink and was staring at him. Sunny wasn't going to like what he had to tell her.

"She's staying at my place for a few days."

"Why?" The softly spoken word hung between them.

He could tell her that Anna had no place else to go, that she knew no one else in the city. "Because I asked her to."

"Why?" she asked again. She'd made no secret of the fact that she'd been hoping for more between them than friendship. But he'd been honest, too. He wasn't ready for the kind of relationship Sunny wanted.

He took a sip of his drink, sending his co-anchor a warning look over his glass.

"I wanted to," he finally answered. It was the only part of the truth she'd care about.

She nudged her drink away. "How well did you know her in California?"

"Well."

Breaking eye contact with him for the first time since the conversation began, Sunny said, "Oh."

Jason sipped his drink, waiting. Knowing Sunny, she wasn't going to give up that easily. He'd known when he invited Anna home that Sunny wasn't going to like it. His relationship with her had started out as a publicity stunt. She was to be full of light sexual innuendoes and lots of personal approval as they worked together on the air, the idea being that if she approved of Channel Sixteen's new co-anchor, so would her loyal viewers. And if viewers tuned in to see a little chemistry between Sunny Lawson and her new co-anchor, so much the better.

In silence they ate their meal, lobster for Jason, crab salad for Sunny. He'd have enjoyed the food a lot more if it wasn't sharing space with the rock in his gut. His relationship with Sunny was important to him, in more ways than one. Just not the way she wanted most.

When Jason had first come to town, not knowing a soul, he'd been only too willing to spend a lot of time with Sunny, to be seen about town with her, appear in all the right places with her on his arm—all in the name of business. She was a beautiful woman, and with her sharp mind, good company, too. But as they'd gradually grown more comfortable together, their relationship had become more than business. After three months of sharing dinners with her, working with her, drinking with her, Sunny had become a good friend.

She wanted to be his lover.

But as beautiful as Sunny was, as tempting as he

found her, Jason did not intend to take her to bed. Sunny wasn't looking for a no-strings-attached affair, and he wasn't sure he'd ever want more than that with a woman again.

There was his job to consider as well. He cared about his job. A lot. And he had to work with Sunny. Though he'd given the show a much needed ratings boost, Channel Sixteen News had been hers long before he'd come along.

She waited until he'd pushed his plate away. "When's she leaving?" she asked.

"I don't know."

He couldn't give her any more than that.

"Are you sleeping with her?"

"No."

"Do you intend to?"

It was on the tip of his tongue to tell Sunny that whether or not he slept with Anna was none of her business. But because she was a friend, because it was the truth, he answered her. "No."

Her shoulders relaxed. "Does she know that yet?" she asked in the voice that had made her famous.

"She's pregnant, Sunny." And then, when he saw the horror in her eyes, "The baby's not mine."

"Oh," she said. "Good."

Picking up her abandoned fork, she attacked her half-eaten salad with gusto and he waited while she ate, well aware of how beautiful she was, of the male eyes watching her appreciatively, of the envy surrounding him in the elite little restaurant. Well aware, too, that Sunny was his for the taking. He wondered if he'd eventually give in and take her to his bed without love. Good sex could go a long way toward covering up what wasn't there.

"You ready?" he asked as soon as she finally laid down her fork.

"Yes," she said, standing and waiting while he settled the check.

Any other time she'd have argued over whose turn it was to pay; tonight, she was claiming the right to have him buy her dinner. Jason didn't miss the message she was sending him. He was hers and she wasn't giving him up.

He could have told her she didn't have a damn thing to worry about where Anna was concerned. His housemate already had a man in her life. And she'd probably be running back to him just as soon as she remembered who he was.

CHAPTER SIX

ABBY AWOKE with a start. Cold sweat trickled down her back and she sat up, looking around her small bedroom in the back of the beach house. Something was wrong. Engulfed in fear, she slid soundlessly from the bed, eyes glued on the open door in front of her. Her own safety didn't matter, not until she assured herself that her sisters weren't hurt. She hadn't heard anything, but she never ignored her instincts. She'd awoken for a reason.

Slipping out her door and into the room immediately to her right, she saw the empty bed. Audrey's bed.

As reality crashed in, a cold calm settled around Abby's heart. Out of a lifetime of habit, she checked the rest of the cottage. But when she found it empty, as empty as her life, she lay slowly down on the kitchen floor, welcoming the coolness of the tile against her cheek, aware only then of the tears running down her face.

God, she hurt. Was going crazy with the pain. Not because she wasn't strong enough to shoulder it. She'd been feeling for three all her life. Whenever her sisters were in need, she knew. When one suffered, they all three suffered. They'd felt each other's thoughts—seemed to share a single soul. Just as they'd all shared a remarkable comfort in each other. The most agonizing heartache became less unbearable simply because it was shared.

But not anymore. Abby was alone now. And this solitary pain was much harder to bear than any she'd known before. Why was she still sensing things that no longer existed? Feeling bonds that had long been broken?

She ached so badly she wished she'd just die and be done with it. And no one knew she felt this way. Which was the worst part of all. For the first time in her life, no one knew.

ANNA FLEW out of bed before she was fully awake, running down the loft stairs with only one thought in mind. To get help. She had to get help.

Jason caught her by the shoulders just outside his bedroom door.

"Anna! What's wrong?"

"Let me go!" She fought his hold. She had to get help.

He held her captive. "What is it, honey? What's happened?"

She heard the concern in his voice, but she couldn't take time to explain. "I've got to get help!" she cried, still struggling to break away from him.

"Why? Are you in pain?" He pulled her closer, turning her face up to his.

His blue eyes bore into hers, full of worry—and something more. Something that reached down to soothe away the panic that had spread through her while she slept. She stared back at him, speechless, wondering how she could possibly explain her frantic urgency when she didn't understand it herself.

"Anna?" He continued to watch her.

She shook her head. Was she losing her mind?

"I..." She looked away, embarrassed, afraid. Confused.

"What frightened you, honey?" His voice was soft, understanding—and yet so very masculine.

"I... It was just..." What? How could she tell him without sounding crazy?

"Were you sleeping?" he asked, leading her over to the couch.

She nodded.

He sat down beside her, still holding on to one of her hands as he reached up to brush the hair from her face. It was a damp tangled mess.

"You just had a nightmare," he said gently. "Dr. Gordon warned us this might happen."

Still silent, she nodded again. Let him think that was all it was. Let her try and believe it.

"Were you dreaming about the crash?" he asked.

"Yes." She forced the word and barely got a whisper. That was how her dream had started, anyway. But there'd been more. Something that when she'd awoken hadn't vanished with the dream. Someone calling out to her, frantically, painfully, needing her so desperately she still felt the echo of it singeing her nerves.

Jason pulled her into his arms. "You're shivering," he said. "Are you cold?"

Shaking her head, she burrowed her face against him, realizing his chest was bare only when her cheek pressed against the warmth of his skin. *Please, God. Make me not be crazy,* she prayed, too weak to pull away from Jason even though she knew that snuggling against him wasn't right.

He settled back into the couch, cradling her. "Talk to me, Anna."

She wanted to. God knew she wanted to share everything with this man. These past few days, she'd been traveling the streets of New York with him on a so far fruitless search for her identity. Living with him, watching him on the news, hearing on the television show what he'd neglected to tell her himself—that his partner considered him the day's best catch—had so intensified her inappropriate attraction to Jason that being with him had, in some ways, become pure hell.

And in other ways, it seemed so natural. Jason knew her even if she didn't know herself. He knew what foods she liked best, what colors. He knew when she was bothered, when something amused her. Through him, she was gaining back bits of herself.

"Did I used to talk to you?" she asked now, allowing herself just a few seconds of touching him, of taking advantage of the strength he was so willing to share with her. Then she'd move, put the length of the couch between them, just as their lives pushed them apart in every other way.

"More than you talked to most people, I guess," he said. He'd considered her question carefully.

Anna was glad she didn't have to look at him. "Was I a pest?"

"Hell no!" His response was immediate, the first personal response he'd given her without first carefully choosing his words. "It used to drive me crazy the way you'd keep things to yourself," he continued. "If anything, I wished you'd open up more."

"I didn't talk much, huh?" Anna smiled. "Somehow that doesn't surprise me." In fact, this discovery felt gloriously right, familiar. Finally. Something felt familiar.

Jason tightened his hold on her. "You talked, Anna. Just not always about the things that mattered."

And what might those things have been? Maybe if she'd talked more, her mind wouldn't have needed to run and hide.

"Were we close, Jason?" She wanted to think that, though they hadn't been lovers, at least they'd been friends. Good friends. The kind of friend you could run to when the world was too much to bear.

Jason didn't answer. She'd whispered the words, so perhaps he hadn't heard.

As she lay there, her mind taunted her, playing absurd guessing games with his possible thoughts. How did you tactfully tell someone she wasn't your favorite person? Especially when that person was sitting half on top of you, helpless with need. How could he say that she'd been a difficult person to like? That while she was nice enough now, she'd been a pain in the ass in her other life? Or worse, how did he tell her that he'd tried his best to steer

clear of her because of the embarrassing unrequited
crush she'd made so obvious?

"Not as close as we are now," he answered after
such a long time had passed she'd been certain her
question had gone unnoticed.

Listening to his heart beat, she thought about his
answer. *Not as close as we are now.* She wanted to
ask him to explain, but was afraid to push him too
far. She was afraid of his answer. Was something
the matter with her that made it hard for people to
get close to her? Had she been the type of person
that someone good and decent like Jason wouldn't
want to be close to?

The damn black hole that was her mind tormented
her with its silence, frustrating her, angering her.
What the hell had happened to her? What had driven
her to running away from herself?

"Is that why I didn't contact you when I came to
New York?" The warmth of his arms gave her the
courage to ask.

"There was no reason you should have," he said,
his voice even, as though he was reporting the news.
"You didn't even know where I lived."

She continued to lie pressed against him, the darkness loosening her tongue. "Did I know you'd
moved to New York?"

"You knew I was going to."

"You didn't tell me goodbye when you left?"

"No."

So they must not have been all that close. "Did
you tell my sister goodbye?"

"Yes," he said, still reporting impassively. "I

saw her before I left. You'd gone down to San Diego. She said she'd say goodbye for me.''

Which made perfect sense.

The warmth of Jason's hands radiated through the thin silk of her gown, and as she relaxed, Anna was suddenly too aware of them clasped just beneath her right breast. He was wearing nothing but a pair of thin cotton shorts, hastily donned, if the undone drawstring at the waistband was any indication.

And as she studied that waistband in the shadows, Anna noticed something else, something that sent her heart slamming against her ribs. He was aroused.

Her throat felt dry; her nipples tightened. She could move just a little bit lower and his hands would slide over her aching breast. Just a little bit lower...

''Do you have any idea who the father of my baby is?'' Her words crashed into the intimate silence that had fallen around them. She had to keep her mind on what mattered, or she was going to make a terrible mistake. One she wouldn't be able to live with when she regained her memory—and her life.

''None.'' The word was clipped, his hold on her loosening.

''Are you just saying that, or do you really not know?''

He sat up on the edge of the couch, setting her away from him, leaning forward with his hands clasped between his knees. ''I had no idea you were seeing anyone.''

''But—''

"It's late, Anna," he interrupted. "No more questions tonight, okay?"

"Just one more, Jason, please." She had to know. Especially after the way she'd just reacted to him, she had to know.

"What?" He turned to look at her, frowning, his eyes shuttered in the shadows.

"Was I the type to sleep around?"

He jumped up from the couch. "What kind of question is that?"

"Please, Jason," she begged, burying her pride to find the truth that was haunting her, the truth she feared almost as much as she feared never finding it. "Was I the type to sleep around?"

He stared at her silently, a shadow in the dark. But his silence drove her on, her stomach knotting. Was it possible that *she* hadn't known who'd fathered her baby? Even before she'd lost her memory?

"I have to know."

His shoulders relaxed, but the frown remained. "I wouldn't have thought so."

"You don't know for sure?"

"No. I don't know for sure."

IF THEY DIDN'T FIND her place soon, he was going to have to tell her who he was. Traipsing around Manhattan on foot in the hopes she'd notice something she'd missed from the cab had done nothing but tire her—and stretch his endurance so dangerously thin he was actually considering trying a little psychology of his own. He'd been tempted from the first moment he'd walked into her hospital room, when she looked at him with the eyes of a stranger. Tempted to lay her down in his bed, strip away her clothes and talk to her with his body as he'd done so often in the past. He just couldn't believe that once he'd made love to her she wouldn't remember him, wouldn't remember the love they'd shared.

"God, I hate that place," she said, her voice tired, worn. They were midtown, not far from the station, but several blocks from Central Park where he'd had the cab drop them off.

Feeling guilty for pushing her too far too fast in his own selfish need to get her out of his apartment before he did something he'd regret, it was a full moment before Jason saw what she was talking about.

Central Deli and Restaurant.

But she loved deli food. And Central was the best. On East Thirty-fourth Street it was a bit of a jog from the station, but the restaurant was good enough to be one of Sunny's current favorites. So why would Anna hate it?

How did she know she hated it? Jason stopped in his tracks, the flow of Manhattan pedestrian traffic bumping into him, and Anna, too, as he pulled her to a halt beside him.

"You remembered something," he said.

Shock crossed her face, followed almost immediately by a smile that took his breath away. "Yeah," she said, grinning. "I guess I did."

The crowd moved around them, too intent on business to be slowed down by a couple of idiots grinning at each other on the sidewalk. "So why do you hate Central?" Jason asked.

"I haven't a clue." She laughed out loud at the absurdity of the situation.

Jason grinned, taking her hand as they finally had to give in and join the Friday after-work throng. He hadn't realized until that moment how worried he'd been that the doctor had been wrong, that Anna's memory loss was permanent, that maybe there *had* been some brain damage.

"Do you think I lived around here?" she asked him as they reached the end of the block.

"It's possible. We can check the phone book, call places nearby."

"I'll make a list tonight while you're at work."

Galvanized by Anna's small victory, Jason insisted on walking around the block three more times, making sure she didn't miss even a speck of gravel on the sidewalk. She'd been there before. Anything could spark a memory, lead them to her life, get her out of his.

And suddenly he wasn't sure he should push her. She'd remembered something. That was enough for one day. Telling her he had to get to work, he dropped her off at the apartment and took a cab to the station. And immediately called Abby.

HE AND ANNA spent the next morning sitting on his couch, the list of phone numbers she'd made the night before on the coffee table in front of them, taking turns with his mobile phone—but every call they made was another dead end. No landlord in the immediate vicinity of Central Deli had ever heard of Anna Hayden, no one had had a tenant missing for the past several days, not one they were aware of, anyway. No one recognized her description.

But Anna wouldn't be daunted. "I remembered that place, Jason," she said late that morning. "I *did* have a life here and I'm going to find it."

Jason couldn't help but admire her persistence, her surge of confidence springing from one small victory.

"Then get back on that phone, woman."

She picked the phone up and started to dial, but stopped. "You telling me what to do?" she asked, her eyes glinting with laughter.

"Not if you don't want me to." She never had liked to be ordered about; gently directed by Abby always, but never ordered.

"Good, 'cause I make my own decisions," she announced, dialing the next number on their list.

They were the sweetest words Jason had ever heard her utter.

THEY FINALLY HIT pay dirt midway through the afternoon. Jason had run through his introduction by rote, already hearing the negative response on the other end of the line before realizing he hadn't received one. The brisk woman wouldn't confirm that Anna was one of her tenants, said she managed so many buildings she couldn't keep track of who lived in them, but she agreed to look at her records.

She called back five minutes later, telling them to

meet her at a brownstone in Gramercy, not too far from Central Deli.

A SATURDAY-AFTERNOON lull hung over the city, streets filled with more shopping bags than briefcases, but the traffic was steady, cabs honking, cars zipping in and out of spaces they should never have tried to inch through. And suddenly Anna wanted to stay right there, enjoying the sun on her skin, and watch the people, wonder where they were going and why. Anything but walk the two more blocks to the life that was waiting for her.

She wasn't going to be able to stand it if this was another dead end. If the apartment wasn't hers. And she was scared to death about what might happen if it *was*. Would she remember it? Remember everything? Was she ready to face whatever she'd run away from?

Did she want to go back?

Living with Jason was the only life she knew. And after just a few days, it was a life she was happy with.

So what if it wasn't real?

And what if she discovered her old life and still didn't remember it? If the apartment was hers and none of it was familiar? Could she carry on without any memories? Did she have any choice?

Butterflies swarmed her stomach as she and Jason approached the building. They'd covered the last few blocks silently, and Anna couldn't help wondering what he was thinking. Was he thanking his lucky stars that he was about to be rid of her?

She had to admit that as much as she liked living with him, as secure, as welcome, as he'd made her feel, she hated having to rely on him. Hated him knowing she had to rely on him. Hated being nothing more than a charity case.

She climbed the steps to the brownstone, praying the apartment they'd come to see was hers.

But what was she going to do when Jason left her there all alone?

CHAPTER SEVEN

ANNA HATED the apartment. Brown vinyl furniture, scarred tables, not even a view out the one tiny window. The only redeeming things about the place were its tidiness and gleaming wooden floor.

"I don't recognize any of it," she said, feeling like a trespasser in a stranger's home—a stranger's life. But Mrs. Walters had recognized Anna, had shown them Anna's name on the mailbox just before she'd given them the key to the apartment. She'd left before Anna could ask the woman any questions but not before making it clear that Anna could stay only as long as she wasn't a bother to anyone—they weren't in the health-care business—and as long as Anna paid her rent.

"Relax, Anna," Jason said. He was standing by the nook that served as a kitchen, watching her. "You rented it furnished and you've only lived here a couple of months."

Relax. She'd just been made to feel like some kind of freak by her landlady, she didn't recognize a single stick of furniture, didn't like it either. Somehow she didn't think this was a relaxing situation. Damn him and his optimism, anyway. What did he know about losing all knowledge of everything you'd been, everything you'd ever hoped or dreamed to be? What did he know about letting yourself down so badly?

Crossing to the far corner of the apartment, Anna flung open the closet door, revealing a sparse row of uncomfortable-looking cotton shorts and shirts. She hated the clothing more than she hated the furniture. "Did these come with the place, too?" she asked, doing her best to stave off an attack of panic with a show of anger.

It was bad enough that nothing was familiar, but she didn't even like the stuff she was seeing. What if she didn't like the woman she'd been any better?

Jason crossed the room, dismissing the clothes with barely a glance as he took her by the shoulders. "You must have wanted a change when you came to New York," he said, holding her gaze with his own. "You never wore shorts."

She wasn't ready to be mollified. Not even by him. "It's not a good change."

"So don't wear them," he said, rubbing her shoulders. "But stop being so hard on yourself."

More than his words, the look in his eyes spoke to her, telling her he believed in her, that he knew she'd make it through this awful time.

But how could she believe in herself when her loss of memory was proof of her inability to handle her life?

"It's been almost a week, Jason. Don't you think I should be getting somewhere by now?"

"Dr. Gordon said it could take a while. You remembered the deli. That's a start."

And with that she would have to be satisfied. Except she didn't feel satisfied at all. Looking around, she tried to see the room from another perspective, as if this were all happening to someone else. How should a woman in her situation react? What should she do? What was the answer?

She just didn't know.

A perfunctory search of the apartment turned up a checkbook with a balance that would see her through several months; there were lots of Saltine crackers stashed in a drawer of the end table by the pullout couch, in the bathroom cupboard, in the single kitchen cupboard with a couple of cans of soup to go with them. The only other personal items were a laptop computer Jason said she'd used to keep her personal finance records, and a beautiful music box shaped like a castle. Jason listened to the tune, rewound it and listened again. He seemed more than casually interested in the box, almost as if surprised to see it there; but when she asked him about it, he merely shrugged and said she'd received the box from a friend.

And—in a table drawer—a personal address book. Shaking, afraid to open it, she stared at the flowered cover.

Eyes closed, she held the book to her breast. Between its covers lay details of her life, people she'd known. And suddenly she couldn't open the book quickly enough. Scanning the pages so urgently she almost tore them, her gaze flitted from one entry to the next, until she reached the last page.

"Nothing," she said as the book fell from her

fingers. "I don't recognize a single name, not a place, not a number. I don't even recognize the handwriting." Her eyes burned with tears, her heart with failure.

"I've never seen this before," Jason said. She heard him pick up the book, riffle through the pages, and just didn't care. She was a great big nothing. The father of her baby could be listed there, and she wouldn't even know it.

"They're all from back home," Jason said, having reached the last page of the book.

"You know them?"

"Every one of them."

"We were that close that you knew everyone I knew?"

Setting the book on the end table, Jason pivoted away from her. "We ran in the same circles, shared a lot of mutual friends," he said. "This book looks new, as if you copied those numbers all at the same time."

She'd noticed that, too. Every entry was in the same ink, the handwriting neat.

"And I never met a person, made a phone call, wrote down an address since coming to New York?" she asked. She couldn't help the bitterness she heard in her voice. It was as if she didn't even exist anymore.

"You had a planner you kept things in," Jason said as if just now remembering. "Everything from business cards to appointments. You carried it in your purse."

"Which was lost in the crash." She was not having a good day.

After knocking fruitlessly on the doors of her immediate neighbors—they were either not at home or said she'd kept so much to herself they knew nothing about her—Anna and Jason stood awkwardly in her apartment again, surrounded by furniture neither of them recognized. And then there was nothing else to do but say goodbye. Jason invited her to spend one last night at his place, but precisely because she was tempted, she declined his offer. It was Saturday night, and he was sure to have his pick of beautiful women with whom to spend it. His beautiful co-anchor, Sunny Lawson, for one. The woman had undoubtedly been more than patient.

Jason accepted her refusal easily, almost insultingly easily, but Anna couldn't blame him. Instead, she chastised herself for being hurt, made certain he saw none of her uncertainty as she waved to him at the door and kept herself well hidden as she watched him all the way down the block through her one small window.

Then, desultorily, she made another search of her apartment, acquainting herself with where she kept the silverware and napkins, what kind of makeup she used, her few pieces of jewelry. She added her locket, which she'd been keeping in the inside pocket of her new purse, to the box containing her other jewelry. And then pulled it right back out again, dropping it into an envelope before placing it back inside her purse.

Dr. Gordon had warned her about depression, so

she continued to poke into drawers, touching her things, trying to get a sense of the woman she'd been, pretending that she cared. But she still felt as though she were trespassing in a stranger's life, one she couldn't identify with, one she wasn't sure she even wanted to know.

First thing tomorrow she was going shopping for some more dresses. Right after she packed up every last pair of shorts for the Salvation Army.

Finding the key to her mailbox in a corner of the kitchen drawer, Anna went down to check her mail, retrieving only a couple of bills and some solicitations. She returned the wave of a small dark-haired woman coming out of a door down the hall from her before locking herself back inside her apartment, making sure to secure all three locks as Jason had instructed.

The entire episode ate up fifteen minutes of an evening that stretched beyond eternity. With the walls of the small apartment closing in on her, increasing the agitation that already drove her day in and day out, she sank onto the couch, telling herself to relax, to hold on, to be patient and let her mind heal itself. Yet the future loomed ahead of her, a dark specter in the night, frightening her with its blankness. What was she going to do with the rest of her life? What was she going to do tonight, and tomorrow, and the day after that?

She had no idea where she'd worked, if she'd worked, but judging by the size of her checking account, work wasn't going to be of pressing concern anytime soon—she was going to be receiving a settlement from the city, as well. Besides, it wasn't as if she'd be much use to anyone at the moment, not having the slightest idea what she could do or memory of any training she'd had. And there was always the chance that her employer would view her exactly as her landlady had, a burden to be pitied. Nothing more.

For now, work was out.

Her stomach tightened, the horrible fear looming darkly over her again, consuming her. What was she going to do if she never remembered? And what was going to happen if she did? What horrible things would be there waiting? Would she still not be able to handle them? Would she flip out? Have a breakdown? Go mad?

She thought about calling Abby. About California. About going home. At least there she'd have someone to talk to. Someone to take care of her. Someone to commit her if she went over the edge.

And she thought about Jason. His tall athletic body. The way his eyes always made her feel warm, special. His laugh. His charm. His arousal the other night.... And she thought about Sunny Davis in his apartment, maybe that very moment.

She thought about the child she carried, the conception that had vanished from her memory as if it had never been. The man whose baby she carried. Then she started to cry. Was he out there somewhere thinking she'd deserted him? Or had he deserted her? Would he think her a weak fool for having a mind that checked out as it pleased?

Did *she* think herself a fool?

Anna stopped crying. Stood. Paced her small living room. And faced the truth. She did think herself a fool. And worse. She hated herself for refusing to deal with her life and escaping into this…emptiness. Hated the weakness, the cowardice surrounding her condition. But worst of all, she hated herself for wishing she could run back to Jason, bury herself in his arms and never remember at all.

HE BOUGHT HER groceries, called her four times a day, asked her to breakfast, to lunch, and beat the hell out of a racquetball while convincing himself that he was just being a friend, that he wasn't getting involved. That he'd be able to walk away.

He always had, hadn't he? Every time his mother called, he was there for her, no strings attached. No expectations. No recriminations when his birthday rolled around, Christmas, sometimes even a year or two with no word from her. Helping was what a man did. What a man *should* do.

"Jason?" He'd known it was Anna on the phone even before he answered it Tuesday morning. She was the only one who would dare call him before noon. In recent months, as his nights stretched till dawn, he hadn't been awake much before then.

"I found a file box in the back of the closet," she said. She was sounding stronger each day, taking control of her life. He admired the hell out of her. "There's this pay stub, just like you said there might be, from a place called Old World Alterations. It's in Little Italy."

Grabbing his keys off the coffee table, Jason said, "I'm on my way."

THE PLACE WAS a modern day sweatshop. Standing with Anna on the sidewalk outside the building that gray New York day, Jason stared with horror at all the women crammed into the small space, some sitting at sewing machines, others in hard-backed chairs, stitching by hand. No one spoke. No one smiled. But their fingers flew, racing to finish one job only to start another.

Sick to his stomach at the thought of Anna sitting in there like that, working as though she was a slave, Jason turned away. He'd seen enough. If Anna had worked there, she would no longer. He'd pay her damn rent if he had to. She wasn't going back in there.

Except she was. She reached for the door handle. "Anna."

She dropped her hand and turned, surprised, almost as if she'd forgotten him.

"Do you remember being here?" he asked her.

She shook head distractedly.

"Do you know if I can sew?" she asked him.

The way she said it was so odd he had to ask, "Why?"

"I feel like I can sew," she said slowly.

She was remembering. "You can."

Someone bumped into her and she stepped back along the wall of the building. "Am I any good?"

"Very." She'd made money—a lot of it—sewing

up Abby's designs for a line of children's wear that sold in exclusive shops all over Southern California.

Frowning, she looked at the women. "I don't think I like it," she said, sounding perplexed.

A sigh eased through Jason, releasing a spring of hope. He'd always suspected that sewing wasn't what Anna wanted to do, rather, what she did for Abby. But she'd never before admitted as much—even when he'd confronted her about it before leaving for New York. Perhaps, just perhaps, her memory loss was doing something for her he never could, getting her to know herself.

"Let's go in," Anna said. Her mind was obviously made up. She was going to follow up on this lead. Jason went with her inside.

"Anna!" The accented male voice came from someplace in the rear of the shop. "You've come back to us!"

Anna froze inside the door, immediately wary, though she had no idea why. The man sounded friendly enough. He'd been sitting at a desk and now he jumped up and came forward, weaving his thin body between the sewing machines.

Several women looked over at her behind his back, smiling tentatively, but then bowed their heads and resumed their work before she could return their smiles.

"I can't believe you've come back to us," the man said. Ignoring Jason, he reached for Anna's hand, kissing it before pulling her forward.

Anna wanted to slap him. In fact, the urge was so strong she had to move away.

She tried to concentrate on what he'd just said. He couldn't believe she'd come back. As though he hadn't been expecting to see her again. "I don't work here anymore?" she asked.

"Of course you work." He winked at her. "I give you lots of work!"

Jason stepped forward so that he stood between Anna and the man.

"You know about the subway crash," he said, his usual charm nonexistent. Anna had never seen him like this before.

"Oh!" The man hit his palm to his forehead. "It was you!" He looked at Anna. "The Anna they say was hurt. She was you?"

Anna nodded.

"And you still don't remember?"

Anna shook her head before realizing she was under no obligation to tell this man anything.

"My poor Anna," he said. "Come here and let your Roger make it all better." He tried to pull her into his arms, but Anna held back.

"My Roger?" she asked, managing little more than a whisper. Jason was frozen beside her.

"Of course you don't remember, but not to worry. I will remember for both of us." He grabbed Anna again, holding her close as he whispered, "What we had was good, no?"

Nausea overwhelmed her. It was all Anna could do not to be sick all over the man's dirty white shirt.

"You were so good, my little Anna." He kissed his fingertips.

Had she actually slept with this creep?

Oh, God. Was it his baby she carried?

With a quick look at Jason's horrified face, she dashed for the bathroom, getting there just in time to lose her breakfast. Hunched over the toilet, she heaved until she thought her ribs were going to break, but nothing could take away the sick feeling washing over her.

How could she go out there? Jason had heard the man. He'd obviously reached the same conclusion she had. And was disgusted. How could she ever face him again? How could she ever face herself?

Finally she rose, wetting a piece of paper towel under the sink and holding it against her burning face. If this was the life she'd left behind, she'd rather die than go back to it.

"Anna?" Jason's voice came through the door.

"Anna?" Roger's suggestive calling of her name nearly sent her back to the toilet.

"Ohhh, go away," she cried softly to herself, and opened the door.

"You're still sick from your crash?" Roger asked, not quite as enthusiastic once he got a look at her pale face.

All Anna could see was Jason, standing in front of the other man, his eyes searching her face intently. "You okay?"

She shook her head, silently begging him to get her out of there, to make the nightmare go away.

The phone rang and one of the women answered it, calling Roger to talk to someone named Baker.

"I'll be right back," he said to Anna as he walked off.

"Pssst."

Anna looked at Jason. Had he said something?

"Pssst."

A woman over by the door was trying to get her attention. Jason motioned Anna ahead, and they eased their way to the front of the shop.

"You no work here no more," the woman whispered in fractured English. She stared at the pair of men's slacks she was hemming by hand, her fingers never missing a stitch as they flew along the dark material.

Anna didn't respond, afraid to draw attention to the fact that the woman was speaking. But she nodded, hoping the woman would understand that she was listening.

"Quit, six, eight weeks ago. Very sudden. No one say why."

Exchanging a glance with Jason, Anna nodded again.

"Boss, he like you. Not like he like good worker." She lifted the pants to her mouth, cut the thread with her teeth and looked out the window.

The conversation was over.

Roger could still be heard in the back of the shop, speaking rapidly in a foreign language, glancing out every now and then, making certain Anna was still there. Jason grabbed Anna by the arm and pulled her out the door of the shop into the gloomy morning. She hurried silently beside him as he led her down the street, eager to put as much distance as she could between her and the disgusting slimy man whose touch had made her want to curl up and die.

The man who could very well be the father of her baby.

JASON DIDN'T SLOW down. Not even after they'd traveled enough blocks and made enough turns to have lost the bastard should he *have* followed them. He continued to walk simply because he didn't know what else to do. He had to think, to make sense out of the past half hour, consider the woman he'd known and loved for more than two years and somehow find the truth.

"Am I carrying his child?" Anna's cry was so distraught passersby on the sidewalk stopped and stared.

"No!" Jason said, pulling her against him, sheltering her from a young man who was sending her furtive looks over his shoulder.

"How do you know?" she asked more softly. He could hear tears in her voice. Tears and something else—a distress so deep he knew she'd never recover if her fear turned into truth.

"I know you." But did he? "You'd never have gone for a man like that, Anna. Never."

The Anna he'd known wouldn't have. But the Anna he'd known would never have slept with another man only six weeks after leaving his bed. Or left Abby, either.

CHAPTER EIGHT

NEITHER OF THEM had an appetite for lunch and, at Anna's suggestion, headed back to her apartment. She had to search it again, tear it apart, look through everything she could find for something that would prove Roger was not the father of her child. Jason helped her look, but found nothing.

She had books—lots of those—blank computer disks, they even found the name of the obstetrician she'd made her first appointment with, one she missed the day after the subway crashed.

Getting out the phone directory, Jason started calling alteration shops in the area. None of them had employed or ever heard of Anna Hayden. Anna contacted the phone company, the electric company, asking for the job information recorded on her billing records. Old World Alterations.

"The first person someone calls after changing jobs usually isn't a utility company," Jason pointed out when she hung up the phone for the second time.

Anna felt like crying. She could feel the tears welling behind her lids and forced them away. On top of everything else, she wasn't going to cry on him. Jason hated tears.

Her head shot up, her heart beating against her ribs as she stared at him.

"What?" he asked.

She shook her head, flooded with confusing emotions, glee, fear, a sense of helpless foreboding left from the morning's ordeal—and hope. Grabbing her shoulders, Jason pulled her closer, holding her gaze. "What, Anna? You look like you've seen a ghost."

Her tears won the battle, trickling down her cheeks, but she smiled up at him, grateful beyond anything she'd ever known to have this one precious memory. This connection. To him.

"You hate tears," she said.

She laughed at the astonished look in his eyes. The delight. And was puzzled by the shadows that immediately followed. "You remember me?" he asked, letting her go.

She shook her head, still smiling in spite of his puzzling behavior. "Just that you hate tears." She really had known him before. Not that she'd ever doubted his word, but it was just so damn good to know something simply because she knew, not because she'd been told.

He nodded. "You're right. I do. Or I did. Until a friend pointed out how ridiculous I was to feel threatened by a simple expression of emotion." He continued to study her, his hands in the pockets of his chinos.

"Why would I know such a thing?"

"We went to see *While You Were Sleeping*. Your sister balled like a baby and I got on her case for it."

"*While You Were Sleeping?* Is that a movie?"

He nodded, still watching her.

"Why'd it make her cry?"

"Because all the woman in the movie wanted was to be part of a family and yet, in spite of her efforts, she was always on the outside looking in."

Sounded to Anna like something that might have touched Jason, as well, knowing what she did about his lonely childhood.

"So who had the guts to tell you how ridiculous it was to feel threatened by tears?"

"You did." He turned away from her. "In Abby's defense."

For the first time in days he was measuring his words again. There was more to that story. He just wasn't telling her. But at the moment she was so giddy with her proof of his place in her life she couldn't worry about the secrets lurking just beyond her grasp.

She remembered knowing Jason.

HER NEWFOUND REMEMBRANCE, minute as it was, had a disturbing repercussion. Sitting on her couch, munching an early dinner, Anna watched Jason on the six-o'clock news that evening. She took pride in how he looked in his navy jacket with the station's emblem above the pocket; only Jason's broad shoulders could look that good. She loved the way his eyes crinkled when he smiled, approved of his witty repartee and generally felt privileged for knowing personally one of the city's most sought-after bachelors. And was shocked at the proprietary nature of her feelings.

When Sunny Lawson laid her perfectly manicured fingers on his forearm, Anna wanted to claw her eyes out. Afraid of the vehemence of the feeling, of what it meant, she forced herself to think about all the reasons Jason needed a woman like Sunny in his life, why, as a friend, she, Anna, had to hope they'd be very happy together. Why she had no business feeling jealous over a man she wasn't free to have. Even if she wasn't living in this half world of no memories, she had no right to Jason. She was bound to another man—and to the child she'd created with him.

Making herself watch Jason and Sunny together, Anna tried not to care. But no matter the logic of her reasoning, she couldn't stop her chest from tightening, her skin chilling, the butterflies invading her stomach.

And the more she panicked, the more panicked she grew. Was she so unstable that she was going to fall apart at everything? The woman she was now had only known Jason a matter of days. She couldn't possibly care for him so much that merely seeing another woman touch him was ripping her heart out.

But Jason was all she had. The only person she knew. It was natural for her to feel a bit possessive, she thought, trying to reassure herself. She just had to make certain she didn't get carried away with her possessiveness.

Jason had other friends. He played racquetball. One time when she'd been at his place, he'd received a phone call from a buddy of his in California. She wasn't the only person in his life by a long shot—wasn't even the most important person in his life.

Suddenly, out of nowhere, Anna was struck with the need to talk to Abby. Jason wasn't the only person in her life, either. He wasn't even the only one who cared. She knew Abby had been keeping in close contact with Jason. He'd told her so.

Picking up the phone with shaking fingers, Anna realized she didn't even know Abby's number. She refused to be daunted, dialing the operator, instead, requesting the area code for Oxnard, California, dialing long-distance information, only half-aware that she knew exactly how to do so. Yes, there was a listing for Abigale Hayden. Anna scribbled while an automated voice intoned the number.

She dialed the number quickly, giving herself no time to change her mind. She'd only talk for a couple of minutes. She just had to connect with someone who knew her, who hopefully loved her, unconditionally, as family was meant to. Someone who would still love her if Roger was the father of her baby. Someone who would love her even if she found herself hopelessly, dangerously attracted to another man. Someone who knew Jason.

But before the phone rang even once, Anna hung up, remembering Dr. Gordon's warning not to contact her family. And even more, his admonition to learn to trust herself. She'd had a real live memory that day. She couldn't give up now, couldn't let herself down. As the doctor had reminded her more than once, she'd requested a year away from her family for a reason. And that reason might very well be connected to the vacation her mind had taken.

She had to learn to trust herself. Regain some faith in herself. And that was going to take time. She had to take back control of her life or live forever like this—in a world without color, without depth, without memories.

Turning off the television set, Anna grabbed one of the many books stacked on her closet shelf, drew a hot bath and ordered herself to settle in and read. To focus her mind on something else for a while, to think about somebody else's problems. She made it through only a couple of pages before realizing that she'd read the story before. She couldn't remember how it ended, but she knew she'd read it.

And several hours later, as she lay in the middle of the pullout bed, snuggled in her nightgown under the covers, and finished the book, she couldn't help replotting the ending. And that was something she'd done before, too.

HE SHOULD HAVE learned his lesson, but Jason couldn't seem to stop himself from spending most of his free time with Anna. She was like a drug, an addiction, had been since the first time he'd ever met her. He was also thinking about her too much, preoccupied when he should have been focused—on the racquetball court, at the station, out with Sunny. But he couldn't just desert Anna. Not now. Not when she needed him. Not when her eyes lit up every time he walked into the room. Not when she said his name in that husky voice. Not when he...

It couldn't lead to anything. She had other priorities, people who came before he did in her life, in her heart. But where was the harm in helping her? He was a strong guy. He could handle it, he assured a couple of his buddies from California when they phoned. He was fine, he told his mother when, for once, she remembered to call to wish him happy birthday.

What he couldn't handle, couldn't accept, was walking away from a friend in need.

And Anna was a friend in need, he told himself the following Saturday. She needed a day out of the city. A day of freedom when she could be the same as everyone else around her, carefree, enjoying herself. A day at the beach. He wanted to take her somewhere that might spark a memory—of him, of the love they'd shared. They'd been on a beach the first time they'd made love. And the last time.

His Jaguar was waiting for him, sleek, its white paint gleaming, the leather seats cool in the dark of the garage. Flipping the switch to put the top down, he waited for it to curl into the back of the car, securing the leather cover around the entire mechanism. Jason counted on very little in his life, invested his heart stingily, but he cared about his car. It was the one thing he'd really wanted that he'd had the power to get, to keep. He'd worked hard, demanding from his career what he couldn't demand from his personal life, fighting for the top spot in a competitive field, settling for nothing less. The Jag was his reward. And his reminder.

Anna had loved his car. She'd loved the wind blowing through her hair, unconcerned when the long strands became tangled because of her refusal to pull it back, laughing out loud when he pressed the accelerator to the floor, the thrill of speed turning her on.

"What a gorgeous machine!" When he collected her Saturday morning, her eyes lit up just as they'd used to. "Why haven't I seen it before now?"

She had. And she'd run her hands along its smooth contours just as she was doing now. "The closest garage I could find is fifteen miles away from my apartment," he said, opening her door for her.

She climbed in and he shut the door, asking, "You have your swimsuit?"

"I'm wearing it." Pulling down the top of her dress, she showed him.

Yep, she was wearing it. A tight-fitting one-piece black affair that showed him the cleavage he already knew intimately. Suddenly it was his turn to appreciate a sleek body. Except that he couldn't run his hands along this one the way she'd done moments before. Not anymore.

"You'll let me drive it sometime, won't you? After I get my new license?"

Jason froze, halfway around the car, staring at the back of her head. She finally turned, frowning at him.

"What?" she asked. "I'm a great driver." And then, "Aren't I?"

"Yeah, growing up near L.A. you have to be, but what makes you think I'd let you drive my car?"

She shrugged. "You're a nice guy."

Giving some inane reply, Jason continued on to his side of the car, sliding into the driver's seat with the ease of practice. For a second there he'd thought she'd remembered. In the old days, back when they loved each other, her driving his car had been a standing gag between them. She always wanted to. He always let her—and was nervous as a ninny sitting beside her the whole time. But she'd always made it up to him in the most glorious ways. More than once, before they'd ever made it out of the car....

"I met this girl in the hallway yesterday," Anna said, breaking into his thoughts as he headed out of the city. "Maggie Simmons."

"Someone you knew before?" He downshifted, trying to ignore the feel of his hand brushing against her leg. He moved over to the right lane.

"Not well." Anna frowned. "Like all the others she said I kept mostly to myself."

Jason nodded, content to listen to her. She'd been giving him hour-by-hour accounts of her day ever since she'd left the hospital, sharing more of her thoughts with him in the past two weeks than in the two years they'd been lovers. He would gladly have spent the rest of his life listening.

"Has it ever occurred to you that I'm not a very friendly person?" she asked.

Keeping his speed moderate so he could hear her, Jason considered her question. God, he hated the secrets between them. Not just the things she couldn't remember, but his lies by omission.

"You were always private, honey, but never unfriendly," he said, weighing his words. He wasn't a doctor. How the hell did he know how much he should tell her? And how, loving her as he had, did he stomach keeping the truth from her?

They drove silently for a while, Anna's expression smoothing as the Jag ate up the miles, putting more and more distance between them and the city.

Anna at last broke the silence. "Maggie told me something kind of odd."

"What's that?"

"Well, she's pretty sure I haven't worked in the past six weeks because I was always home."

"Nothing too odd about that if you were having troubles finding a job you wanted. It's not like you couldn't afford to take a little time off."

"My money isn't going to last forever."

Jason acknowledged the truth of that with a shrug. She was getting a settlement from the city, though not enough to live on for the rest of her life. But she had lots of time to worry about earning her keep and more pertinent things about which to worry.

"Anyway, Maggie said sometimes I'd come home carrying full garbage bags like some kind of bag lady." Anna said the words hesitantly, stealing a glance at him as if to assess his reaction.

Jason chuckled. "Surely you aren't thinking you were a bag lady."

"Of course not!" Anna said indignantly. "But you have to admit, it's odd."

"Only because you don't seem to have several garbage bags worth of stuff in your entire apartment."

"Oh, well, that's the other weird thing." Anna's hair flew about her face, brushing his shoulder as she turned her head toward him. "Apparently, after bringing in the bags, I'd be home all day, sometimes several days in a row, and then I'd leave again, carrying the same full bags."

"And what do you make of all this?"

"I did people's laundry?" She grinned at him.

Jason grinned back. "Where, in the tub?"

"I had a bird-sitting business and was smuggling in birdcages?"

He hooted with laughter. "You're afraid of birds."

She frowned at him. "Why on earth would anyone be afraid of a poor defenseless creature like a bird?"

"You saw Alfred Hitchcock's movie *The Birds* when you were little."

"And?" she prompted.

"Swarms of birds practically take over a town, and they attack people. It gets pretty ugly."

"I wonder why a little girl would be watching such a thing?"

He'd asked the same question when she'd first confessed her childhood fear. It was the first time she'd told him anything about growing up with only her sisters for guidance. The three had spent hours in front of the television watching programs they never should have seen, waiting patiently for the parents they adored to get home from work. There had been times when they'd fallen asleep, still waiting.

She wouldn't like the answer any better than he had.

"I wasn't there," was all he said. "Anyway, it wasn't birds. What else can you suggest?"

"I liked to shop, but suffered from buyer's remorse?"

Her stories got wilder the farther they drove. She was the bagman in a smuggling ring. A drunk—the bottles empty when she carried them back out, of course. A thief with a conscience, stealing and then returning what she stole. By the time they'd parked and gathered the cooler and blanket from the trunk, Jason had almost forgotten the troubles they'd left behind. For a moment out of time he had his Anna back.

Following Jason, Anna took a deep breath of the salty ocean air. "I love the beach, don't I?" she asked, but she didn't need the confirmation. Something else she just knew. Like she knew she was a good driver. Things were coming back. Too slowly, to be sure, but how glorious to begin to know herself. To really know the person in whose body she lived.

"You had a cottage on the beach," Jason told her, coming around the car.

Had she stayed there alone? she wanted to know, but didn't ask. She wasn't going to ruin this time with him by worrying about things she had no control over. Not today.

The sand felt like heaven between her toes. So familiar. So good. She could imagine herself lying in it, the grains closing around her body like a glove.

"Let's build a castle," she said suddenly, plopping down close to the water.

Dropping the blanket and cooler, Jason joined her. "Watch out," he warned, settling in as though he expected to be there awhile.

"Whatever for?" Anna asked. How difficult could it be? Anyone could see that all you needed was the right mixture of water and sand to construct just about any shape you wanted. It didn't take a memory to pile up a bunch of sand.

Jason pulled off his shirt, threw it down and stretched out on it, his elbow in the sand, his hand supporting his head. "Just wait and see."

He looked resigned, expectant. And gorgeous.

"Did you play sports in school?" Anna forced her eyes back to the job at hand. The sun was hot enough without her thoughts making her even hotter.

"Quarterback of my high-school football team," he said, clearly pleased with himself.

She wasn't surprised. His body was a work of art.

"Did you go to college?"

He nodded. "On a swimming scholarship. Care to race me?"

Anna grabbed a cup out of the cooler, packing it with sand. "In a minute. Let me finish this," she said.

"That'll take more than a minute."

She didn't care if it took all day if it meant he'd

still be lying there beside her. Her stomach was doing flip-flops just looking at him. But she couldn't make herself stop stealing covert glances.

"What school'd you go to?" she asked, making room for the small tower that had to go on one corner of the castle.

He'd gone to USC, had a masters degree in communication, could ski as well as he swam, spent summers playing beach volleyball and had lost his virginity when—

"What?" he snapped, sitting up when she asked that last question.

"Sorry," she said, using both hands to dig her moat. "It just slipped out."

When it came to Jason, she had sex on the brain. She was praying that was because she didn't have much else there at the moment. But she wasn't convinced.

"Sixteen."

"Hmm?" she said, trying her best to concentrate on the sand castle.

"I was sixteen. She was a present from my father. He was supposed to have taken me skiing for my birthday, but had to fly to New York on business at the last minute."

"Some present."

Had that woman been worth being ditched by his father? To some guys, probably so. Anna wasn't so sure about Jason. His priorities were different. People were important to him. Commitment, loyalty were important to him. This was perfectly clear to her, even after having only known him less than two weeks. Why else would he be continuing to help her if not for his loyalty to her family?

Remembering what he'd told her about his youth, Anna wondered if he'd ever come first in his parents' lives. Hadn't they seen what a special person they'd created? She couldn't imagine not wanting to spend every minute she could with her baby as it was growing up, whether he was a model child or not. Life passed so quickly.

"She was actually kind of nice," Jason added almost as an afterthought. "I dated her for a while, until I realized that just because she was seeing me didn't mean she wasn't also working as a prostitute."

Anna didn't want to hear any more about it. She was sorry she'd ever asked.

"I'm sorry, Jason," she said, knowing the words weren't going to do anything to dispel the memories she'd roused.

"Don't be." He filtered a fistful of sand through his fingers. "It was a long time ago. And hey, for a kid with adolescent hormones, great sex isn't anything to scoff at."

"That's some castle!" A young couple strolling down the beach stopped beside them, interrupting just as Anna was getting jealous of a seventeen-year-old memory.

"One of her more basic attempts," Jason said.

The girl leaned down, marveling at the nooks and crannies. "Basic! She's an artist!"

Anna dug her moat a little deeper, hating the attention she'd inadvertently drawn to herself.

"Gee, lady, you're good!" a little boy said.

One by one, people of all ages came over, little kids who wanted to make a castle, too, their parents, assorted couples, several teenagers, even an old codger down on the beach with his metal detector, looking for Lord only knew what kind of treasure. But they all had one thing in common—shared amazement at Anna's creation.

Jason being Jason struck up a conversation with just about every one of them as they wandered over. Anna, feeling tongue-tied and uncomfortable, marveled again at his charm, his talent for making people feel at ease.

Embarrassed by the continued attention, she finally suggested they break out the lunch he'd brought along. But before they opened the cooler, she insisted on moving as far down the beach as she could get from the castle she'd made.

"I had no idea I was going to cause such a stir," she said. Looking back at it, she couldn't help but be proud of her work. She really was good. She'd had no idea.

"I did."

"I've done this before, huh?" she asked. She should have known something was up by Jason's reaction when she'd first sat down in the sand.

"Your sand sculptures have won prizes," Jason said, helping her to spread their blanket.

Anna laughed. "Get out of here."

"Kids used to knock on your door just to ask you to come out and play in the sand."

She froze, her hand half in and half out of the

cooler. She couldn't tell if he was pulling her leg or not, and it was suddenly important to her that he wasn't. For the first time since she'd awoken in this nightmare, she was discovering something about herself that she liked—a lot. She wanted to be the kind of person little kids knocked on the door to play with.

"Did I?" she asked.

"Of course."

Satisfied, feeling better than she had in days, she tucked her sandy damp dress beneath her and sat down to lunch.

She'd discovered a talent. She'd made a sand castle. She'd had fun.

CHAPTER NINE

BEDRAGGLED BUT SMILING, Anna climbed the steps to her apartment late that afternoon, meeting Maggie in the hallway.

"Looks like you had a day at the beach," Maggie said, pointing at Anna's damp and sandy dress. In spite of the bathing suit she had on, she'd never taken the dress off. She'd been too aware of Jason's half-naked body to be comfortable undressing with him so near, and too self-conscious of the fact that, though she wasn't yet showing, there was a baby growing inside her. She'd also seen that look in his eyes again.

"Jason took me," Anna said, smiling shyly at the other woman. She'd told Maggie about her amnesia when they'd met the day before, and also about Jason's rescue of her from nowhere land.

"You guys have dinner?" Maggie's short curls bobbed as she spoke, giving the impression that she was always on the move.

"No." Anna felt her stomach rumble even as she said the word. She may not feel pregnant yet, other than the occasional bouts of nausea, but she was hungry enough for two. "I imagine Jason had a date."

Maggie grinned. "It's so cool that you know him," she said.

Anna nodded, a little uncomfortable with Maggie's brash way, not sure how to respond. But she welcomed the woman's friendliness just the same. Especially when again faced with a lonely Saturday night of trying not to picture Jason with another woman. Anna and Jason spent days together. Never nights. She assumed he had less platonic ways to spend his evenings off than with a pregnant, confused family friend.

"So how about dinner? I made spaghetti and there's plenty," Maggie offered.

Anna shook her head instinctively and then stopped. "I'd like that," she said. "If it won't be too much of a bother."

"No bother at all. I'd love the company."

THE TWO HAD DINNER together twice more that next week. Once at Anna's. The other time at Maggie's. Maggie wanted to be an actress and waited tables four nights a week to make ends meet while she spent her days traipsing from one audition to the next. Anna didn't see what Maggie saw in her, a woman with no past, and feared sometimes that the only thing that kept Maggie coming back was pity. And yet Maggie's friendship felt genuine.

"Do you know if I was dating anyone?" Anna asked Maggie the following Thursday night. They were sitting in Maggie's apartment, and though she itched to tidy up some of the clutter, Anna liked being at her friend's place.

Maggie nodded, helping herself to another piece of the pepperoni pizza they'd ordered. "You mentioned having a date once or twice."

Suddenly not hungry, Anna asked, "Did you ever see the guy?"

"Yeah." Maggie frowned. "Once. I'm not even sure if it was the same guy each time. I just assumed it was. You weren't quite as easy to get to know back then."

"From what I can tell, I was a really private person," Anna admitted. "I'm not really sure how to go about the friend thing."

Except that she knew she wanted Maggie's friendship. She looked forward to their evenings together, to having another woman around to talk to, laugh with.

"Relax." Maggie grinned. "You're doing fine."

"WHAT DO YOU DO during the day?" Maggie asked on Wednesday of the following week. They'd gone to a deli around the corner for dinner and were on their way back to the brownstone.

"I walk in Gramercy Park." She might have hated her apartment, but she adored the gated park, she'd discovered, which was for residents' use only. "And I read a lot." Hearing herself, Anna was embarrassed by how boring her life must seem to her actress friend.

"That's all? I'd go nuts." Ever dramatic, Maggie rolled her eyes and pressed a hand to her chest.

Anna supposed to someone like Maggie it sounded like a prison sentence, but to Anna, this time was a gift; she could feel herself growing stronger with every day that passed—although she suspected it wouldn't be long before she was going to have to find something to do. One could only sit around getting strong for so long. Then you had to do something with that strength. Trouble was, she had no idea what she wanted to do. What she *could* do. Other than sew—and build sand castles. She didn't want to sew, and building castles was a bit difficult in the city.

"I also see Jason," she said, hating that she was actually trying to win Maggie's approval with the admission. It was more important that she approve of herself.

"Now that I could handle." Maggie grinned. "You guys an item yet?"

Anna laughed, embarrassed. "Of course not."

"Why not? He's gorgeous. You're gorgeous. A match made in heaven."

"I'm pregnant." Anna couldn't believe it when she just blurted the words.

Maggie stopped in her tracks, staring openmouthed at Anna. "Pregnant?"

Anna nodded, watching her friend, wishing she'd kept quiet. But she was going to be starting to show soon, and if she planned to continue this friendship, Maggie was going to have to know.

"How?"

Anna shrugged. "The usual way, I suppose," she said, echoing words she'd heard from Dr. Gordon.

"You mean you don't remember?" Maggie's

eyes widened, her New York accent more pronounced than usual. "It happened before...?"

Nodding again as Maggie's words trailed off, Anna started walking again. Maggie followed.

"Then you don't know who the father is?" Maggie asked, turning to watch Anna.

It sounded so horrible the way Maggie said it. Anna shook her head.

"Wow."

Exactly. But at least now Maggie knew.

"So how often you seeing Jason?" Maggie asked a few moments later.

"Almost every day."

Maggie stumbled. "You're kidding!"

"It's nothing, really," Anna said. But it was. She cherished every moment of her time with Jason. "We're just doing the tourist bit. He's only been in this city three months and with the new job and all hasn't done any sight-seeing yet. And it's not like I remember any of it even if I have seen it."

"You're touring the city with him and you call that nothing?" Maggie screeched. "You know how much I'd give for one lunch with someone like him?" She clearly thought Anna needed some brain readjustment. If only she knew. Anna was glad to see their brownstone just up ahead.

"It's completely platonic." If you didn't count the way her body had a mind of its own every time she was with Jason.

Maggie harrumphed. "Maybe you simply haven't figured out yet that he's nuts about you. A guy doesn't spend that much time with a girl unless he wants in her pants."

"Maggie!" After several days in Maggie's company Anna was still sometimes shocked by the other woman's New York bluntness. "And he's not nuts about me," she said. He couldn't be. Period. "He's just a friend. I think he feels sorry for me."

"Real sorry," Maggie said sarcastically. "Has he asked you up to his place yet?" Her question was accompanied by a sly lift of her eyebrows.

"I lived there for three days."

"I mean since then," Maggie said with exasperation.

"No. And he doesn't come to my place, either," Anna said before Maggie could ask. "We go out in public, in broad daylight. That's the way one tours the city."

"Just wait," Maggie said. "He'll ask you up to see his etchings."

"Trust me, he saves his etchings for other women, Maggie. I never even see him after two or three in the afternoon."

Maggie gave a disappointed sigh. "Have it your way."

"It's the way it is." The way it had to stay.

"So what's he like?" Maggie asked, stepping sideways to avoid a little boy on a bicycle.

Anna smiled. "I don't know... Charming. Intelligent. Nice."

"You go out with a man like that and you call him *nice?*"

Anything else she might see in Jason she couldn't

admit to herself, let alone Maggie. "He *is* nice." He was still taking pity on her, wasn't he? Although, if she was to be honest, there'd been more than one time since that night in his apartment when his interest in her had seemed like anything but pity. There was that peculiar look in his eyes...

"He's also to-die-for gorgeous, every inch male—even his eyes can knock you for a loop if you let them."

So Maggie had noticed. "He's just a friend, okay?" Anna couldn't think of him as anything else. To do so would be emotional suicide. If not now, then certainly when she regained her memory of the man whose child she carried.

"And he takes you out every day?"

"Not every day, but a lot." Anna was growing more and more uncomfortable with Maggie's questions. "We're seeing Manhattan one block at a time."

"You're in love with him, aren't you?" Maggie said suddenly, stopping at the steps of their brownstone.

"Of course not!" Hadn't Maggie been listening? "I'm not, Maggie," she added when her friend still looked unconvinced. "We're just friends."

"Well, if you're not in love with him, you should be." Maggie persisted. "Take a chance, girl. A relationship with that man would be...*incomparable.*"

Somehow Anna knew that, her lack of anything to compare it to notwithstanding. But that changed nothing. "Maggie, I'm pregnant."

"So?"

"So, the baby's not Jason's."

"Does he know?"

"Of course."

"Then what's the problem?"

"The problem is that there's a man out there I don't remember right now, but who I loved enough to make a baby with."

"Maybe. Maybe not."

Anna prayed every day that she'd loved her baby's father. She didn't want to be the type of woman who'd get pregnant for any other reason. If she hadn't loved the man... The very thought terrified her. Because if she hadn't loved the man, she could be carrying the child of a creep like Roger. Or a man who'd forced her...

"Besides, what would Jason want with someone like me?" she asked, wishing she'd just stayed home that night. She'd really been having a good day.

"Have you looked in the mirror lately, girl?" Maggie asked. "You're nuts if you don't try to make it with this guy."

And suddenly, as much as Anna loved having her new friend around, she felt the strongest urge to turn and run. To get as far away from Maggie as she could go. Her chest felt tight, every breath a struggle as, standing outside in the balmy New York evening, walls started closing in on her.

She couldn't let herself be talked into something she felt was wrong. She had to make her own decisions. Even if it meant that Maggie didn't want to be her friend anymore.

And as for what Maggie'd suggested, what kind of man would Jason be if he was willing to settle for someone like her? Someone who came to him, not only memoryless, but pregnant with another man's child?

A man who didn't love her, that was what he'd be. Because with the way he'd grown up, never coming first in his parents' lives, there was no possibility he was going to allow himself to settle for second place again. And second place was all she had to offer.

WAITING TO DRIVE across the Verrazano Narrows Bridge onto Staten Island Saturday morning, Jason smiled to himself. Life had a way of slipping in surprising little twists and turns that made the impossible almost seem possible. He would never have believed a month ago that he'd be joining a queue of summer tourists with Anna at his side. He wouldn't have believed she'd ever be at his side again, period.

As usual she was wearing one of her lightweight, sexy-as-hell dresses, though one Jason had never seen before—something she must have picked up on one of the shopping expeditions she'd told him about. He approved of her choice. The colors were bolder than she usually wore. So many little changes.

"I saw Dr. Gordon yesterday," she said, her long hair wind-tousled. "His wife had her baby last week—a little boy. Both are home and doing fine."

"Good for them!" Jason tried to inject the same

enthusiastic note he'd heard in Anna's voice into his own, in spite of the surprising flash of jealousy that flared in him. So the doctor and his wife shared something he and Anna didn't share—a child. The best of both of them in one package. He could almost picture the little towhead he and Anna would have had. But it wasn't to be. Still, he had more today than he'd had a month ago. It should be enough.

"So what did he have to say about you?" He stole a sideways glance.

"He says my confidence is growing."

"It is." Three weeks ago Anna had relied on him for everything.

The sun highlighted the gold in her hair. "I asked him about calling Abby."

Jason froze. So the bond the triplets shared *was* reaching her even now?

"What'd he say?" Not yet. He wasn't ready yet.

"That to rock the boat at this point could very well cause a setback," she reported. "He still says it's best if I remember on my own."

"And he's confident you will?"

Anna stared straight ahead as Jason inched his Jag closer to the bridge. "Absolutely. According to him all these little things coming back are just the beginning."

"Like the sand castle."

"Yeah." She paused, frowning. "You know, I had the oddest sensation last night, almost like a memory, but it wasn't that tangible."

"A feeling?"

GET A FREE TEDDY BEAR...

You'll love this plush, cuddly Teddy Bear, an adorable accessory for your dressing table, bookcase or desk. Measuring 5½" tall, he's soft and brown and has a bright red ribbon around his neck – he's completely captivating! And he's yours *absolutely free*, when you accept this no-risk offer!

He wanted so badly for her to remember their love. And dreaded the day when she did. He didn't really hold out any hope that he and Anna would ever be together again. So much more than her sister stood between them now.

"Yes, a feeling—that describes it as well as anything," she finally said.

"What happened?"

"Maggie was nagging me and suddenly I got really claustrophobic." Anna was still frowning, still watching the traffic inching ahead of them. "I mean, I really resented her for a minute there. I enjoy Maggie's company a lot, but I've got to make my own decisions."

If only the old you could hear yourself now, my love.

"There's nothing wrong with that." Jason pulled the Jag closer to the suspension bridge.

She shrugged. "I don't know, maybe I overreacted, but I've got precious little control over anything right now. At least let me control my decisions."

"You're not overreacting, Anna. It's just like Dr. Gordon said. Trusting yourself means trusting your own decisions."

"You're right, of course." She twisted in the seat to face him. "And a good friend. Thanks."

Hold that thought, he urged silently. He wasn't so sure how happy she was going to be with him when she remembered everything.

"You know, it's odd," she said a few minutes

later. "But lately I've been more at peace with my amnesia."

"Yeah?" So she was okay with this, too, the two of them living in the here and now, in their own little world?

"It's just that when I get these feelings, they're so strong, you know? I didn't simply not appreciate Maggie's nagging. I had to physically restrain myself from running away from her. For a second there I thought I might pass out or something."

Looking her over carefully, Jason asked, "Do you feel okay now?"

"Of course. Fine." She brushed her hair back from her face. "But it makes me think that maybe I do need this time to heal from whatever happened. The intensity of some of my reactions scares me."

"You're afraid of remembering?" *Oh, Anna, if only I really knew the extent of our problem here. If only I had all the answers.*

She looked away, out her side of the car. "Sometimes."

Thankful for the traffic that kept them at a standstill, Jason turned her to face him, holding her chin in his hand, forcing her to look at him. "That's nothing to be ashamed of, Anna."

He could see the tears welling in her eyes as she searched his gaze. Relaxing his hold, he moved his thumb along her jaw, needing to kiss her more right then than at any other time he could remember.

"Thank you," she whispered.

"For what?" *Wanting to kiss her senseless?*

"Knowing me so well."

Oh. That. In her other life she'd been able to read him just as clearly. "It's the truth, Anna. Fear is natural."

"Are you ever afraid?"

Her eyes implored him for the truth, looking for reassurance. Dumbstruck, Jason sat there staring at her. He used to be afraid sometimes, back when he still counted on his parents to be parents. He could remember being at a football game, afraid as the quarters went by that his father wasn't going to make it to see him play again. Afraid that he'd go to his mother's house, after four days at his father's, only to find he'd lost his bedroom. But sleeping on couches hadn't been so bad, and that was all so long ago, back when he'd depended on other people for his happiness.

And fear?

He continued to stare at her—until a horn sounded behind him. Jerking away from Anna, he put the car in gear and shot forward. He was concerned. Concerned she'd remember everything. Concerned she wouldn't. Concerned about the baby she carried, about the man who'd fathered it. Concerned she was going to see his own misrepresentation of their relationship as a betrayal, in spite of the doctor's advice. Because parts of him saw it that way, himself. Concerned he'd never again be able to hold her in his arms, lose himself within her honeyed depths. Concerned he'd never be home again. That he'd carry the ache of her loss with him to his grave. Yeah, he was concerned.

He was not afraid.

CHAPTER TEN

STATEN ISLAND deserved better. Its beautiful shore-
lines, magnificent rolling hills sprinkled with grand
homes, and miles of trails waiting to be explored
didn't receive even a tenth of Jason's attention. He
was too distracted by Anna's nearness. They visited
Conference House, a stone manor that had served as
the only site of a Revolutionary War conference. But
while noteworthy, if one cared to take notes, the
Revolutionary War was far in the distant past—and
Anna was the present.

He took her through historic Richmond Town,
visited the Staten Island Institute of Arts and Sci-
ences and debated with her about the exhibits, com-
paring them to pieces they'd seen at the Museum of
Modern Art earlier in the week. He was challenged
by her thinking, pleased with her new openness—
telling him what she thought rather than leaving him
to guess—and entranced by her laughter. At her request, he walked with her through innumerable gift
shops. She pointed out trinkets, commented on like-
nesses to things they'd seen, bought a deck of cards.
All he saw was Anna. All he heard was Anna. All
he wanted was Anna.

And she wanted him, too. He'd been her lover for

almost two years, her friend before that. He knew when Anna was turned on.

They toured the Alice Austen House Museum that afternoon and then it was time to go home, to get away from Anna before darkness spread over the city, cloaking them in its intimacy. To avoid temptation.

"Let's stay for dinner," he heard himself say, instead, as they climbed back into the car.

After a full day of being with Anna, Jason wasn't ready to reenter the real world, temptation be damned. "I saw a pamphlet back there." He indicated the cottage that housed the pioneer photography collection they'd just viewed. "It advertised waterfront dining just a few miles from here."

Anna stopped, her seat belt pulled out but not yet fastened. "Don't you have a date?"

The question sounded so wrong coming from her. "No."

"Why not? It's Saturday night."

Because, after a two-year commitment to her, one he'd expected to last forever, he had no desire for other women. "Never got around to asking."

She studied him closely. "But you *are* dating someone, right?"

For a woman who wanted him, she was doing a damn good job of convincing him she didn't. "No, Anna, I'm not currently dating anyone."

"But you have to be!"

He wasn't sure it was panic he heard in her voice until he turned and read it in her eyes loud and clear. Just then a family walked by the convertible, staring at them; Anna looked down at her lap. Starting the Jaguar, Jason roared out of the parking lot and sped along Hylan Boulevard past the Gateway National Recreation Area, turning off at the first semiprivate cove he found along the shore. He stopped the car and stared out at the ocean.

"Now, you want to tell me why I have to be dating?" he asked.

Anna hadn't said a word since he'd left Austen House. She still didn't.

His gut turned hard as a rock when he saw the hunted expression on her face. Reaching over, he took her hand. "Anna?"

"You get this look in your eyes sometimes." Her words were a mere whisper on the ocean breeze.

He waited for her to continue, fully aware she hadn't pulled her hand out of his grasp.

"I recognize the look, Jason." Her own eyes burned with heat.

Shit.

"And?"

She gazed at him, shook her head and got out of the car. A breeze from the ocean whipped her dress up, swirling the thin material about her thighs, reminding Jason of the first time he'd seen her. As then, he had no choice but to follow her. Down the small copse to the beach beyond.

But the laughter that had been in her eyes when he caught up with her that first time was nowhere to be found now. Sandals in hand, she just kept walking, her face a mask.

"I feel like such a fool," she said.

"Why?" He was the one making a royal mess of things. He had the facts. He knew better.

"Because if I'm wrong…" She stopped walking, turning to look at him. "Except I'm not, am I?"

He shook his head. "I want you, Anna, if that's what you mean."

Looking away, she started to walk again, silently. Jason could only keep pace with her, waiting, watching. She had to make the decisions.

"Why now?" she asked suddenly. "Why not when I knew you before?"

Okay, Dr. Gordon. What now? "I can't answer that, Anna," he said, carefully weighing his words. She was going to remember their past someday— along with today. "Except to say that I see things in you now that weren't there before."

"What things?"

"You're more independent," he said, strolling slowly beside her on the deserted stretch of beach, the late afternoon bringing a chill to the air.

"Really?" She seemed pleased.

"Really." He smiled at her. "And stronger, too."

"I don't feel very strong."

Grabbing hold of her hand, Jason stopped her, reaching up to brush her hair back from her face, his hand lingering on the softness of her cheek.

"Is it so very wrong to admit that we're attracted to each other?" he asked.

Winning her heart a second time hadn't been what he'd had in mind at all, but what kind of fool would turn his back on this chance?

Jason withstood her gaze as she stared up at him.

He wanted her. She wanted him. And for now, he and she were all that existed.

"Yes," she finally said, breaking eye contact with him. She took his hand and held it against her cheek. "It's very wrong, Jason."

"Why?"

She dropped his hand and continued her trek up the beach. "You know why."

She wasn't talking about her amnesia. "Because you're pregnant."

"That's a start."

"I'm sure you're not the first pregnant woman to have a romance."

Dropping her sandals, Anna plopped down in the sand, scooping up a handful and letting it run through her fingers. "And when my memory comes back?" she asked, her voice stronger, bitter. "What if I discover I love someone else?"

"And what if you don't?"

He sat down beside her, and took her hand. "Anna, would it help if I tell you that I won't hold you to anything? That you call all the shots? That if, once you remember, you choose someone else, I won't stand in your way?"

The longing in her eyes as she stared silently up at him was all it took. All reasoning, all conscience vanished. With the familiarity of having loved her before, he lowered his mouth to hers.

ANNA WAS LOST at the touch of his lips. He felt so right in a world that had been nothing but wrong. Her mouth opened to his automatically, as if possessing a mind of its own. And because her body seemed to know exactly what to do when she hadn't a clue, she listened to it.

Easing her back onto the sand, Jason moved over her, sliding one leg between hers, molding their bodies to a perfect fit, his lips caressing hers all the while.

Like a starved woman, Anna returned kiss for kiss, finding in Jason's arms everything she'd been looking for—a sense of home, and a strength beyond anything she'd ever be able to muster on her own. Fire, too. Fire that ignited a matching flame in her veins. One that threatened to consume her if she didn't have more of him.

His hands, never still, caressed her body, pleasuring her in ways she'd never imagined until finally, blissfully, they found her breasts. Not just cupping them, as she'd longed for so many times over the past weeks, but moving back and forth, back and forth across her hardened nipples, sending shock waves of sensation through her.

"So perfect," he whispered against her lips, continuing to torture first one breast and then the other with his light caresses, only ceasing when Anna arced her body, pressing his hand more firmly against her aching breast.

"So full," he said.

Anna fell back to the sand, turning her head, breaking the kiss, pushing him away with both hands. Yes, they were full. Fuller than normal, or so she'd been told. Because she was pregnant.

"Anna?" Jason's voice sounded drugged, or as if it came from far off. "What's wrong, honey?"

"I'm sorry," she said when she could speak. Rolling away, she sat up a few feet from him, hugging her knees to her throbbing breasts.

It took him a minute. She saw his struggle, saw the cords in his neck tense as he tried to compose himself. Eventually he, too, sat up, his hands on his knees as he stared silently out at the ocean.

"Did you remember something?" he finally asked, his voice level, resigned.

Not in the way he probably meant. "Yes."

He flinched, but gave no other indication that he'd heard her, strengthening Anna's resolve to let things go no further between them. Because Jason wasn't going to protect his heart. With his eternal optimism he would enter into the relationship with high hopes. But if the worst happened, if she suddenly remembered another man, one who already had her undying love, Jason would simply allow her to walk away from him.

Even though he knew that doing so would kill him.

"I remembered the baby," she said. She owed him complete honesty. If they were going to salvage their friendship, one that had become as essential to her as the air she breathed, they had to talk openly about this.

"And his father?" Jason asked, still deadpan, still gazing at the ocean. If he hoped to convince her he didn't care, he'd failed miserably. Or maybe it was himself he was trying to convince. One thing was clear, he wasn't going to try to urge her to forget whatever it was she'd remembered.

"No, Jason." She shook her head. "Just the fact that I'm pregnant."

He looked at her then, relief in his eyes. "That's all?"

Nodding, Anna gave him a sad smile. "I don't know what I did in the past, Jason, but the person I am today, the person I'm learning to live with, the person I have to like, can't make love without commitment."

"I don't have a problem with making a commitment," he said.

"I know."

He shifted over until his thigh pressed against hers in the sand. "So what's the problem?"

"*I* can't make any commitments, Jason," she said, not bothering to hide her pain from him. At least it told him she cared. "Until I know what promises I've already made, I'm not free to make any more."

He didn't move away. Didn't move at all. Just sat staring out at the ocean.

"I'll understand if you'd like to take me back to Manhattan and forget you ever knew me."

He was silent so long she wasn't sure he was even still listening to her. Not that she blamed him. All she'd done was take, take, take since he'd first walked into her hospital room. Strength, money, peace of mind, time. He'd given them all freely. And she had nothing to give in return.

"No chance of getting naked, huh?" His outrageous words dropped into the silence and suddenly Anna felt giddy with relief. He was going to get them through this.

"None," she lied.

"Then my next choice is dinner on the waterfront."

"But what about—"

"Anna," Jason interrupted, taking her hand, "look at me."

She did. When he gazed at her like that, she couldn't look anywhere else.

"I understand, and it's okay," he said, enunciating every word. "When your memory returns, we'll have this discussion again. Until then, I'll wait."

Her eyes wet with tears, she touched his sweet handsome face. "What did I ever do to deserve you?"

"Someday, when I have you in my arms, I'll tell you."

She prayed that someday she'd be able to take him up on his offer.

HE CALLED ABBY much later that night. He'd finally dropped Anna off sometime past midnight, walking her to her door but not asking to come inside. It wouldn't have taken much to get her to acquiesce and, once inside, to bed her. But then he'd have been as bad as Abby, overriding Anna's decision with his own. He had no choice but to respect her judgment.

But damn, doing the right thing felt like hell.

All things considered, they'd had a great evening, almost like the old days—laughing, simply enjoying being together. Being able to feast his eyes openly on her had helped. There was more honesty in their relationship now. And for the time being, he could live with that. Was determined to have this chance—and to be prepared to walk away.

Abby's phone rang so long he was ready to hang up, a bit relieved to see that Abby had found something to do with her Saturday evening besides sit at home.

"Hello?"

The voice that answered, just as he was putting the receiver down, barely resembled his old friend.

"Abby?" he asked, frowning.

"Yes?"

"Am I interrupting something?" Did Abby have a man there? Wonder of wonders. He'd never known the oldest Hayden girl to bring a man home.

"No. I'm just sitting here."

"Alone?"

"Yeah."

Oh. "Something good on the tube?" He remembered some cozy evenings back when Audrey was alive. Abby would make popcorn and coerce everyone to sit down and watch some show or other she was sure they'd all enjoy. And they usually had.

"Nah."

"You working up something spectacular to introduce in the fall?" He wasn't sure how Abby kept coming up with ideas for her children's-wear designs fast enough to keep her growing clientele happy.

"No. Just sitting."

"Anna saw the doctor yesterday."

"And?" She sounded almost afraid to ask. Suddenly Jason wondered if he and Anna weren't the only ones frightened of her memory.

"He's happy with her progress, her growing confidence."

There was another long pause and then, "How is she, Jason?"

"She misses you."

"Oh, God, I miss her, too…" And that was when Jason heard the tears Abby had been trying to hide. She'd been sitting in that cottage on the beach all alone on a Saturday night, crying.

FIFTEEN MINUTES after hanging up the phone Jason was still sitting on his couch in the dark—his thoughts far from pleasant. While he'd been convinced that Anna would only be free to live a full life if she could separate her identity from Abby's, he'd also honestly believed that in the long run Abby, too, was going to be happier. He was no longer so sure.

Hell, what did he know? He'd never been a part of a relationship of the sort Abby, Anna and Audrey had shared from birth. Had never really been part of a family.

Maybe being together was the way the sisters were meant to be, the only way they could be happy. Maybe there was a greater reason for their multiple birth than simple genetics, a connection stronger than physical resemblance and blood ties. A connection beyond understanding.

A connection that threatened him more than anything else in his life.

He'd been so sure that he'd had all the answers, that he knew exactly what the problems were between Anna and him. But looking back now, he was seeing something else. Something that sickened him. Could he possibly have been jealous of the closeness Anna shared with her sisters? Had his New York job offer merely been an excuse to make her choose, once and for all, between her sisters and him? Had he been so shallow, so immature?

God, he hoped not.

And if he had? And Anna had seen through his righteous indignation to the selfish man beneath? And Anna remembered?

Breaking out in a cold sweat, Jason dropped to the floor. One. Two. Three…

CHAPTER ELEVEN

JASON WAS ON THE PHONE first thing the next morning, Sunday or no. He couldn't wait anymore. He had to know what he was up against. He had to find the father of Anna's child.

She may have to remember on her own, but nothing said he couldn't find out in the meantime. Not only would he be better prepared to help her deal with the memory, especially if it was distressing, but he, too, would be better protected. Knowledge was power. And Jason needed all the power he could get.

Calling his contacts in California, as well as the fact-finding sources he'd encountered since coming to New York, felt good. Right. At least he was doing something. He couldn't fight what he didn't know. And he planned to fight.

Unless it turned out that Anna truly loved the man who'd fathered her child just weeks after Jason moved out of her life. In that case he'd walk. A thing much easier done sooner than later.

Again, he had to know.

He also put down a retainer on one of New York's best private investigators. If anyone could find out who Anna Hayden had been sleeping with, Smith Whitehall could. A Harvard graduate, the man not only knew how to turn up dirt in a bottle of glass cleaner, he was smart.

And then Jason set out himself, visiting all the places he would expect Anna to visit upon arriving in New York, showing her picture around, asking questions. He'd have sent out an all-points bulletin on the evening news if he could have found a way to do so without humiliating Anna.

"Yeah, I've seen her," a clerk in a bookstore close to Gramercy Park told Jason late Sunday afternoon. "Not lately, though."

"Was she ever with anyone?" Jason asked casually, his heart pounding. *Say no. Say yes. Say she didn't love him.*

"Nope." The clerk shook her head. "Always came in alone. Always bought a lot of books, though. Fiction, but nonfiction, too. Art-history stuff. I suppose she could've been buying for two."

Nodding, Jason thanked the clerk and walked out. He was getting nowhere. New Yorkers were a tough bunch to crack, too concerned about their own backs to notice other people. He'd spent an entire day traipsing the town for nothing. An entire day he could have spent with Anna.

Shit. He was losing it, big time. And all for a woman who'd already sent him out of her life once. Once home, Jason changed into cotton shorts and a T-shirt, grabbed his racquetball gear and headed for the club. He'd stay until midnight if that was how long it took to beat some sense into himself.

He knew better than to look to anyone else for his personal happiness, to need to be the most important person in another's life. Knew all the inherent dangers of doing so firsthand. Had, as a boy, lived with the fear of rejection as his constant companion. He wasn't going to be afraid again. Not ever.

ANNA INVITED MAGGIE to go secondhand-clothes shopping Tuesday evening. She'd seen Jason that day and was too restless to be content with her own company. Being with him was better than ever—and worse. It was ten times harder to keep her desire under control when she knew he wanted her, too.

"What do you want with used stuff?" Maggie asked. She was sitting on the only counter in Anna's kitchen eating Anna's last apple.

"It's got character," Anna told her. Besides which, it was cheap and she needed some more dresses. With the baby on the way, Anna was growing more and more aware of the limits of her bank account.

"You've already got plenty of character," Maggie said, surprising Anna with her praise.

"You think so?"

"You might've lost your memory, but even you have to know that much," Maggie said. "And you've got looks, too, dammit. If I didn't like you so much, I might have to hate you."

"So you'll come?" Anna asked.

Begrudgingly Maggie followed Anna into three different shops, grumbling when Anna bought exactly what Maggie told her not to buy, more of her "flower child" dresses as Maggie called them.

"You need some shorts, girl," Maggie said. "Show off your legs."

"I need dresses," Anna countered. "To hide my belly."

"No kidding?" Maggie looked at the part of Anna's anatomy in question. "You're starting to show?"

"I don't know. I'm three months along and I'm starting to look bloated. It's embarrassing."

Maggie laughed. "What're you gonna do when you're big as an elephant?"

"Don't," Anna groaned. "Let me get used to bloated, first." And let her not think about four or five months down the road. Who knew where she'd be then, who she'd be, or with whom. It scared her witless every time she thought about it. So she tried not to.

"I sure wish I knew what I used to do," she complained to Maggie on the walk home. "I'm getting restless."

"Which means you're getting better," Maggie said. "You've got that computer on your dresser—can you type?" she asked. "You could get a part-time job as a secretary or receptionist or something. Lord knows you have the looks for it."

"I'm not even sure how to turn the thing on," Anna admitted. And she hadn't wanted to admit to Jason yet another failure, another thing she no longer knew. Plain and simple, she'd been too proud to ask for help.

"Even I know that much," Maggie said over her

shoulder as they climbed the steps of the brownstone. "Come on, together we can figure it out."

ONCE MAGGIE HAD the laptop open and on, Anna
suddenly took it from there. There were no con-
scious memories, but she knew how to move about
in the first couple of programs fairly well. She spent
the rest of that evening fooling around with the computer, surprised to find how many things she just
automatically knew to do.

She'd just discovered her personal financial file
the next morning when the telephone rang. Assuming it was Jason, she grabbed it up on the first ring.

"Hi!" she said. She couldn't wait to tell him that
she had an account in a bank in California with
enough money to see her through a couple of years,
baby expenses included. Then she'd have to go to
work. But, God willing, by then she'd have regained
her memory.

"Hello, yourself, sexy lady."

Anna froze, wanting to drop the phone back in its
cradle and pretend she'd never picked it up. But as
horrified as she was to hear Roger on the other end
of the line, she had to know why he was calling her.
Was he going to claim his child? Expect visitation
rights?

"What do you want?"

"You know my voice," he said a little less enthusiastically. "Does this mean you've recovered
from your unfortunate affliction?"

He made her sound like some kind of half-witted
freak. "My memory hasn't returned yet."

"It's been three weeks and one day since you were so naughty and ran out on me, Anna. Are you ready to kiss and make up?" His voice was oiled with sickening innuendo. "I promise to take good care of you."

"Never."

"I see you've still got a lot to learn, Anna. Lovers' tiffs aren't meant to last forever. Come back to work, let me take care of you, and you won't have to worry your pretty little head anymore."

"Never," she repeated. Still fighting the urge to slam the phone down, Anna hung on. Did he know about the baby? Surely, if he was the father, she'd have told him about the baby. The woman she was now certainly would have.

"But, Anna, it's summer! We can go to the beach," he said, as if coaxing a child. "I'll take you down the coast, just you and me. No one will know about you." His voice lowered. "You won't have to use your mind at all."

Yeah, but she could guess what she would have to use. She'd rather die.

"I'll make you happier than you've ever been," he said confidently, as if he actually thought there was a chance she'd go away with him.

"I'm pregnant, Roger."

"Son of a bitch! You threatened me with a lawsuit for stealing a little kiss and here all along you were screwing some other man?"

"I didn't sleep with you?" Anna asked, almost dizzy with relief.

"You aren't going to pin your bastard on me, you

little bitch. Other than that one kiss, I never touched you—''

Anna clicked the off button on her mobile phone and laid it calmly beside her computer.

Two seconds later she picked it back up, dialed automatically and held her breath, praying he was home.

''Jason? He's not the father!'' she cried the minute he picked up his phone.

''Who isn't?''

''Roger. He called just now. I never slept with him.''

''Why'd he call?'' Jason didn't seem to be sharing her joy.

''He wanted me to go to the beach with him.''

''If he calls again, you let me know,'' Jason said. ''We'll get him for harassment.''

As thrilled as she was at the protectiveness in his voice, Anna stomped her foot.

''Didn't you hear me?'' she practically hollered. ''He's not the baby's father.''

''I didn't think he was, Anna. You'd never sleep with a jerk like that.''

Anna was grinning when she hung up the phone after promising to be ready to accompany Jason to lunch in half an hour. He'd had a lot more faith in her than she'd had herself. She was damn lucky he'd been in New York when that subway crashed.

A WEEK PASSED and there continued to be no word on a man in Anna's life. Jason hung up from his daily call from Whitehall, frustrated as hell. No news was supposed to be good news. But in this case, it was still just no news. Because it was beyond doubt that somewhere out there was a man who'd impregnated Anna. She was starting to show. Not obviously, probably not at all to someone who wasn't as intimately acquainted with her body as he was. But when he'd slid his arm around her on their walk through Gramercy Park the day before, he'd felt the difference.

It had bothered him so much, this evidence of another man's having touched her, he'd dropped his arm, then contented himself with simply holding her hand. And for the first time since Staten Island, he'd broken his promise to himself and to her. He'd kissed her goodbye. He hadn't lingered, just a quick peck. Because he'd had to leave his mark on her like some macho jerk. An insecure one at that. The fact that she'd clung to him made him that much more of a heel. That kiss hadn't been about loving. It had been about jealousy, plain and simple.

So for the fourth time in three days it was back to the gym for him. To things he could control, things he was good at, things he could count on. But for the first time in months he lost a match.

JASON WAS LATE. Which wasn't all that unusual. Anna, on the other hand, had been pacing her small apartment since fifteen minutes before he was due to arrive. It was this way a lot recently, her nerves stretched tight with impatience. It had been two weeks since the night she'd finally admitted to the restlessness that was slowly consuming her. She was

sick and tired of sitting around storing her strength
and waiting for her mind to heal. She needed something to do.

When Jason called, saying that he'd gotten caught
on the phone, that it would be another forty-five
minutes before he'd be by to take her to Chinatown,
she almost snapped at him.

She sat down at her computer, instead. Jason was
a saint, and there was no way she was going to take
her growing tension out on him. But she'd already
played the few games installed on her computer a
hundred times apiece. She was bored as hell.

Desultorily flipping through the directory of her
hard drive, she found several files she didn't recognize, having really explored only program files to
this point. She clicked on the first unfamiliar file. It
contained only a series of unreadable formating
codes. As did the second, third and fourth.

She clicked on the fifth file, surprised when her
word-processing program opened up. What she saw
was entirely readable. And there was a lot of it, paragraph upon paragraph. Her heart started pumping
furiously, butterflies swarming in her stomach as she
scrolled through the pages.

She closed her eyes, frightened suddenly, wishing
she could turn off the machine, return to the tedium
of sitting and waiting. Something safe. Something
she was sure she could do.

But the words continued to flow in her mind,
words she recognized. Exciting her, balancing her
panic. She couldn't exit the file, couldn't turn off

the machine, couldn't get up and walk away. She had to read.

Starting with the first page, she read every word, knowing some of them *before* she read them. It was a story. A compelling one. Of a young man...

And Anna knew this man better than she knew herself. Knew his desires and goals. Knew his fears. Even his hobbies. She knew because she'd admired him most of her life.

The pages were the beginning of a book, a biography. The story of John Henry Walker, a nineteenth-century New York artist whose tragic life was filled with triumph. A man who, orphaned at a young age, grew up in squalor, an unwanted ward of the state. A man whose first wife was killed by outlaws, whose baby girl died of tuberculosis. A gifted impressionist. A loving husband, a revered father. She'd come to New York to research his story.

She was so engrossed in her reading, she didn't hear Jason's knock on the apartment door. Until his knock became a pounding accompanied by his voice calling her name.

"You won't believe it!" she cried when she threw open her door.

"Are you okay?" He looked her over swiftly.

"Better than okay. Magnificent! Terrific! Oh, Jason, I know why I came to New York!"

His face drained of color and he shut the door behind him. "You remembered everything?"

"Yes. No!" she grabbed his arm, dragging him over to the computer. "I haven't regained my memory, just a small part of it. Look!" she cried exultantly, pointing at the screen.

Jason looked from her to the computer screen and back again, as though wondering if she'd finally flipped her lid completely. "It's a paper of some sort," he said.

"It's a book, Jason!" She could hardly contain her excitement. This book was a huge part of her, of who she'd been before the accident. "I remember writing it!" She tapped the computer screen. "This is why I came to New York!"

"You wrote it?" he asked, clearly shocked.

"Yep!" She *did* have a worthy endeavor. "It's about an American artist—an obscure American artist—named John Henry Walker. Some of his work is still on display here in New York."

"John Henry Walker?" Jason asked, frowning. "You had a print of his hanging in your cottage in California."

Anna was so relieved to hear that she almost cried. She wasn't losing her mind. She was remembering. "I think I like art."

"You minored in it in college," Jason said.

"I have a college degree?"

Jason's glance was shuttered suddenly, as though he was remembering he was supposed to be watching what he told her. "You earned a B.A. in English," he finally said.

Leaning over, he looked more closely at the words covering the computer screen. "Is this finished?"

"No." She shook her head. "I don't remember

how far I was into it, but judging from the number of pages, it's only about half-done.''

Scrolling through the pages, he asked, ''You haven't read it all?''

She grinned, shaking her head again. ''I just found it half an hour ago.''

After reading a couple of paragraphs, Jason went back and read the first two pages.

''This is really good,'' he said, turning to look at her.

''You think so?'' She'd thought so, too, but she still put more stock in his opinion than her own.

Jason straightened, pulling her against him and kissing her full on the mouth. ''I know so,'' he said.

As if suddenly realizing what he was doing, where he was, the temptation that was even now blazing into flames between them, he set her gently away. ''If you'd like, I can take a copy of this with me and print it out for you at the station.''

Though she missed his warmth, Anna was too grateful for what she'd discovered to mourn for things she couldn't have.

''Great! Sure. If it's not too much trouble,'' she said, still practically dancing with excitement. She couldn't wait to immerse herself in the life of the man she'd admired most of her life. To read the whole book, or the finished portion of it, anyway.

Finally she had a little piece of the real Anna Hayden.

THERE WAS A MESSAGE from Smith Whitehall waiting for Jason when he stopped home to change before work that afternoon. The man had a lead, was chasing it down and would call back. Jason flipped off the machine, the day suddenly bleak. This was not good news. And yet it was the news he'd been waiting to hear. The question was, was he ready to hear it? Was he ready to give Anna up?

But then, how could he give up what he didn't have to begin with?

HAVING GONE into the station early enough to print out Anna's manuscript, Jason was sitting on the couch in his dressing-room-cum-office reviewing the day's stories.

"You're here!" Sunny came into his office without knocking. She was wearing one of the short tight skirts she always wore on the air, her white silk blouse displaying a fair amount of cleavage.

Jason nodded, continuing to read, hoping she'd get the hint and leave him alone.

"What's the occasion? Lately you've barely gotten here in time to go on," she said, her tone a little resentful.

"I've been busy, Sunny. You know that." He wasn't in the mood for a showdown with his partner.

"I know." Her voice softened as she sat down close to him on the couch—too close. Running one perfectly manicured finger along his arm, she laid her head against his shoulder.

It wasn't the first time she'd cuddled up to him. In fact, he'd probably encouraged the closeness a time or two. But it wasn't enough. He had to resist the urge to shrug her away from him, to jump up off the couch and put as much room between him and Sunny as he could. He didn't want her touch. He wanted Anna's.

Still, a small part of him wanted to wrap his arms around Sunny, place his mouth on hers and ease the ache that had been burning inside him for weeks. Maybe even find a moment or two of forgetfulness.

But although she might be able to ease his physical ache, it would only be momentary. And the self-loathing that was sure to follow would be far worse than the original problem. If all he had was himself, he was damn sure going to be someone he could be proud of.

"Why don't you come back to my place after the last show tonight?" she invited softly.

"Sunny—"

"I'll even make breakfast in the morning," she interrupted. For Sunny that was major. She hated to cook.

"I need to get home tonight." He had a manuscript to read.

"Why?" Her finger strayed higher, moving toward his chest. "Don't you think it's time our relationship progressed a little?"

He braced himself against her practiced seduction. His body had been too ready for too long not to be tempted by the beautiful woman beside him.

"We're friends, Sunny. Good friends. I never intimated that we'd be more," he reminded her.

"It's because of that woman you're helping, isn't it?" she asked, sounding jealous.

He didn't want to think about Anna. Thinking

about her only made the ache worse. The ache Sunny was offering to ease. One she wanted to ease.

"I'm not seeing her tonight, if that's what you mean," he said.

"Then why not come home with me? It's not like you two have anything going, right?"

He shifted slightly away from her before he threw good judgment to the wind and drew her onto his lap. "We're friends." Unfortunately the new position had her breast pressing against his arm.

"But you don't owe her anything."

She was right of course. The person he owed something more to was himself. He had to look at himself in the morning. He wanted to like what he saw. And using Sunny for his own selfish release wasn't something he'd be able to look upon too fondly, no matter how he tried to rationalize.

"She has nightmares sometimes," he heard himself explaining. "I told her she can call—"

"She calls you in the middle of the night?" Sunny sat up, her eyes reflecting her hurt as she pushed away from him.

Jason wondered how a face could be so beautiful and make him feel so uncomfortable at the same time. "Once or twice."

"So how much longer are you going to be at the beck and call of this poor family friend?" she demanded.

All trace of desire fled. "You make her sound like some dim-witted hanger-on," he said, biting down on his anger.

"Your words, not mine."

Jason stood, walking to the door. "Let's get one thing straight," he said. "Every woman should hope to be as smart and courageous as Anna." He held the door open for Sunny to leave. "If you can't accept that, then we have nothing more to say."

Sunny rose—graceful, classy and way too disappointed as she walked slowly toward him. "You *are* involved with her, aren't you."

"No," he said. "I've just known her a long time, and I admire the heck out of the way she's handling this whole thing."

But while Sunny seemed to accept his denial for now, Jason wasn't so easily convinced. He might not have fallen in love with Anna all over again, but if his instant defense of her was any indication, he was starting to care more than he wanted to. With that in mind and considering the call from Whitehall that afternoon, he needed to take a serious look at what he was letting himself in for.

LATE THAT NIGHT, after two hours of engrossed page turning, Jason set Anna's manuscript carefully down on the coffee table in front of him. She was good. Better than good. Anna possessed a talent for pulling the reader so completely into the story, that Jason actually thought the man's thoughts, hoped his hopes.

As he put down the manuscript, Anna's earlier words rang in his ears. She'd come to New York to sell this book—not to see him.

CHAPTER TWELVE

EXCITED, NERVOUS, a bit frightened, Anna stood outside Jason's apartment building at nine o'clock the next morning. She'd never just popped in on him, hadn't really planned to do so now. But she was on her way to an ultrasound appointment, and she didn't want to go alone.

Her fear wasn't logical. Seeing the child growing within her wasn't going to tell them anything about the conception. Still she was frightened. She really wanted Jason to go with her. But could she ask him to do this? Considering their encounter on the beach on Staten Island, was it fair of her to ask?

And yet, considering his willingness to accept her, pregnant and all, was she really out of line to want him there?

Time continued to tick away, people stared at her as they passed her on the street, and still she couldn't make up her mind. Looking around her, she noticed a phone booth a couple of buildings down. She'd call him. Should have called him before she'd ever left home.

He answered on the fourth ring, and the first thing Anna could tell was that he'd been asleep. The second was that he wasn't in the best of moods, though he did try to cover that up.

"No, Anna, don't apologize," he said quickly. "I told you to call me anytime. Is something wrong?"

He sounded concerned. Anna felt a little better.

"Not really," she said. She still had an hour before her appointment. There was time for him to get dressed and accompany her. But should she bother him?

"Did you remember something?"

"No." Should she ask? Would he want her to? "I just..."

"What?" He still sounded sleepy.

"I have an ultrasound appointment this morning. I just wondered if you wanted to come along," she said quickly.

"Are you having problems?" he asked.

"No, not at all. It's strictly procedure." This was a bad idea.

"It doesn't hurt, does it?"

Not unless you considered her uncomfortably full bladder. "No."

"What time's the appointment?"

She heard the hesitancy in his voice. As if he wanted to come. And at the same time didn't. She should never have called.

"Ten-thirty."

"I'm sorry, honey, but you'll have to go without me," he said. He didn't sound sorry—more like relieved. "I have a meeting at the station at eleven."

"That's all right, Jason. It was no big deal," she said, embarrassed, trying not to feel hurt. Jason had

already gone above and beyond the call of duty.
She'd been wrong to expect him to step into the
shoes of a man he'd never met, a man who might
very well appear at any time and claim them. And
her.

THE LIGHT on her answering machine was blinking.
Dropping the bag of groceries she'd carried in, Anna
hurried to the machine. She'd been so busy writing
the past several days she'd hardly seen Jason at all.
She missed him. A lot.

Jabbing impatiently at the button, she waited
through three beeps to hear his message, hoping he
wanted to take her to lunch. Monday was broccoli
soup day at the deli. Not only was she lonely, she
was starving, too.

"Hello, Anna dear." The unfamiliar deep bari-
tone startled her. "I'm sorry to have missed you.
Business is going to keep me here much longer than
I expected. I'm in Italy this month and part of next,
and then back to London for more meetings." More
than his words, the regret and genuine affection in
the man's voice spoke to Anna. With both hands
she rubbed the swell of her belly. "I'll be in touch
the second I'm back in New York, my dear," the
voice continued, "with great hopes you'll still be
free to take up where we left off. Until then, happy
writing."

The machine re-wound, clicking off, and Anna
stood there staring at it. She had no idea who the
man was or where they'd left off. Remembered
nothing, felt nothing at hearing his voice. But she

was suddenly, sickeningly afraid he'd fathered a child he knew nothing about. By the sounds of things he'd been in Europe awhile. Possibly before she'd found out that she carried his child?

Oh, God. Her unattended groceries scattered, the frozen foods melting on the hardwood floor, Anna sank to her knees and wept.

"YOU LOOK like a rag."

Anna chuckled wanly, taking the chain off her door to admit her friend. "Thanks, Mag," she said dryly. "I can always count on you to cheer me up."

"Hey." Maggie held up her hands, sauntering over to sprawl on Anna's couch, her feet resting on the arm. "You're the one who invited me to dinner." But Anna saw the concerned glance her friend gave her on her way past. She sat down in the chair at her computer desk, needing the support for her back.

"You cry when you're preggie and the kid comes out a grouch." Maggie grabbed an apple from the bowl on the coffee table that Anna kept specifically for her.

"There was a message on my machine today from some guy in Europe," Anna blurted. "He's there on business and says he hopes we can take up where we left off." She had to tell someone, and she couldn't bring herself to talk to Jason about it. "I think he might be the father."

Maggie sat up. "Yeah? Wow, that's great!"

Anna nodded, wishing she felt half as excited as

Maggie about the news. What she felt was a bone-deep dread.

"So you remembered? Recognized his voice? Something?"

"No." As hard as she fought them, tears filled her eyes again. "Nothing happened, Maggie."

"It's okay, kid." Maggie's voice was uncharacteristically gentle. "You know the doc said it'll take time. When you're ready, you'll remember this guy."

Anna shook her head. "I don't want him to be the father of my baby," she whispered, ashamed, frightened, as lost as she'd felt in the hospital after the crash.

She needed Jason.

Maggie set her half-eaten apple back in the bowl. "So what makes you so sure this guy's it?"

"He almost has to be, doesn't he?" She rested her chin on her hands. "There's nobody else beating down my door."

"Still doesn't make him the daddy."

No, it didn't. But this man, whoever he was, was the only logical choice. She'd apparently been seeing him. And she was sure she wasn't the type to date two men at once.

"He must have money if he's got business all over Europe," Maggie surmised.

"Yeah." But though Maggie clearly saw this as a plus, Anna didn't care.

"He's probably that guy I saw you with," Maggie said, frowning. "He was always wearing natty suits. Seemed real important."

"What'd he look like?" If the man had fathered her child, she should at least learn the color of his hair.

Maggie shrugged, picking up her apple. "Tall, thin, dark hair. Fortyish."

Twelve years older than I am. Seven years older than Jason. Old enough to have a nearly grown family of his own. Maybe past the time in his life when he wanted to start a new family. She started to cry again.

"Buck up, kid!" Maggie said. "You don't owe the guy anything."

"If he's my baby's father, I do!"

"That's a big 'if,' and no, you don't. He took off for Europe without you, right?"

Anna nodded.

"And he only *hopes* you'll be free when he makes it back, right?" Maggie took another bite of apple, chomping contentedly.

Anna nodded again. It all seemed so hopeless. The baby didn't even seem real yet, and here she was, having to accept a complete stranger as its father.

"There you have it, then." Maggie tossed the apple core in the trash. "You guys obviously don't have a commitment at all."

"We have one big commitment," Anna said, rubbing her stomach. "He just may not know about it yet."

"A baby's a responsibility, Anna, not a commitment," Maggie said, her voice more serious than Anna had ever heard. "Say you get your memory back, you remember the guy, the baby's the result of one night with a little too much champagne, a little too much loneliness—no love. You gonna marry the guy?"

"No." Surprised at how quickly the answer came to her, Anna suddenly felt better than she had since she'd listened to that wretched message. No one could force her to do anything she didn't want to do.

"He may not want to marry you, have you thought of that?" Maggie tossed out the question.

She hadn't. Feeling incredibly stupid, Anna realized she'd never even considered the possibility that the man wouldn't expect her to marry him.

Jason's image as he'd kissed her on the beach on Staten Island filled her mind. He'd wanted her then, baby and all. Was it possible that things could work out for them? Someday?

"Of course, when you get your memory back, if it turns out this guy is the father and you do love him, it's good that he called," Maggie said cheerily.

Maggie's words plummeted Anna straight back into the depths. She had nothing to give to Jason. Not while there was still a possibility she was in love with a man she couldn't seem to remember.

OTHER THAN BRINGING HER a new printer, reams of paper and extra diskettes, Jason stayed away from Anna for six days. Long enough to win a racquetball tournament at the club and to drink himself into a celebratory stupor with the guys afterward. Long enough to convince Sunny he hadn't fallen in love with his old family friend. To gather his defenses about him. To drive himself completely crazy with wanting Anna, with worry.

She was pregnant and virtually alone in one of the most dangerous cities in the world. And she had no memory of her life prior to the past seven weeks.

He'd planned to wait until he heard something concrete from Whitehall before spending any more time with Anna, but the lead the man had mentioned was on simmer because a contact was on vacation. Finally Jason couldn't stay away any longer. He still hadn't come to terms with her pregnancy, with the other man in her life. Still wasn't certain he could stop himself from falling for her all over again. But he was sure of one thing. The past week had been hell. So while he still could, he wanted to spend as much time with Anna as possible.

Feeling guilty, he rapped on her door Tuesday morning. He'd been wrong to leave her on her own so long.

No answer.

Jason rapped again. Harder. She didn't usually leave the apartment in the morning. Though she'd never outright admitted it, he knew she was still suffering from occasional bouts of morning sickness.

The vacant look on her face when at last she opened the door changed to instant welcome when she saw who was standing there.

"Jason!" Throwing her arms around him, she hugged him tightly. His arms came around her automatically as he gloried in her softness, ignoring for the moment the evidence of her pregnancy.

"I'm sorry, Anna," he felt compelled to say. "I didn't mean to desert you." But he *had* meant to. And he'd been wrong.

"No, Jason, don't be sorry." Her sweet smile tore at him. "I understand. You have things to do." Smoothing the frown from his brow, she said, "It's okay, really."

"How are you?" he asked, still holding her. He couldn't seem to let her go.

"Fine. Especially now that you're here. I've missed you."

"I missed you, too."

Looking into her big brown eyes, seeing the desire there, he either had to kiss her or get away from her.

He couldn't kiss her. He had to keep enough distance to retain his sanity when they eventually found the man who'd slept with her.

Seeing her computer blinking over her shoulder, he let her go and crossed to it. "You've been working?"

She chuckled. "All the time."

"It's going okay?" His gaze met and settled on hers. Damn, she looked good. Her hair was tousled, her face was devoid of makeup—exactly as she'd looked waking up in his bed.

"Ideas are flowing so fast I'm afraid of losing them," she said, grinning.

She was doing fine. Just fine. Jason was glad, relieved. Whatever happened, Anna was going to be okay.

"You want to go out for breakfast?" He had to

get out of her apartment. She was too close, too tempting. He couldn't stop thinking about Staten Island.

"Sure." She grabbed her purse. "So, what've you been doing besides working?"

What could he tell her? That racquetball had been more important than seeing her? That he'd taken Sunny out several times?

As easy as Anna was making it, Jason couldn't just pretend that there hadn't been a problem, that there wasn't still a problem. She might not remember their relationship, but he did. And the one thing that had made it so different, so remarkable, was the complete honesty between them.

"Staying away from you." The words were out of his mouth before he could stop them.

"What?"

"I've been avoiding you."

Anna's purse hit the floor. Her face white, she sank onto the couch, her eyes stricken. She didn't say a word. Just looked at him.

"I was wrong." The confession didn't make him feel any better. Her either, apparently.

"To the contrary, your reasons were probably quite valid." Her calm impersonal tone cut him to the quick.

This was Anna when she was hurting the most. She'd perfected the art of covering up. *Don't let it show.* He could almost hear the ingrained words repeating themselves in her head.

"Valid or not, avoiding you wasn't the answer." He sat down beside her, taking her hands in both of his, holding tight when she tried to pull away. "But we have to talk about this, Anna."

"Why are you doing this?" she asked. "Why do you hang around, keep coming back?"

That was easy. "Because I care."

Her gaze searched his relentlessly. "As an old family friend?"

"No."

"Oh." She looked down at her lap. He looked, too, and was surprised to see how much larger she'd become in just six days.

"I tried to stay away. It didn't work."

Anna nodded, feeling stupid. She'd had no idea. All the while she'd been working, content with the knowledge that Jason was just a phone call away, he'd been contemplating changing his number.

Jason's hand suddenly moved, and Anna flinched as it covered the swell of her stomach.

"Don't." She pushed his hand away, embarrassed. She would have given anything for Jason to have been the man who'd put the child there.

"Do you want me to go?"

Her gaze flew to his. "No!" she said. And then, more softly, "I care, too, Jason. A lot." Frightening as the admission was, it was also a huge relief.

Bringing his hand back to gently caress the baby again, Jason said, "We have to talk about it, Anna," He tapped her stomach with one finger. "This little guy's a part of you."

"She's a girl." He was right. They couldn't keep pretending the baby didn't exist.

His hand stilled. "You know for sure?"

She nodded. "I found out last week during the ultrasound."

Not only wasn't it fair to either of them to keep pretending the child didn't exist, it wasn't fair to her daughter. Something shifted in Anna's heart as she finally allowed herself to acknowledge the tiny being inside her. She was bearing a child. And a part of her was very very glad.

"Was everything all right?"

"Fine." The baby was growing right on schedule—which made Anna about fifteen weeks pregnant.

"I'm sorry I let you down." He was troubled. And that troubled Anna.

"Oh, Jason, don't," Anna said, laying her hand on top of his. "You've done so much for me. There's no way you've let me down."

Jason's gaze held hers, seeking what she didn't know. But she knew when he found it. He smiled at her, squeezing her hand.

"Have you thought of names?"

Hell, no. She'd barely thought of the child as real until two seconds ago. She shook her head.

"What happens next?" he asked, rubbing her stomach again, staring at it as if he could actually see the little girl growing inside.

"Not much for a while," she said, her eyes misting with tears as she watched him. Oh, God, why couldn't it have been him?

"I continue my monthly checkups clear up until the last month," she continued. "Take my vitamins, get fatter."

"This isn't fat," Jason said, almost sounding like a proud papa for a moment as he continued to rub her stomach. One thing she'd learned about Jason over the past weeks, something she greatly admired, was how completely he jumped into everything he did. He'd decided to acknowledge her baby, and now she couldn't get him away from it.

Unfortunately his fingers weren't just communicating with the child in her womb; they were sending erotic messages to her.

She forced herself to concentrate on his original question—the months ahead. "If I can find a partner, I'd like to take childbirth classes."

If she'd been looking for a way to stop Jason's attentions, she'd found it. He pulled his hand away, sitting stiffly beside her, not touching her at all.

The ensuing silence screamed with the offer he wasn't making.

"What about after she's born?" His quiet words fell into the awkwardness she'd created. "Have you thought about what you're going to do?"

Anna shrugged. "I guess that all depends on where I'm living."

"Where?" He turned to look at her, shocked. "You're thinking about leaving New York?"

If his stiffness a moment before had hurt her, his dismay now made up for it.

"I meant whether I'm still living in this vacuum or in the real world."

And there was the crux of their problem. The past weeks, the time they'd spent together, the relationship they were building—none of these were real.

Taking her hand, Jason pulled her up and into his arms. "I want to be a part of that world, Anna."

No more than she wanted him there. Still… "Nothing's changed," she whispered. She wasn't free to make promises, no matter how badly she wanted to make them.

"Just tell me you won't disappear without a word. No matter what happens, what you remember or when, you'll come to me first? Talk to me about it?"

His request was fair. It was even one she could grant. "Of course."

He smiled at her, kissing her lightly. "Then there *is* a commitment we can make."

"Yes?" She was desperate enough to listen, even knowing he was wrong.

"We can promise each other the present."

It wasn't at all orthodox. It solved nothing, as the present became past with each new minute. "I promise you my present," she whispered, her eyes welling with tears as she looked up at him.

"And I give you mine."

Jason offered to attend the childbirth classes with her.

WHITEHALL'S LEAD turned out to be nothing—wrong person, wrong place. They knew from questioning Anna's landlord that Anna had been accompanied by a man on at least one occasion, but hadn't managed to find out anything about him. Jason had already questioned all of Anna's neighbors himself, knew what a dead end that was. On a hunch Jason had Whitehall check every literary agent in New York, but a month later, nothing was still all they had.

Sitting in Anna's apartment one Tuesday in mid-September, waiting for her to finish getting ready for their lunch date, Jason wasn't even sure he wanted Whitehall's answers. Anna was nineteen weeks pregnant. In all that time, no one had shown up on her doorstep. Maybe their luck would hold out for another fifty years.

"Jason! Come here, she's awake!" Anna called from the bathroom.

He was up in a flash, striding across the apartment as fast as the cramped quarters allowed. He'd missed the last two times. He wasn't about to miss a third.

"Where?" he asked, reaching for her belly the second he was in the door.

"Here." Stretching her dress across her stomach, she took his hand, placing it just under her left ribs.

Jason waited, feeling Anna's heart beat, but nothing else. Damn. Did the little girl somehow know it was him? Had she recognized his voice when he'd walked in the room?

Waiting impatiently, refusing to budge until Anna's daughter gave in, Jason continued to cup Anna's stomach. *Come on, darling, move for me,* he encouraged silently.

The flutter against his hand startled him so much he pulled back instantly. Shocked, he looked up into Anna's laughing eyes.

"Put it back, silly." She grinned, guiding his hand to the right spot.

"It's amazing!" Jason said seconds later. Until that moment the life forming in Anna had been a source of pain to him. Suddenly the child was nothing but incredible joy.

His gaze met Anna's, the wonder, the awe of life's creation passing between them there in her cramped little bathroom.

"I wish she were yours," Anna whispered softly.

Not as much as I do, sweet Anna. Not nearly as much as I do.

Unable to say a word, Jason broke his own rule and leaned down to kiss her.

THEY WERE FINALLY READY to leave the apartment when her phone rang. Still tingling from the shock of Jason's kiss, Anna fumbled with the receiver, nearly dropping it before getting it to her ear.

A woman's voice greeted her in German. It sounded harried, apologetic and wonderfully familiar.

"Rosa!" Anna said. *"Guten Tag."*

The older woman spoke rapidly, apologizing profusely in her native tongue for disturbing Anna, aware that Anna was writing, that Anna would call if and when she had some extra time for sewing. But Rosa was in a terrible bind. Just had two seamstresses come down with the flu and had a whole series of jobs due out that week. Please, could Anna help her just this once? She didn't have anyone else to call.

Anna assured Rosa that of course she'd be glad to help and was halfway through her commiseration with Rosa's predicament before she noticed the odd way Jason was looking at her. That's when she realized she herself was speaking fluent German.

And just as suddenly she knew that she'd studied German because she didn't want to study Spanish. Though what relevance that piece of information had was completely lost on her.

Quickly explaining her condition to Rosa, she asked for directions to Rosa's shop, saying she'd be by later that afternoon to pick up a batch of jobs. Rosa started to cry when she heard what Anna had been through, trying to retract her request for help fearing that she was putting too much on Anna's shoulders, but finally giving in when Anna assured Rosa that she'd welcome something extra to do.

Rosa did, however, insist on bringing the sewing to Anna. She couldn't get away that day, but she'd come by first thing the next morning.

"Rosa?" Anna asked, just before she hung up. She just had to know one thing, she explained. Did she pick up her sewing in garbage bags and return them the same way?

"*Ja.*" Rosa went off on another spurt of German, worrying about Anna, assuring her she'd do anything she could to help.

Maybe Rosa would know who Anna used to consort with. Maybe she'd be able to help Anna find out who'd fathered her child.

CHAPTER THIRTEEN

ABBY NEVER CALLED anymore. Jason dialed the beach cottage for the third time that week, frowning when he realized he was the only one keeping in contact these days. The past months were taking one hell of a toll on Abby.

She answered on the fifth ring. "Yes?"

"What, you can't say hello anymore?"

"Jason!" There was a little more life in her reply as she recognized his voice. "Nothing's wrong, is there? You just called two days ago."

"Everything's fine," he quickly told her. He knew it was hell for Abby being so far away when Anna—the sister she'd spent her entire life caring for—was going through such a difficult time. Jason understood, which was why he called so often.

"I felt the baby move today," he told her.

"No kidding!" It sounded like Abby might even be grinning. "Is Anna getting huge, then?"

"Not yet, but she's definitely showing."

"Will you send me a picture?" The wistful tone was back.

Jason agreed readily, then said, "She had a call today from some German woman who owns an alterations shop. Anna had been doing piece work for her.''

"That's one mystery solved.''

"Anna spoke to the woman in fluent German.''

"She remembered her German?''

"Not only that, she told me over lunch that she remembered studying it because she didn't want to study Spanish.''

Silence thrummed over the line. Jason had expected Abby to find the news encouraging. Slowly but surely Anna was remembering.

"I never knew she didn't want to learn Spanish. I just thought she liked German,'' Abby finally said. It sounded as if she was crying again.

"What's wrong with her not liking Spanish?'' Jason asked, lying back on his couch, exhausted. Tired of trying to find answers that didn't seem to exist.

"I made all three of us sign up for it,'' Abby finally said. "Living so close to Mexico, with so many Spanish-speaking people, I thought it would be good for us to be fluent.'' She stopped, took a deep breath.

Jason waited.

"Both my sisters agreed, but the first day of class, Anna didn't show up. She'd gotten Mom to change her schedule at the last minute. They just told me she really liked German.''

"Maybe she did.''

"Or maybe she was trying to get away from me even then.''

"She wanted to think for herself, Abby,'' he said

softly, the back of his hand over his eyes. "Not to get away from you."

"I'm not so sure."

"I am."

"Because she wouldn't leave me to move to New York?"

It hurt to hear her say it even after all this time. "That's one sure sign."

"Did you ever think that maybe we're the real reason for Anna's amnesia?" Abby sounded as worn-out as he felt.

"That she needed to find her own identity, you mean?" he asked. Of course he'd thought of it, they'd all discussed it—he, Abby and Dr. Gordon. But while the doctor had seen that as a contributing factor, he'd been sure there was more going on with Anna than an identity crisis. Something far more disturbing.

"No. I mean, maybe by forcing her to choose, we forced her to escape, instead."

Sitting up, Jason frowned. It was past midnight. He was beyond playing mental gymnastics with Anna's sister. "I don't follow you."

"Think about it, Jason. If Anna loved us both equally—shared an equal though different bond, an equal loyalty—we both betrayed her by forcing her to choose one bond over the other. To make one of us happy, she had to desert the other. For someone as intensely loyal, as deeply committed as Anna, it was an impossible situation."

Abby had had a lot of time to think. And what she said made sense.

"So how do we get her back?"

"Wait. Just like the doctor told us," Abby said, sounding more like the bossy woman Jason had grown to love. "It's when we have her back that it's our turn to go to work. We can't make her choose anymore, Jason."

"You're prepared to give her up?" Jason asked.

"Are you?"

"Of course not."

"Then how can you ask it of me?" Her voice was barely above a whisper. But Jason had no trouble hearing her message. *Or of Anna?*

"I'm an ass," he said, finally seeing what he'd done all those months ago. He'd let the insecurities he thought he'd left behind years before overrule his good sense. Anna was an identical triplet whose bond with her sister had grown as necessary to her as breathing over the years. Moving her to New York wouldn't have changed that. It would only have made Anna miserable. Just as miserable as Abby was now.

And because he was a jealous fool, feeling shut out by a bond that was stronger than anything he'd ever known, anything he could ever share, he'd laid down an ultimatum.

"I'll quit my job, move back to California," he said, surprised to find that he wasn't as upset as he should have been at the thought. He'd been so proud when the offer had come in.

Or had his excitement been charged with the knowledge that he now had a legitimate excuse to force Anna's hand, to make her prove she'd forsake all others for him? To get her away from her sister?

He didn't know. But one thing was for sure—the job alone had not made him happy. He needed Anna. And although he'd sworn he'd never again allow himself to come second to a woman he'd committed his all to, wasn't second still better than nothing? If he knew going in not to expect any more than that?

"Jason?" Abby's voice was oddly hesitant.

"Yeah?"

"Don't quit your job yet."

"I'm not going to lose her again, Abby."

"You may not have a choice."

He'd thought Abby was on his side. All these weeks she'd been encouraging his involvement with Anna. "We were meant to be together, Abby. She may not remember our past, but she's fallen in love all over again."

"And how's she going to feel when she remembers the choice we forced on her? Do you think she's going to be fond of either one of us?"

He didn't know. Dammit, he didn't know. "The move back to California should settle that."

"Maybe. But where's her guarantee it won't happen again?"

"She'll have my word. Besides, life never carries guarantees. Anna's smart enough to know that."

"There's another possibility. What if, when she remembers, there's another man she loves more?"

Her words sliced into him and he couldn't answer her. *God, did she hate him this much?*

"I'm worried about you, Jason," Abby finally whispered. She was crying again. "You're the best there is and you're getting in too deep."

"You'd rather I just walked away?"

"No." She sniffed. "I'd rather you just marry her before she comes to her senses."

The thought had crossed his mind.

"But I know you. You won't do anything even remotely so dishonest."

"Thanks for that, I think." God, he'd never felt so weary of spirit. Why did he go on? But with Anna still within reach, how could he not?

"I wish you weren't so damn honest. Because when Anna remembers who the father of her baby is, she may very well choose him even if she loves you more. And knowing you, you're going to let her go—and that just might kill you."

"You think letting her go now is going to hurt any less?"

"Just be careful, okay?"

"Yeah." He'd be careful.

If only he could figure out how.

"OH MY! HOW DID THAT happen?" Rosa exclaimed in German, standing in Anna's doorway the next morning. The plump gray-haired woman was staring at Anna's stomach.

Anna looked down, too, as if she might find a spot on her dress, something she'd spilled. But her head remained bowed. "I don't remember."

Rosa didn't seem nearly as bothered as Anna was by the humiliating admission. "I'll bet it was that nice man you brought with you sometimes," Rosa said pleasantly, her old-fashioned brown dress crinkling as she walked by Anna to set her bag of sewing down beside the couch.

"I brought someone with me?" Anna asked. Her embarrassment fled in light of possible answers to questions she'd almost given up asking.

"A man, yes," Rosa nodded. "He was tall, nice-looking, if you like them skinny. Older than you."

Sounds just like the man Maggie described. Anna looked blankly at Rosa; she didn't remember this man at all.

"Clark, you called him," Rosa told her.

Clark. Anna felt sick to her stomach. She didn't want him to have a name. She'd wanted Maggie to be wrong, to have imagined the man. *And the voice on the answering machine?* She'd erased that.

"He had dark hair?" Anna heard herself ask. But she didn't want to know. Didn't want this man to exist.

"Yes, he did." Rosa's heavy, flat-soled shoes against the hard wood floors sounded like cannon shots as the woman approached Anna again. "You remember him?" she asked.

Anna shook her head, shame washing over her. Not only did she not remember this man, she didn't *want* to remember him, didn't even want him to exist.

Rosa clucked when she saw the stricken look on Anna's face. "Oh, he'll understand, dear. He was always so nice to you, carried your bags, took you nice places."

Anna tried to smile at the older woman, all the while feeling more and more trapped. Tied up in so many knots she'd never get out, never be free.

"Sounds like I spent a lot of time with him," she said, and knew she hadn't hidden her distress very well when Rosa took her hand and led her to the couch.

"A bit, I think," Rosa said. "But don't you worry about it now, dear. You just rest here." She pulled the blanket off the back of the couch, laying it over Anna's legs. "You've got that little one to think about now."

Yes, she'd think about the baby. And Jason. The past was past. She was living in the present. A present she'd promised to Jason.

BECAUSE DRIVING in the country was one of Anna's favorite things to do, Jason took her out most weekends. He loved to see the smile on her face as they sped down quiet country roads.

"I feel so free out here," Anna confessed one Saturday in early October.

He glanced over at her, seeing her hair falling about her shoulders in a golden halo. "You don't feel free in the city?"

Shrugging, she said, "My problems are there."

"You shouldn't worry so much, Anna." Jason frowned. "Dr. Gordon gave you a great report just last week."

"I know." She nodded. "And it's not even worry so much as it is feeling trapped by my own mind."

He was happy with their present. A small part of him wished she, too, could be satisfied with just today, although he knew he was asking the impossible.

And were he to be completely honest with himself, he'd have to admit he was only happy with the present because he refused to consider the future. But ignoring it was getting harder and harder.

"Do you want to start asking questions? Call Abby?" he asked.

Anna took a long time answering him, telling him without words of the battle taking place within her. He needed to do something to help her. But he sat beside her, instead, completely helpless.

Finally, shaking her head, she said simply, "No."

"Then we'll wait."

"Are you disappointed in me?"

The car swerved as Jason stared at her. "Good Lord, no!" How could she even imagine such a thing?

"You don't think I'm a coward for wanting to wait?"

Jason pulled to the side of the road and stopped. Then he took both her hands in his and leaned over to kiss her gently. "You're the farthest thing from a coward, Anna Hayden," he said, kissing her again. "You're brave—" another kiss "—and strong." He brought his lips to hers one more time.

"Strong enough to hear the truth?" she asked when he finally pulled away from her.

"Strong enough to make your own decisions." He sat back in his seat, still holding her hand. "And for the record I think you've made the right one."

Her eyes clouded. "Because you don't think I'm ready?"

"Because I trust Dr. Gordon, and he thinks you're going to remember on your own."

Jason's heart jumped when she pulled on his hand and planted a big kiss on his mouth. "Thank you," she said, smiling as she let him go.

"You're very welcome." Jason ran his finger along her cheek. She was so beautiful, his Anna. Except that she wasn't his Anna. At least not yet.

"TELL ME MORE about Jason Whitaker," she said later that afternoon when the Jag was headed back toward the city.

"What do you want to know?" This was one of the hardest parts for him, looking at the woman he'd shared his heart and soul with and having her act as if she'd only known him for a few months.

"Why are you still single?"

The flippant answer that came automatically to his lips froze when he glanced at her earnest expression. She cared about his answer.

"You know about my last relationship," he reminded her.

"The woman who turned you down?" She was frowning.

Guiding the Jag around a curve, he studied the landscape. "Mm-hmm." Such a beautiful day—and so filled with land mines.

"What about before her?" Anna asked. "You're thirty-three—you had to have had some other relationships." Her husky voice drew him.

"I lived with a girl my last couple of years of college." Which was something he'd never told her before.

"What happened?" Her eyes shimmered with ready understanding.

"She could never get over her first love, a guy who left her at the altar to marry a woman almost twice her age."

"I'm sorry."

Jason shrugged. "I was young," he admitted. "Just made a bad choice." He grinned at Anna. "I didn't really love her, anyway—at least, it only took me about a week to get over her."

Anna smiled back at him, connecting with him the way she used to when they'd had entire conversations without ever saying a word.

"So what about after her?" Anna asked.

"There was only one other serious relationship...." One the old Anna had known all about. In fact, he'd met her the day it had fallen apart. He'd only spoken three words to Anna that day, but her smile had carried him through a very difficult afternoon.

"She wasn't in love with someone else, too, was she?" Anna asked.

Jason shook his head, welcoming the lights of the city ahead. "Nope. The law was her first love."

"She was a lawyer?"

"A defense attorney."

"Oh." Anna sounded almost intimidated. "So what happened?"

"My grandmother died. Sheila chose to bail a new client out of jail rather than accompany me to the funeral. The guy didn't want to wait a few hours. I decided then that I didn't want to wait around anymore, either."

"I can't believe she did that!" Anna's eyes were wide, just as they'd been the last time he'd told her this story. "Did she know your grandmother?"

"My grandmother introduced us."

THE INSTRUCTOR Anna wanted for her childbirth classes, a woman who came highly recommended by Dr. Litton, already had a full roster during Anna's last trimester, leaving Anna the choice to take the classes during her second trimester or take them from someone else. Anna chose to take the classes early, starting in mid-October.

His leather jacket over his arm and nervous as an expectant father, Jason showed up at Anna's apartment half an hour early the first night of classes, extra pillows in hand.

"These okay?" he asked, thrusting the pillows, still in their packaging, at her when she opened the door.

"Fine." Anna grinned. "Any pillows would have done—I only have one."

She looked great, her long-sleeved brown flowered dress matching her eyes. She was going to be able to get through her whole pregnancy without having to buy maternity clothes. Her loosely cut dresses came in handy for more than the freedom of movement she'd always claimed from them.

"Where's Maggie?" he asked, looking around when Anna disappeared through the open bathroom door. Maggie had laughingly promised to send them off with a glass of champagne. Jason had hoped to have more than one.

"She got a job!" Anna called, coming out of the bathroom with a tube of mascara in her hand. "She's playing a female cop in an NBC pilot. She flew to California this afternoon."

As happy as he was for Maggie, Jason was sorry to see her go. She'd been a good friend to Anna. And he'd really been counting on that champagne.

HIS FANTASY WORLD shattered the minute they walked into the classroom. It wasn't until he saw the size of the stomachs of the women who were in their third trimester, saw how far Anna had yet to go, that he was forced to acknowledge the dangerous pretense he'd embarked on. And the small hope, that chance in a million that Anna was carrying his child, that the doctor had been six weeks off on Anna's due date, died a very painful death.

But because everyone, Anna included, was watching him, waiting for him to take his place beside her, Jason didn't give in to the impulse to bolt. Like the mature grown man he was, he sat down beside her on the mat and proceeded to learn how to help her bring another man's child into the world.

Unfortunately mature grown men experienced agony right along with the rest of them.

THAT FIRST CLASS introduced a new intimacy into a relationship already on the verge of becoming far too personal. Feeling like a wanton woman, Anna started to flood with desire at the merest glance from Jason, at the unexpected sound of his voice on the telephone. And every time he helped her practice for the birth of her daughter, every time she lay back and lifted her pelvis for him to shove a pillow beneath her, she ached with the need to pull him down on top of her. More than one time she had to bite her lip to stop herself from begging him to make love to her.

Instead, she directed her emotion into the biography she was writing, pouring her longings onto the page, her frustrations, her desires, knowing that if nothing else came from this nightmare time of her life, she was writing a good book.

In the evenings she sat, drained, watching Jason on the news and sewing for Rosa.

Then one afternoon toward the end of October, a letter came in the mail from a literary agent in Manhattan. It seemed she'd sent three chapters of her manuscript to the agency back in June. They liked them. Enough to want to see the entire manuscript as soon as she could send it.

It wasn't a sale. But it was more than she'd even dared hope and her spirits soared.

Coming down long enough to dial Jason's number, Anna hung up in disappointment when he didn't answer. He'd been invited to take part in a celebrity touch-football game that afternoon to benefit homeless shelters in the city, and she'd hoped he would already have arrived home.

She tried again between newscasts that evening and finally reached him when she was half-asleep late that night. He was as delighted as she'd known he'd be, and more, he sounded proud. Even invited her out to dinner on the Upper East Side the next night to celebrate. But only after she promised that when she was a famous celebrity, she'd still remember him.

As if she'd ever forget him.

Anna hung up with a huge grin on her face. Amnesia or no, she felt good about herself. She'd built a new life. A happy life.

Lying on her side in bed, cradling her unborn child, Anna finally had the courage to admit what she'd been hiding from for months. She didn't want to remember anymore, didn't want to find the father of her child. She didn't care if she'd loved him before the accident—she didn't love him now. And the reason she didn't love him was that she was passionately in love with Jason Whitaker.

But the admission didn't bring her relief. Instead, she started to cry, stopping herself only when she remembered Maggie's words about crying women having grouchy babies. Not that there was any truth to that. Still, her sobs couldn't be good for her daughter, this tiny being who was a hundred percent dependent on her, Anna, to give her a good life.

Could she do that? Her chest tightened. Until she found out who she was, what did she have to offer this child? Not even a father. And what if, when she remembered her past, she found herself irrevocably bound to another man?

What if the past she was running from turned out to have been immoral, or so painful she couldn't face it?

Until she knew what she'd done, what she'd been, she wasn't free to love Jason. Nor fully equipped to be a mother to the child who'd be arriving in less than three months.

Tossing and turning, Anna finally drifted off, but only after forcing herself to practice the breathing techniques she and Jason had been working on. But sleep, when it came, brought, instead of relief, only more nightmares.

HER HEAD POUNDING, she called Dr. Gordon first thing in the morning. Wasn't there something more he could do? Because until she got her life back, she couldn't go forward.

No, the doctor told her. The most she could do for herself was just relax. Allow her mind whatever time it needed to heal itself. Getting upset was only going to slow the process. She should take heart from the memories she'd had, resting assured that the remainder would follow. In the meantime concentrate on her book, on shopping for baby things—on relaxing.

Unfortunately the doctor saying so didn't make it happen.

LIKE SOME DIRTY TRICK, more than three months after he'd hired Smith Whitehall, Jason finally got some answers on Halloween. Jason was sitting in his office an hour before he was due on the air, going over the day's stories, when his phone rang.

Whitehall had a name for him—Clark Summerfield. The eldest son of a family with old money, a New York businessman with fingers in numerous financial pies, he'd been dating Anna for several weeks before being called out of the country on business. There was no evidence that Summerfield and Anna had ever slept together, no indication of nights spent at each other's homes or records of any hotel stays. However, Whitehall was certain Summerfield was the only man Anna had seen on a personal basis since arriving in New York—and there was no one in California at all, not since Jason.

Cold with dread, Jason spent the next half hour calling several of his New York contacts, needing factual and frank character assessments of Clark Summerfield.

The accolades came in almost immediately. Clark Summerfield was a prince. A widower for many years, he had no children, worked hard, although he didn't have to, and attended every family get together. He donated heavily to charities. Before Anna, he'd often been seen escorting his mother or unmarried sister to business functions. He'd celebrated his fortieth birthday the previous spring. His only fault, if you could call it one, seemed to be his workaholic tendencies.

And the fact that he wasn't the least bit athletic. Anna loved sports. Or at least, she'd always been eager to watch Jason's various athletic ventures.

So, his rival had a name. A damn good name. A damn good life. One that in other circumstances, he could see Anna being happy with. Summerfield was a man Anna could love.

Jason went on the air, he exchanged quips with Sunny, even had dinner with her in between shows. And he did it all with a frozen heart.

For the first time in a long time that night Jason went home and did some serious drinking. He hoped the alcohol would warm him up a bit, make him feel again. And maybe it did, because by the end of the evening he felt as if he had died and gone to hell.

But if he had, his rival was there with him, taunting him. Clark Summerfield. New York's number-one catch. Hell, maybe America's number-one catch. And, it seemed, Anna's sweetheart.

Sometime around three o'clock in the morning, six or seven whiskeys under, he started to think. If Summerfield was the father of Anna's baby, wouldn't she have told the man? And wouldn't he, respectable responsible man that he was, have stood by her? Married her?

Or was this guy's image a sham? Had he simply used Anna and then deserted her in her hour of need? Conveniently finding it necessary to wheel and deal in Europe for the next several months.

Had this been the blow that had done her in?

No, if Summerfield was that much of a jerk, someone would know. Anna wouldn't have been the first scorned woman. Men like that left a trail of them.

So maybe he'd left before Anna had known she

was pregnant. Maybe she hadn't had a chance to contact him before the crash had wiped away all evidence of his existence.

And maybe Summerfield wasn't the father, after all. As good as Whitehall was, wouldn't he have found some evidence if Summerfield and Anna were lovers? Even if they'd only had sex once? Of course, they could have done that in the car or on the beach....

It was also possible, based on the lack of any other evidence, that Anna's mysterious lover had died. Perhaps that was the tragedy she was running from. No. Whitehall would definitely have been able to determine that.

Perhaps the guy was running from something himself, purposely covering his tracks. Maybe he'd been a swindler, a professional crook who changed identities and ate nice girls like Anna for bedtime snacks.

So what if the man never turned up? What then? Jason couldn't base his future on what ifs. Was it wrong for him to want to come first in someone's life? No matter how hard he'd tried, he'd always played second fiddle—to his father's career, his mother's second marriage, her new daughter, his college love's other man, the law, even to a prostitute's career. He'd been eating leftovers his entire life.

But weren't leftovers better than starving? And the bottom line was, did he have any choice? He'd been in love with Anna Hayden since the first moment he'd seen her. He had a pretty good idea the

feeling wasn't going to disappear now, just because
his head told him he'd be safer not to care.

Dizzy with the circles his thoughts were running,
Jason finally fell across his bed, still half-dressed,
just as dawn was breaking over the city. One fact
remained. The father of Anna's child wasn't here.
Jason was. And possession was nine-tenths of the
law.

HE WAS GOING to lose her. In the cold light of day,
his head pounding in protest, Jason had to face the
truth. Clark Summerfield was the only logical choice
for the father of Anna's baby. He simply wasn't
aware of the child he'd created. When he was, a man
like Clark would ask her to marry him immediately.
And Anna, loyal as she was, would marry him out
of duty. Wouldn't she?

Or would she?

Anna had changed, was sticking up for what she
wanted. Would that new determination extend to re-
jecting what she didn't want?

Summerfield was in Europe during Anna's
greatest hour of need. Which meant he must not
know anything about the crash or her amnesia. Had
he known, he'd have flown home to see her through
this difficult time. But if there was commitment between them, wouldn't there also be communication?

And if there were no commitment...

Jason had won her love once. While the field was
clear, he at least had to try again. But he'd do it
with his eyes wide open, knowing the risks. No
more pretending.

CHAPTER FOURTEEN

JASON SENT HER FLOWERS. They arrived Saturday afternoon just before his phone call asking her out on a date. An official date. Dress comfortably, he told her. They were going on a cruise around the harbor.

At six and a half months pregnant, Anna didn't have any idea how she could feel sexy and romantic, but when she opened the door an hour later, when Jason looked at her as though he'd like to make love to her right there on the floor, she'd never felt sexier. Dressed in a long-sleeved ankle-length flannel tent with a thick cardigan sweater on top, she felt like every man's dream centerfold. Maybe pregnancy made your hormones rage.

The cruise was idyllic, quixotic—and deserted. No one else was crazy enough to cruise around the harbor at night on the first of November. But snuggled against Jason in the wool blanket he'd brought, Anna couldn't think of anything more romantic.

They ate assorted cheeses accompanied by a homemade French loaf and grapes, popping them into each other's mouths, licking the juice from each other's fingers—and lips. Jason drank wine, Anna, mineral water. And they talked. About the world.

About people. About life. Jason believed in so many
of the things she found most important. Family.
Loyalty. Commitment.

After they'd eaten he pulled her back against him
on the secluded bench. The blanket enveloping them
in their own private world, he linked his hands beneath the swell of her belly, holding her and the
baby both.

Happy, drugged with the night, the romance, she
snuggled into him, content to remain as she was forever.

The baby moved, her little foot dragging across
the bottom of Anna's stomach.

"She's awake, Mama," Jason whispered in her
ear.

"It's 'cause she knows you're here." Anna was
convinced that the baby recognized Jason's voice,
his touch. These days she seemed to become active
whenever he was around.

Jason laughed, following the baby's progress with
one hand, poking her gently, playing with her. Anna
didn't see how any moment could be more perfect.

"There's a daddy position open if you're interested." The words slipped out before she could stop
them.

And she wished she had when she felt Jason
stiffen behind her. "I'm not her father."

She was spoiling the most perfect evening of her
life, but she couldn't stop herself. When she'd
awoken in that hospital all those months ago, she'd
had to start fresh, fill the horrible void that was all
she knew. She'd created a new life for herself, a

good life, and that hadn't come easy or without a fight. If convincing Jason they were meant to be together took another fight, so be it.

"Not biologically," she said, placing her arms over his, keeping his hands on her belly. "But in every other way—in my heart and, I believe, in hers—you're already her father."

"And what happens to me when you find out who her father is, when he returns to your lives claiming what's rightfully his?" Jason's words weren't an accusation; that wouldn't have hurt so much. They were resigned.

It was time to speak up or lose him forever. "He doesn't matter anymore." The confession was difficult to make, not because she wasn't completely certain of its truth, but because it left her so vulnerable. "He can't matter," she continued, her voice breaking. "Because I'm completely in love with you."

Jason's heart soared. Which made the plunge to despair that followed all the more painful. He didn't doubt that she believed what she was saying. But how could she possibly be sure of her feelings without a yardstick to measure them by?

Then, too, she'd claimed tearfully to love him when he'd asked—okay, demanded—that she come to New York with him. Yet less than two months later she'd become pregnant by another man.

"You don't know how desperately I want to believe you," he finally said, her honesty deserving the same from him.

She turned to face him, clearly shocked. "You don't believe me?"

Jason kissed her slowly, tenderly. He'd always been able to show her so much more than he could say.

"I believe you feel that way now," he said when he raised his head.

"You don't think I know my own heart." Her head fell against his chest, and her gaze turned to the bay.

"You know what's there now, Anna, but what about when it fills back up with all the emotions you've forgotten?" He couldn't believe her words, couldn't count on them. He'd only get hurt. And he couldn't go through that again.

Her silence wasn't a good sign. He had to help her see that they had to know for sure. "I'm here," he said quietly into the darkness. "I'm the only one here." He chose his words carefully, needing her to understand. "But we have to face the fact that somewhere there's another man about whom you could have felt the very same way."

"How do I convince you he just doesn't matter anymore?"

"Until you remember him, you can't, Anna," he said, his voice strong. He wasn't going to let her sway him on this. He couldn't. It would kill him to believe her now, only to have her regret her decision when her memory finally returned. "Until you remember what it is you're giving up, you can't know if you want to."

"And what if I don't ever remember?" Her question fell between them, a question they'd both asked themselves a hundred times. A question neither one could answer.

JASON CALLED Dr. Gordon first thing Monday morning. He rushed through pleasantries, assuring the doctor that Anna was fine, the baby was fine, he was fine, and then got straight to the point.

"What are the chances that Anna will never remember?" When was it time to tell her the truth? At least about them. To tell her that she'd opted not to marry him when he'd asked her last spring. To give her at least those facts and then let her decide if she still wanted him to be the father of the child she carried. If she still wanted him.

The doctor was silent so long Jason was almost afraid to hear his answer. "You know something I don't know?" Jason finally asked him.

"No," Dr. Gordon said, the word drawn out. "I'm just not sure I can give you any percentages, Jason." He paused. "Of course there's always been a possibility that Anna won't ever regain the memories she's lost."

"Does it grow stronger as time passes?"

"No."

"So five years from now she could be sitting in a restaurant or driving down the road and suddenly have it all come flooding back?" Five years' worth of living, of loving, only to lose it all?

"Or it could come in little snatches, just as it's been doing."

"I want to marry her, Doctor."

"I'm not surprised." Dr. Gordon sighed. "But I can't tell you I think it's a good idea right now. Too much still rests in the balance."

"It's not fair to Anna, is what you're saying," Jason stated flatly. He'd already reached that conclusion himself. It was just convincing her he was having troubles with. "How can she make such a lasting commitment when she doesn't know what she's leaving behind?"

"Exactly."

The doctor was only confirming what he already knew. And it sounded just as hopeless coming from someone else.

"It also wouldn't be fair to you, Jason," Dr. Gordon continued.

"I'm not worried about that." He brushed the doctor's words aside. He'd given up on fair a long time ago. Now he simply kept himself safe. If he didn't count on anything, didn't look for things that weren't there, he'd be fine. "I'm just not sure I can convince Anna to wait another five years to start living her life."

"You'd have a hard time convincing me if I were in her position."

"She says she isn't going to wait until she's eighty and then, when she's too old to do anything but die, decide that her memory isn't coming back." They'd been her last words to him the night before when, in her apartment, they'd had a replay of the conversation from Saturday night. Jason had a feeling that they'd continue to replay it until he gave in.

"She has a point."

"So you think I should tell her about her past? At least about my part in it?" he asked, hopeful for the go-ahead. It was his only chance.

The doctor took a moment to think, but his answer was disappointing. "I really believe it's too soon, Jason. She's a strong woman, stronger now probably than she ever was before, but we have to remember that none of us knows what she's running from, what prompted her amnesia."

"And you don't think she's strong enough to handle whatever it is even now?" Because Jason did.

"Probably she is strong enough. But if she no longer wants to remember, if she no longer has any reason to try, you might be committing her to permanent darkness." He took a deep breath. "She's growing increasingly more frustrated. Her determination to know her own mind is becoming all-important, her need to make her own decisions stronger than ever. These are all signs of imminent recovery. I can't urge strongly enough that you give her more time."

Jason could find nothing in the doctor's words he could fault. "I'll give her until the baby's due," he said. "If she never remembers who fathered her child, if she never remembers the circumstances that led to her amnesia, I can live with that. But I'll never be able to live with myself if we bring this child into a relationship based on a lie."

There would be no argument on that point.

THE NIGHT SUNNY argued with him on the air, Jason knew he had some other decisions to make. His co-anchor, knowing he'd been seeing a lot of Anna, was trying to get his attention.

"Lighten up, Sunny," he said softly during a commercial break. Cameramen were milling around, someone from makeup came over to blot the perspiration on Jason's brow. Now wasn't the time for a showdown, but he hated to see Sunny humiliate herself on the air. She was a damn good newscaster. And she'd been a good friend.

"I don't know what you're talking about," she said, her voice sweet enough. But she wasn't as relaxed as she sounded. He watched her tap the end of her pencil on the desk in front of them.

"Will you at least agree to wait until we're in private?" he asked.

Sunny's assistant came forward to adjust the collar on Sunny's blouse. "Wait for what?" Sunny asked when the girl stepped away.

"I promise we'll talk, Sunny. Tonight. Right after the show." He smiled at the technician who adjusted his mike.

"The show. Sometimes I wonder if that's all you've ever cared about," she said. "Well, don't forget, I helped make you, Jason. And if all it took was my opinion, my acceptance, to gain your entrance into this town, then my opinion can just as easily guarantee your exit."

"Five seconds!" The voice boomed from the darkness in front of them.

Feeling sorry for Sunny, Jason braced himself for a difficult second half. His ability was one thing he was sure of. If she thought she had any power over his career, she had an eye-opener ahead of her.

ANNA WATCHED the news that night, Friday, almost a week after her cruise with Jason, feeling restless and bothered. She'd become used to Sunny Lawson's proprietary air with Jason, or told herself she had, anyway, but that night, either Anna was even more insecure than she thought, or Ms. Lawson had turned up the heat.

Busy with the little overalls she was stitching—a pattern she'd drawn herself and cut from an old newspaper—Anna hadn't noticed anything all that unusual about the first half of the newscast, other than an occasional uncharacteristic barb from Sunny. But during the second half of the show, Sunny not only touched Jason, she actually rubbed his arm a time or two. She was acting like a woman confident of her man's affection, confident her overtures would be accepted.

Licking her lips, Sunny smiled sexily at Jason as she told him they'd have to discuss their differing opinions on a recent parochial-school levy in a more private venue. Everyone watching was meant to know that the last thing Sunny and Jason would be discussing was school levies. That they'd be too involved in more...physical pursuits to discuss anything at all. Anna stabbed herself in the thumb.

Jason had explained about Sunny months before, assuring Anna that any personal relationship he and Sunny pretended to share was just that—pretend. He'd told her about the publicity campaign the station had devised to introduce him to his New York viewers. He'd told her how Sunny had become a friend, someone who's company he enjoyed. Not someone he wanted to have as a lover.

Anna knew all this. She even believed it. So why did Sunny's hand on Jason's arm make her feel so small, so insignificant?

SUNNY FOLLOWED HIM to his dressing room. Shutting the door behind her, she helped herself to a drink from the sideboard, fixing him one, too. Liquid courage.

"Lillie's having a mystery party next weekend on the yacht," she said, settling back against the smooth leather of his couch. Lillie was Sunny's best friend and a bit too shallow, too materialistic for Jason's taste.

He stood at the desk, the drink she'd brought him untouched. He didn't loosen his tie and didn't remove his jacket. He simply stood, not saying a word.

"It's from four on Saturday till whenever on Sunday."

He remained there, unmoving, unbending, by the desk. In his professional life, at least, he was in control. Always. He'd accept nothing less. And he had the feeling Sunny was actually trying to issue him an ultimatum.

"We're invited." She was no longer looking at him, drinking her martini more quickly than she should.

He still said nothing. Did nothing.

"If you pick me up at four-thirty, we should get there late enough to make an entrance."

He wondered where Sunny had gotten the idea that he'd ever change his mind about them. He'd been clear from the start that a friend was all she could expect him to be.

"I'm sorry, Sunny, but I can't go."

Her gaze shot up, locking with his. "Of course you're going," she said with an attempt at a laugh.

"No, I'm not." Jason enunciated the words carefully.

"Don't be stupid Jason." She set her glass down, stood, came over to the desk. "Didn't you hear me earlier?" She placed her hands on his shoulders, leaning her body into his. "The show's mine. You want it, you take me."

"Don't do this to yourself, Sunny," he said, pleading with her to come to her senses before she did irreparable damage to their relationship.

As she pulled away, the look she gave him was a mixture of desperation and hurt. "I'll have you moved to weekends," she blustered.

"I don't think so."

Picking up the phone, Jason dialed the station manager's office.

And less than two minutes later hung up.

"You play nice or take weekends," he said. "The choice is yours." He didn't wait around for Sunny's reaction—or her decision.

DURING THE LAST childbirth class they watched a movie of a woman giving birth. Anna decided one thing instantly. Jason definitely wasn't going to be there for the birth. There was no way his first sight of her naked was going to be like that. She couldn't get out of the class fast enough, away from the chattering couples, the cheery instructor.

Wonder if she'd be feeling that cheery if it were her going through the ordeal, Anna thought sourly, her head bent as she walked out to hail a cab.

"Wasn't that the most amazing thing you've ever seen?" Jason asked, catching up with her at the curb. "Here, honey, put this on before you catch a chill." He handed Anna the coat she'd left behind in the classroom.

Amazing? She snuggled into her coat. "Thanks."

Lifting her chin and looking into her eyes, he asked, "You okay?"

Anna's glance fell. Hell, no, she wasn't okay.

"Anna?"

His gorgeous blue eyes were warm with understanding. He knew.

"I'm scared," she admitted, her breath misting in the cold air between them.

Silently cupping her face with his hands, he lowered his head to kiss her, the touch of his lips a distraction, a reassurance, a reaffirmation of how far she'd come, how strong she really was.

"I'll be there with you, honey, every step of the way."

"You promise?" She held his gaze. "No matter what happens between now and January?" She was asking a lot, but dammit, this was one thing she couldn't do alone, no matter how badly she wanted to.

"I do."

His words were promising far more than his attendance at her daughter's birth. They both knew that.

CHAPTER FIFTEEN

JASON WAS IN HIS KITCHEN when the phone rang Thanksgiving afternoon. Anna, having lain her increasingly cumbersome body back against the couch for a minute, reached lazily for the receiver. "Hello?"

"Is this..." A young woman rattled off Jason's phone number.

Instantly on edge, Anna sat up. "Yes."

"Is Jason there?"

"Who's calling please?" She had no business asking, no right to monitor his calls. Suddenly she felt ill.

"Is he there?"

Anna didn't answer. She was too busy trying to see through the haze that was enveloping her. Sunny wouldn't be calling; Jason had told her his co-anchor had taken a cruise for the holiday weekend—with the new man in her life.

"May I speak with him please?" The woman was determined. Anna just wanted to hang up.

"Just a moment," she said, setting the phone down. She felt awful, light-headed. Must have over-exerted herself in the kitchen, but she'd been so determined to prepare a perfect holiday dinner complete with all the trimmings for Jason.

"Anna? What is it?" Jason asked, coming out of the kitchen where he'd been lifting the Thanksgiving turkey out of the oven for her.

"Huh?" she asked, looking up at him. "Oh, nothing... I mean, the phone's for you." She couldn't think, didn't want to think.

"I didn't hear it ring," he said, looking first at her and then the phone.

She lay back, suddenly afraid she was going to be sick. "It did," she finally said.

Forcing herself to concentrate, she listened when he picked up the phone.

"Hello?" A pause during which Anna's stomach clenched again. And then, "Oh! Hi!"

Did he have to sound so cheerful? "Uh, yeah." This with a furtive glance her way.

Intending to lay right there and figure out what this mysterious woman could possibly want with Jason, why he was suddenly uncomfortable with her listening in, Anna was forced, instead, to bolt for the bathroom—giving him plenty of time to have whatever private conversation he wanted.

JASON DIDN'T TELL HER who'd been on the phone. And she refused to ask. He didn't owe her any explanations. Except that she needed one. She fought with herself the rest of the afternoon, barely touching her dinner, right up to the moment he dropped her off at her door that night. She didn't want to know, didn't want to be hurt. And didn't see how she could go another minute not knowing—loving him as she did.

He'd said he was bringing her home early because she was tired, because she'd been so violently ill earlier in the day. And he seemed genuinely concerned. But Anna couldn't help wondering if he had somewhere else to be. Someone else to see.

Not that she'd blame him. She just had to know.

"Who was she?" she finally blurted as he slid her key into the lock, her proximity to her own apartment giving her the courage to face whatever might be coming. If the news was devastating, she only had to make it a few feet to her bed, then slip under the covers and escape.

Jason didn't look at her or even ask who she meant. He obviously hadn't forgotten the call, either. "Nobody," he said, flipping on a light before standing back to let her enter.

Anna's nausea returned. For "nobody" the woman really bothered her, though Anna figured that was understandable. No matter how much she wanted to, she couldn't promise Jason anything, not yet. Maybe never. The phone call had brought home to her just how untenable that made her position.

He had every right to find promises elsewhere.

"There's no reason to lie to me, Jason," she said, standing in front of him, feeling like a beached whale as she imagined how beautiful the other woman surely was.

Helping her off with her coat, he stopped, looking down at her, his eyes serious. "Yes, Anna, there is."

He couldn't have surprised her more if he'd slapped her. "Why?"

THE DESPAIR IN HER EYES finally decided Jason. This had gone on as long as he could let it. If the past needed to be buried, that was just too bad. He wasn't going to let it interfere with the future.

"Come," he said, drawing her over to the couch, aware of how reluctantly she followed. She'd been through so much, his poor darling. And he had a feeling things were going to get worse.

"Anna, how did you feel when you answered that phone today?" he asked. He'd been worried about Anna's violent reaction to the call. And he wasn't the only one who'd worried.

"Well, if she hadn't evaded me so obviously, it probably would have been okay," Anna said defensively.

Oh, honey, if only you knew. He'd never felt so helpless, watching her, not knowing what to say, what *not* to say.

"It's okay, Jason, I understand," she said, obviously misreading the look of pain in his eyes. He hurt for her, not for himself.

He shook his head slowly, brushing her hair back from her face. "No, honey, you don't," he said, ready to take the plunge, and yet not ready.

"Yes, I do, Jason, and it's really all right." She was trying so hard to mean what she said it broke his heart. "I won't hold you to your promise to hang around until the baby's born," she rushed on.

"You've been wonderful to stand by me this long, but you don't owe me anything."

"It was Abby."

Anna's eyes went wide, blank, and she started to shake.

"Oh, God." The words were anguished.

Pulling her against him, rocking her as he held her, Jason told her about the call and the two others he'd made later in the day, both times when she'd been in the bathroom, reassuring Abby that no harm had been done. Abby had miscalculated the time when she knew Anna was due at Jason's. And then realized what had happened and been terrified, knowing that hearing her voice could very well have risked Anna's future health.

What he didn't tell Anna was how devastated that call had left Abby. To have actually spoken to Anna, to have had her on the phone, hearing her voice— and still not be recognized had shaken Abby to the core. Nor did he tell her how worried they still were. Both from Anna's first nauseous reaction to having spoken with her sister, and the fact that Abby's voice hadn't sparked any memory at all.

"I could have talked to her—" Anna's words, thick with tears, broke off.

"You can always talk to her, honey."

She swiped at the tears on her face. "Dr. Gordon says I should wait."

But the doctor's way wasn't working. "And is that what you want to do?" This was Anna's show now.

"I don't know what I want." Her voice broke

again. "Hold me, Jason," she begged. "Please, just hold me."

He did. But his arms couldn't take away the fear. For either of them.

AUDREY. ANNA SAT straight up in bed, looking around at the predawn gray of her apartment as if she'd find someone there. Audrey. She wanted to name the baby Audrey.

Although not knowing how she knew that or why, Anna had never been more sure of anything in her life. *If the baby was a girl, she was to be called Audrey.* Anna was having a real live honest-to-goodness memory. A resurgence of a thought she'd had before she knew the sex of her child, a thought she'd had before the accident.

She'd been walking in Gramercy Park, and she'd just found out she was pregnant. She'd decided to name the baby Audrey if it was a girl. And she'd hoped it was a girl. Surrounding the memory was a feeling that someone would be very pleased about her decision—once she was free to speak of it.

Still frustratingly locked away was why she couldn't speak of it or who would be pleased.

Tempted to call Jason, in spite of the hour, a new worry held Anna back. Something—or someone had been calling out to her more and more often lately. Before it had only been in dreams, like the nightmare she'd had at Jason's just after she'd left the hospital. But in the three days since Thanksgiving, she'd been experiencing the oddest sensations while wide awake, almost as though someone else were there in her mind, calling her name, needing her.

Terrified, she had no idea what to do—and half suspected she was losing her mind, after all. Which was one reason she didn't tell Jason. She couldn't bear to have him see her go crazy. To place such a horrible burden on him.

But there was a second reason she didn't call. She was horribly frightfully suspicious that she was remembering someone—and that the someone was the man who'd fathered her child. Who else would have such an intense emotional hold on her? A bond that was reaching out to her even through her darkness?

Queasy, shivering, Anna burrowed beneath her covers, her arms cradling her child, holding on by the barest thread to logic, to reason.

She only had one thing to focus on right now. One thing that mattered. In only seven weeks she was going to give birth to her daughter. To Audrey.

TO SAY JASON WAS SHOCKED when Anna told him what she planned to name her baby was an understatement. Fortunately she did so over the telephone and he was able to hide his reaction. She was remembering. She had to be remembering. And for that reason alone he didn't tell her the significance behind the name.

He was achingly aware of what the return of her memory would mean. Every day as her baby grew, so did the tension between them. They were living on borrowed time. They both knew that.

Jason was sitting with Anna in her apartment the

first Saturday in December, his leg bobbing swiftly and almost imperceptibly as they watched another movie. They'd been spending most afternoons that way since Thanksgiving, and he had to get out, to do something besides wait quietly for his world to come crashing down around him. He was spending far too much time watching Anna's expression, waiting for the light of memory to come into her eyes. Dreading what would happen when it did.

And today was worse, knowing as he did that, since it was a weekend, he didn't have to leave for work in a matter of hours. That he could stay right there with her as darkness fell over the city. And stay. And stay. Now, before her memory came between them.

"Isn't it about time to buy her some stuff?" He asked, his hand resting on Anna's stomach, waiting for Audrey to wake up.

"I've been looking through catalogs," Anna said, grabbing one from under a pile of books on the coffee table. "I found the furniture I want, but as small as this place is, I figured I'd wait until I was a little closer to my due date before I started getting any of it. I was thinking about looking for a larger place." She'd received her settlement check from the city the week before.

Flipping through the well-worn pages of the catalog, she found the nursery ensemble she'd chosen.

"All that color's great," Jason told her approvingly. The crib and changing table were white with colorful balloon motifs. The baby would only have to open her eyes to be entertained.

"See, there're sheets, receiving blankets, hooded towels, sleepers—everything to match." She pointed to the next page.

Standing up, Jason said, "So let's go get 'em."

"Now?" She looked up at him. They'd just finished lunch. She usually rested after lunch.

"Sure now." He suddenly wanted to do it all, to take part in everything that was yet to be done to prepare for Audrey's imminent birth, and to do so as soon as possible. Because he didn't know from one day to the next if there'd continue to be a role for him to play.

"But where will I put it all?"

Looking around the cramped apartment, Jason could see her problem. And suddenly he had the perfect solution. Or at least as close to perfect as he could get, considering his limited options.

"We'll set it up in the downstairs bedroom in my place. I'll move back up to the loft."

"Your place?" she asked. But she didn't sound at all displeased with the suggestion.

"Sure," he said, grabbing her coat. "I've got the room."

And if he had the baby's things, didn't he stand at least some chance of eventually having the baby? And her mother, too?

"But won't it be a lot of trouble to move it all again?"

Jason shrugged. The possible trouble would be worth the chance to have her stay. "Your chances of finding a place you want before she's born are pretty slim," he said, which was one thing they both knew to be the truth. Waiting lists for New York apartments, at least ones she'd want to raise Audrey in, were a mile long. "You guys can room with me until something comes up."

Neither examined the plan, knowing that to do so would only borrow trouble. Instead, avoiding each other's eyes, they locked hands and went on a shopping spree.

"WE DID GOOD, don't you think?" Anna looked around Jason's spare bedroom on Sunday night, tired but happy.

"We did great!" he said, the pride in his voice sending little thrills clear through her. This was how expecting a child was meant to be. A man and woman, their love electrifying the air between them, filled with anticipation as they surveyed the crib that would soon bear a tiny body, the changing table filled with tiny T-shirts and sleepers, bottles waiting to be filled, diapers to be worn.

"You don't think we went a little overboard?" she asked, looking around them. They'd bought out half of New York in less than twenty-four hours.

"This little one's worked damn hard to get here," Jason said, wrapping his arms around her from behind, his hands spreading over her stomach. "She deserves to have her necessities waiting for her."

Anna grinned at him over her shoulder. "I'm just not convinced that a life-size bear that plays nursery rhymes can be considered a necessity." She covered his hands with hers, leaning back into him, loving the solid strength of his body. A body she'd not yet discovered, and yet felt as if she knew so well.

"Sure it was," Jason said. "He matched the crib."

"And the curtains?" She looked at them, hung at the window to pull out the creases. They were playing a dangerous game. But curtains could be rehung.

"You want someone peeping in at her while she sleeps?" Jason asked.

"On the tenth floor?"

Her gaze locked with his over her shoulder. He'd never actually asked her to move in with him, but they were both talking as if such a move was a foregone conclusion.

"Anna?" Jason's voice was hesitant, unlike him. "If, after the baby's born, we're still where we are now, would you consider making this her home?"

If we're still where we are now. If she was still without half her senses, he meant. If she still didn't know who Audrey's rightful father was.

She should tell him no. She had to tell him no. None of this was fair to Jason, but moving in with him, being a family, was downright cruel.

"For how long?" she whispered when she'd meant to decline his offer. "Not just until I can get into someplace bigger than what I have now?"

She felt him shrug as his arms fell away. Cold, suddenly bereft, she took his hand gladly when he offered it, following him out to the living room.

He sat down on the couch and pulled her down beside him, still holding her hand. His gaze locked with hers.

"I want her here," he said. "I want you both here forever."

Her heart flip-flopped. She'd been living to hear those words since she'd first come home from the hospital with Jason, maybe even before. And then reality set in. "But..."

"Shh. Hear me out." He placed one finger against her lips. "I want to marry you, Anna."

Tears sprang to her eyes. She didn't think it was possible to hurt so much. "Oh, Jason, I want that, too, so much."

He nodded. Swallowed. And then started again. "I can't ask you to do that, Anna. It wouldn't be fair."

"To you," she said, her tears still welling as she held his gaze. "I know."

Shaking his head, he said gently, "To you." He reached up and dried her eyes. "I'd be taking advantage of you if I married you now when you're at your most vulnerable. When you have no idea what you'd be giving up."

"You mean Audrey's biological." It was how she'd come to think of the man.

"Her what?"

"Her biological, as in the biological source of half of her existence."

"He's a man, Anna," Jason said, although she could see what the words cost him. "He's her father."

She couldn't allow him to go that far. "No, Jason." She shook her head. "He's not a father."

As if he knew she was prepared to argue seman-

tics with him all day if that was what it took, he
nodded slowly. "He exists. Someplace in your
memory he exists." A pause. "And there's more."

Frowning up at him, she asked, "What?"

"You have no idea how you felt about me before,
but if your memory returns, that will come back to
you, too. And whether you believe it or not right
now, that memory could very well change how you
feel about me."

Anna's stomach clenched. She hated the sudden
turn the conversation had taken. "Didn't I like
you?" It was something she'd never even considered.

"Yes."

But his eyes told her there was more.

"Was I angry with you?"

"Yes."

Frightened, she grasped his hand more tightly.
No. She didn't want there to be any problems between them.

"Did I have reason to be angry?" she whispered,
her heart thudding.

She'd pretty much decided that she was ready to
deal with whatever it was she'd been avoiding remembering now that she was stronger, now that she
had Jason by her side. She'd never once considered
the fact that he might be part of the problem.

"Yes."

She pulled away from him and then, seeing the
pain in his eyes, grabbed his hand back again. "You
wouldn't ever have hurt me deliberately, Jason, I
know that," she said, the conviction in her words

coming straight from her heart. There were just some things a body knew, no matter what.

Jason acknowledged her trust with a nod, a slow smile spreading across his face. "Never," he said.

"Do you want to tell me this horrible thing you did?" she asked, trying to make light of it.

Jason studied her for a long moment. "Do you want me to?"

No. She didn't. She didn't want to know any of it, to have had a past at all. She was happy with the present. A present they'd promised each other. Why couldn't they just leave it at that?

"What do you think Dr. Gordon would say?" She knew she was copping out even as she said it. But while she'd been convinced she was strong enough to handle the return of her memory, she'd also planned on having Jason to turn to, to help her pick up the pieces.

"He said you're probably strong enough to hear what I have to say."

Her fear increased. "You've already talked to him about it?"

Jason nodded. "I'd planned to tell you, anyway, before the baby's born."

"And he agreed?"

For the first time Jason looked away, and Anna breathed a small sigh of relief. He wasn't sure.

"He advised me to wait. Going by what you've already remembered, your chances of complete recovery are excellent, and so anything we might tell you could hamper that recovery." He said the words in one breath.

"Then I'd like to wait."

"Okay, we'll wait." He didn't even try to convince her otherwise.

"Will you tell me one thing?" she asked, missing the emotional closeness they'd been sharing these past weeks.

"I'm ready to tell you whatever you want to know," Jason said, sounding resigned.

"This thing that made me angry, was it something horrible enough to make me run from myself?"

"Not by itself, no," he said, choosing his words as carefully as he had those first few days she'd been with him. He was going to honor her decision not to be told about her past. "We had a nasty quarrel. The stance I was taking was unfair. But that was all."

Anna started breathing easier.

She grinned up at him. "I can live with that."

"Here? After the baby's born?" Jason asked, his eyes serious.

Anna nodded. She'd learned to trust herself these past months, and Jason's home, in his life, was where she wanted to be. "But if six months after the baby's born I still haven't recovered my memory, I'm going to be expecting a marriage proposal, anyway."

Shocked by her own boldness, Anna nevertheless held his gaze.

"I'll do better than that," Jason said, pulling her into his arms. "You have it now, due and payable six months after Audrey's born."

She wanted the proposal more than anything else. And yet, as part of her rejoiced, another part shivered. So much could happen in the next seven and a half months.

CHAPTER SIXTEEN

JASON HELD ANNA for a long time, reluctant to let her go, knowing that every minute of his time with her was to be cherished as though it was his last. Knowing that every moment might very well *be* his last.

She felt so good in his arms, so right, even pregnant by another man. This time was his. His and hers. And if, with the regaining of her memory, he lost it all, he at least would have had something he'd never had before. Unconditional love. Total commitment. An acceptance of his proposal of marriage. Even if just for today.

Pulling Anna closer, Jason inhaled her natural scent. Anna. His woman. He couldn't get enough of her.

"I love you," she whispered against his neck.

And because this was his moment, he answered her. "I love you, too, Anna." He raised her face, kissed her deeply. "Please remember that."

Her eyes clouded, almost as if she'd heard the desperation he'd thought he'd concealed. Before she could delve into things better left buried for now, he kissed her again, lifting her, settling her on his lap, on the aching hardness he'd grown almost accustomed to these past months.

Or thought he had until she moved against him, creating a friction she'd created so many times before.

Her dress slipped up her body, bearing thighs firm and long and so painfully familiar. He knew every freckle, every shadow there—and other places, too. He ran his hands along one smooth thigh, back and forth, up and down, caressing her, remembering. Until her long legs wrapped around him, straddling him, cradling him.

And he was lost.

With the ease of exploring familiar territory, Jason seduced Anna, knowing where to touch, how to caress, how hard and how soft, how much to tease. He knew because she'd taught him; he'd insisted she teach him. And he'd taught her, too.

Breaking off a long satisfying kiss, Anna drew her tongue down his neck, unbuttoning his flannel shirt as she went. Artfully flicking his sensitive flesh with the tip of her tongue, she ignited him as she'd done so many times in the past, the only difference being that, instead of laughing up at him as she'd done in the days when confidence had made her bold, her eyes were shyly downcast.

And even this turned him on. To seduce Anna all over again, to relive those shockingly erotic days of teaching her how to give him love, how to take it for herself. A gift few men were honored with twice.

Then, as she settled herself more completely against him, things were suddenly different. She didn't fit as she used to. Her stomach protruded between them.

Oh, God. He let go of her thigh. What in hell was he thinking?

"We can't," he said, unable to hide the agony in his voice as he pulled away from her.

She stared up at him, her eyes clouded with passion. "What?"

"The baby." He could barely get the words out. He was struggling to breathe, to hold her calmly, to not lose his control in an agony of want.

Pulling herself farther up his body, she traced his ear with her tongue. Hadn't she heard him? He had to stop. Now.

"It's okay." He barely heard the whispered words through the roaring of his blood.

When he didn't respond, didn't do more than sit there holding her, holding on, she whispered something else, her words sending the blood straight back to his groin.

"I asked Dr. Litton when I saw her last week."

Her announcement stunned him. She'd been that sure? Or, his body throbbing harder with the thought, just that needy? Jason held her firmly away from him, watching her as he demanded, "And?" His hands were shaking with the effort it was taking not to carry her upstairs to his bed.

"I'm still seven weeks away," she said. "As long as it's not uncomfortable and we're careful..." Her voice trailed off as she lowered her eyes.

His own sweet Anna. Bold yet shy. Needy and yet not wanting to ask anything for herself. Even in love. He was going to enjoy teaching her how to ask all over again.

"Then let's be careful, my love." He was already carrying her up the stairs to the loft as he said the words.

ANNA HAD NEVER BEEN so thoroughly loved. Even without a single memory of anything to compare it to, she knew making love had never been so good. Not only did she catch fire everywhere Jason touched, she sensed his love, as well, and a reverence she wasn't sure she deserved but knew she returned with every fiber of her being. She was his totally, completely.

When she sat astride him, lowered herself down on him, she found not only a physical joy beyond anything she'd imagined, but an emotional release she felt she'd been craving for as long as she'd lived.

At first, when it became obvious to her that she knew what she was doing, that a man's intimate touch was achingly familiar, she worried that she might be remembering another place, another time. Another man's touch.

But soon, as Jason stroked and kissed and encouraged her to do the same, she had no thoughts other than Jason. Loving him.

"You're so beautiful," he whispered, every muscle in his body straining with the obvious effort it was taking him to be gentle.

The truth of his words were reflected in his eyes. And in that moment Anna felt beautiful.

"I could get real used to this," she said, watching him, the concentration on his face, the love in his eyes.

"Good."

He held her motionless on top of him and Anna frowned, eager to reach the destination she'd been climbing toward for months.

"Just giving us a minute to slow down," he said, his words coming with an effort. "To prolong the pleasure." Then he gasped, thrusting so deeply she felt the sensation to her fingertips and toes.

There was nothing slow about their loving then.

JASON HAD TOUCHED heaven, confirmed not only its existence, but that it was everything he'd hoped it would be. He held Anna, rolling with her until she was lying on her side facing him, his body still connected to hers. He was home.

"That was incredible," he said, needing her to know that what they'd just experienced hadn't been ordinary at all—not even for them.

"Mm-hmm," Anna said, moving her body against his, getting him aroused all over again.

"You're sure?" he asked, his body already fully hard within her.

She moved with him, giving herself to him completely. For now, this one night, this one time, he knew there was no part of her already reserved, already spoken for. For this one night he was first.

As Jason moved slowly within her, holding her gaze with his own, speaking on so many levels and connecting on every one of them, he couldn't help thinking that their lives would always be like this if she never regained her memory. And for just a second he hoped for exactly that.

But only for a second. Her beautiful brown eyes were filled with love but only a present love. His love had its roots in their past, had a depth hers would always be lacking. It would never be enough. For either of them.

He loved all of Anna—before and after. For both their sakes she needed to know herself, to love herself, too.

SHE'D STEPPED OUTSIDE herself again, was watching as she walked in Gramercy Park, stumbling because she hadn't seen the uneven sidewalk through her tears. She even knew why she was crying. What she couldn't figure out was why she was there all alone.

She'd never been alone before in her life.

And then there were two of her. Only she was in a different park, the ground covered with soft white sand, instead of grass. There was a sand castle nearby and she was laughing. Both of her were laughing at something beyond the castle. Something she couldn't see.

No. Wait. She'd miscounted. There weren't two. There were three of her. And all three were crying. They must know about Jason, she thought. They're all crying because I can't remember anything so I can't marry Jason.

Except that Jason hadn't asked her to marry him yet. This was before the crash. But the tears didn't stop. Had Anna caused all this pain? She wanted to

*tell them she was sorry, but all three ignored her.
They'd reached the end of their endurance, found a
hurdle they couldn't vault.*

*She was losing her mind—but not the pain. It
wasn't ever going to go away. No matter how hard
she cried, how hard all three of them cried, they
couldn't change the—*

With a start Anna sat bolt upright in bed. Remembering wasn't the shock it should have been; it
wasn't even surprising or new. It was a solid wall
of agony. An agony so familiar she knew she'd
never forgotten it, not for an instant. Had been carrying it with her every day since the accident. And
before.

Dr. Gordon had told her an incident, something
deeply important, could very well trigger her memory when she was ready. Making love with Jason
must have been that important. But she didn't think
she was ever going to be ready.

She was Anna Hayden. Of Abby, Anna and Audrey Hayden.

Oh, God. Memories assailed her. Audrey. And
Abby. "Abby!"

Her voice startled her, scaring her, bringing the
nightmare to life. She felt arms steal around her,
allowed them to hold her only because she hurt too
much to fight them off.

They weren't three anymore. "No!" she shouted,
shaking her head, refusing to accept the picture in
her mind. She couldn't bear the memory. Couldn't
go back to living with the pain day in and day out.

But the memories continued, pouring in so quickly she thought she might collapse from the onslaught.

Audrey. Beautiful vibrant laughing Audrey. Still. Terrifyingly unnaturally still. Covered in blood. Her face. *Oh, God.* She saw her identical sister's face. No one else. Only her. She'd been the one to find Audrey out on the beach. Had gone there to build a sand castle.

She'd screamed, could still hear her screams even now. They deafened her, sickened her. Covering her ears, Anna rocked from side to side. No! Stop!

But the pictures, the sounds, the smells just kept coming. She hadn't been strong enough, even then, to handle things on her own, to call the police, to spare her sister Abby at least that much. Instead, she'd stood there shaking and screamed for her. She'd thought that was all she'd done. All those months after the accident, she'd thought all she'd done was stand there and scream, the smell of Audrey's death enveloping her. But that hadn't been all. First she'd rolled her dead sister over. She'd rolled her over so Abby hadn't had to see her face.

"Ohhh nooo, please!" she cried. "Please stop!" She shook her head again and again, trying to dislodge the pictures. Anything to make them go away.

The funeral had been closed-casket. At the time she'd been too thankful to question the decision her parents had made without even seeing their daughter first. Now suddenly she knew why. They'd probably been told...

Rocking, crying, holding herself, Anna was no longer aware of the arms that held her, couldn't feel

anything but the agony. A pain so deep there was
no way to recover, to ever be again the innocent
woman who'd walked out of the beach house that
day.

And Abby. *Oh, God, Abby!* It was Abby who'd
been calling out to her these past weeks. Abby who
was hurting, who was needing her. Abby, who'd
also had a part of her soul destroyed. "Abby!" she
cried. She needed her sister. Needed that part of herself.

JASON JUST HELD ON, sweat running off his body as
he listened to Anna's anguished cries. He'd never
witnessed such suffering, had no idea what to do for
her, how to help, how to reach her. He just knew he
couldn't let her go, couldn't let her be alone when
she came back out of this hell of hers. If she came
back. His throat dry, his body starting to shake, it
hit him that he might be losing her forever.

She'd remembered. Though she'd still said nothing but Abby's name, nothing else could have rent
this much pain from her. But as he sat there holding
her, the memories no longer mattered. Anna mattered. And her torment was breaking his heart.

His helplessness rendering him powerless, he just
held on.

"Shh," he whispered over and over, rocking her,
brushing the tangled hair back from her face. "I'm
here, honey. I'm right here," he kept saying.

Whether or not she could hear him, he kept repeating the litany, hoping that even a trace of the

comfort he had to offer would reach her, help her fight her way back.

"Oh, God."

The anguish in her voice tore at him. It was so hard to believe it was only hours ago he'd heard her crying in ecstasy. Their lovemaking must have triggered her memory. Subconsciously she'd remembered loving him before.

Anna continued to cry out against whatever visions she was seeing, locked all alone in a world he couldn't share.

Why? he asked over and over. *Why her?*

Fighting him again, she kicked the covers away.

"Anna! What is it, honey? Talk to me." He spoke firmly, urgently.

She continued to wrestle with no direction. Then one arm wrapped around his, holding him in a death grip.

"Talk to me, honey," he said again. "Let me help."

Pushing frantically at the hair tangled about her face, she continued to sob.

"I saw her!" she cried suddenly. "I saw her face." And then, as if the admission drained the last of her strength, she went limp in his arms.

"Whose face, honey?" Jason hoped to God he was doing the right thing in making her talk.

"Audrey's. I saw her face." The words were mumbled, as if she'd finally given up.

Unsure whether she was speaking of the baby she carried or the sister she'd lost, Jason asked, "When? Where?" Had Audrey visited her in a dream? He'd never been a big believer in the supernatural, but Anna couldn't be imagining whatever horrors were playing themselves out in her mind.

"That day—" She broke off, started to sob again. "On the beach..." More gasps. "I saw her face."

"What day?" he asked softly. When Audrey was killed, she'd been found facedown in the sand. Anna was remembering something else. If only he knew what.

"The blood!" she cried, and then moaned, burying her face against his chest. "Her beautiful face."

Jason held Anna more tightly, as though by sheer force of will he could erase her mind once again. Anna had found Audrey, but the police had made her leave—made Abby leave—before anyone had touched the body. Neither had seen the extent of the damage caused by the murderer's knife. Unless...

Jason swallowed, took a deep breath. "Tell me about it, Anna," he said, his voice gentle but commanding. He had to get it out of her before she escaped back to a place where nobody could reach her. "Tell me what you saw."

"Her face—" She broke off, sobbing. "I c-couldn't even r-r-recognize her." A spasm of hiccups choked her words. "But I saw her neck...her neck...her necklace..."

Cold to the bone, sickened, Jason knew. Audrey hadn't been found facedown. Anna had seen her and then wiped the sight away. But the vision had remained in her subconscious, preying on her without her even being aware of it, waiting.

"Her n-n-nose was g-gone."

Sick to his stomach, Jason had heard enough. "Shh," he whispered. "I'm here, honey," he crooned.

"Her ch-cheeks and m-mouth..." She tried to breathe, couldn't, tried again, her voice shaking with sobs. "So much b-blood."

Oh, Anna. Beautiful strong silent Anna. You didn't have to do this all alone. We would have helped you.

Suddenly she stopped. Stopped crying, stopped speaking. Stopped breathing. Panic shot through him and he sat up, intending to force his own breath into her lungs until she was ready to take over on her own, a part of him trying to devise a plan that would allow him to be in two places at once—breathing for Anna and on the phone getting help.

He lay her down, her closed eyes scaring the hell out of him. But before he could do more than prop her neck with pillows, a shudder tore through her. She was breathing again. Tears running down her face, she lay completely still and cried.

Unable to bear her pain, Jason reached for her again, and her eyes opened. She looked at him as though only just realizing he was there. "Oh, Jason!" she cried. "Her eyes, they were open and glassy and they weren't laughing at all." Her husky voice was thick with tears, but sounding more like her own.

"Anna. Lovely Anna." He swallowed, exerting every ounce of control he had to hold back his own emotion, cradling her against him.

And then, leaning back to look up at him, she

asked, "You knew Audrey, didn't you Jason? Were you our friend back then, too?"

He nodded, unable to speak. Hadn't she remembered him?

"I'm glad," she said, smiling through a fresh spate of tears. "Oh, God, Jason, how could I have forgotten something like this?"

He didn't have any answers for her. Only platitudes she'd heard before. Leaning back against the pillows, he held her close, surrounding her with strength, with love. It was all he could do.

She cried quietly now, speaking little. "Thank you," she said at one point.

Brushing his hand gently across her cheek, he said, "You don't have to thank me, love."

She nodded, as if accepting the truth of his words.

A long time later, still crying but much calmer, she pulled away just enough to look up at him. "I rolled her over," she said, as though confessing a crime.

"You did the right thing, Anna."

She shook her head. "I couldn't bear to look at her."

"There was no reason to."

She started to cry harder, still so full of raw anguish she overflowed with it. "Death smells awful."

Jason had smelled death once, during his early days as a reporter. He'd never forget the sickly sweet stench that had permeated the air, choking him. He'd been so violently sick to his stomach he'd had to leave the scene.

"I love you, Anna." The words were torn from

his throat. He'd take her pain, her memories, upon himself if he knew of a way.

"I love you, too," she said, sitting up and gazing at him, the love in her eyes still fresh, still new. There was no recognition of the former love they'd shared.

NUMB, ANNA LAY in the bed with Jason, her head on his chest. He'd made her get up, put on one of his shirts, afraid she was going to catch a chill. But he'd taken only a brief moment to yank on a pair of cotton shorts himself before pulling her right back down into the comfort of his arms, the covers close around them.

But still she shook. Her whole body trembled as her mind wandered, stumbled, shied away and wandered some more. So many things, so many memories to revisit. Her childhood, growing up with her sisters. The time she'd broken her arm and Abby had been the one to sit up half the night with her, trying to take her mind off the pain of her broken bone setting in the cast. She remembered the jokes they'd played on their teachers, on their long slew of baby-sitters and nannies. But never on their parents.

Desperate for time with them, the girls had always been perfect angels whenever their parents were around. Except of course when they'd done some stupid kid thing, like the time their parents took them out to dinner at the Beverly Hills Hotel and Anna had spilled her drink on the table and into their father's lap. Or when Audrey had gotten lost at an amusement park, and the nanny of the week had panicked and called her father out of an important meeting.

Anna remembered the time Abby had bloodied Jimmy Roberts's nose for calling Anna a bookworm. The year her mother had surprised them with three birthday cakes—for her three little angels, she'd said. And Anna remembered Audrey, always hugging everyone....

All of these memories and more she shared with Jason, talking long into the night, one memory resurfacing after another. But every memory was tainted with bone-deep sadness. It was over.

"Poor Abby," she said, her eyes welling with tears as she thought of her older sister. Older by twenty minutes chronologically, older by years in every other way. "She grew up so fast." And had lost so much.

"Too fast and yet not unhappily," Jason said. "Abby's a born caregiver."

Anna had to remember that he'd known them before, that some of what she was telling him might not be new to him. But then, why was he still new to her?

She sat up, frowning. "There're still some blank spots."

He nodded. "Dr. Gordon said there might be, that your memory probably wouldn't come back all at once."

Anna started to shake again. "I can't take any more, Jason." She'd rather die than go through another night like last night.

"You're a strong woman, Anna, stronger now than ever before," he said, his hand rubbing her arm, warming her.

And in some ways she knew he was right. She was stronger now. If nothing else, these past months had given her that.

"It's funny," she said. "I remember leaving California. It was just like Abby said—I had to prove to myself I was a complete entity on my own." She chuckled without humor. "I guess I've done that, huh?"

"Absolutely," Jason agreed, his breath brushing the top of her head.

"The shop," she said, suddenly remembering the business she'd built with her sisters, the reason she was such a good seamstress. Knowing, too, that the overalls she'd been sewing for her baby were Abby's design. "I left her all alone with the shop."

"And it's doing just fine," Jason said. "Abby hired a couple of women who love her designs almost as much as she does."

Anna was glad. She'd hated spending her days sewing when her own creativity had been clamoring for release. But she'd owed Abby and hadn't begrudged her sister her chance. Or herself the opportunity to do something for Abby for a change. Even Audrey had done her share at the shop without grumbling.

Frowning, Anna said, "I even remember making my family promise to leave me alone for an entire year." She could picture the scene as if it had happened yesterday. Her parents had been stunned, Abby devastated.

But in the end they'd given her the promise she'd demanded.

"I just can't remember why it was so important," she said weakly. How could she remember hurting her sister so horribly and not remember why she'd done so?

"It'll come back to you, Anna," Jason said. "You just need to be patient."

"And you?" Anna sat up again, staring at him. "Why can't I remember you at all?"

Jason shrugged, breaking eye contact. She couldn't blame him for being uncomfortable. How must it make him feel for her to claim to love him but to have forgotten him so completely?

And then there was the other person she'd forgotten....

"I still can't remember the biological," she said softly. She was frustrated and frightened and so damn tired. What horrors remained to jump out at her? And would she be able to cope when they did?

CHAPTER SEVENTEEN

DAWN WAS BREAKING over the city when Anna finally fell silent. Believing she'd fallen asleep, Jason lay completely still, cushioning her head on his chest. And although he had a lot to think about, to consider, to accept, at the moment only one thought occupied his mind. Anna hadn't run for the telephone—for Abby. She'd remembered and had come through her emotional crisis without her sister.

And then, as if his mind had conjured the action, she sat up, slipping silently from the bed.

"You calling Abby?" he asked, resigned and maybe even a little relieved. She'd made it through her crisis. That was all that mattered. For the rest he'd been wrong. Wrong to expect her to leave a bond that was as necessary to her happiness as food and air. One that had been forged long before she'd even known him. One that had seen her through her entire life, made her who she was. The woman he loved.

Surprised when Anna shook her head and walked past the phone, Jason climbed out of bed and followed her. She'd turned her purse upside down and was shaking out the contents, sifting through them. Pulling an envelope from the pile, she opened it, dumping a chain and locket into her hand. He recognized it immediately.

"I thought it was such an odd shape," she said, holding the locket lovingly in her slender hands. "It's odd because it's only a third of a whole. Put together, the three parts form a heart."

Jason nodded silently, although he knew she wasn't looking at him. His throat thick, he watched Anna, seeing her—all of her—for the first time. He'd thought he'd wanted her to be whole, and all the while he'd been the one tearing her apart. Refusing to see an important part of who she was simply because it was a part he couldn't share.

"Our parents bought the original locket when we were born," she murmured. "They had it cut into three and then made into three separate lockets."

Even with her head bent, Jason could see that she smiled.

"They made us wear them always so they could tell us apart." Her finger brushed over her name.

"As we grew up, the lockets were a sign of our loyalty. We agreed never to take them off." She shrugged. "Other girls had best-friend necklaces. We had our lockets."

He ached to hold her, but didn't.

"It was also a symbol of our own separate identities," she said, telling Jason something she'd never told him before. "We were always part of a whole and yet different, too. I can remember Abby telling us that once when we were little. Audrey had been crying because Abby's locket was bigger than hers. Abby explained that hers was biggest because she was the oldest. Mine was next, and Audrey's was the smallest. That we were the same and yet special in our own ways."

"I didn't know that." Jason spoke for the first time since following her out of the bedroom.

She glanced from the locket to him, as though surprised to see him there. Frowning, she said, "You know, it's funny, but I don't think I've thought of that in years."

She handed the locket to Jason. "Would you help me fasten it?" she asked, holding her hair up off her shoulders.

She wanted him to fasten around her neck the symbol of what had driven them apart, asking him to give her back to the relationship he'd tried to take her from. She was asking him to share her, to know he was never going to be the single most important person in her life.

He fastened the locket.

MONDAY MORNING, just as soon as she was alone in her own apartment, Anna called Maggie.

"Hey, preggie, what's up?"

You were right about Jason and me all along, Maggie. We're lovers now. And it was even better than I imagined. Better than you'd probably imagined. And...I remembered some things. "Your apartment was rented."

"Yeah, well, I don't think I'm coming back."

"You got the job?" Anna asked, happy for her friend.

"Don't know yet, but the pilot's finished and it looks great."

"Oh, Maggie, that's wonderful!"

"I got me an agent, Anna," Maggie said, her usual sardonic attitude slipping. "He says I'm good."

"You *are* good, Maggie." Damn good.

They talked about a couple of other auditions Maggie had been on, and Maggie actually made Anna laugh when she told her about the job she'd lost for a cookie commercial. Maggie as a life-size macaroon Anna couldn't see.

"Where are you staying?" Anna asked when she could finally get a word in. She'd had a crazy idea during the cab ride home this morning.

"A dump on Sunset Boulevard."

Anna paced her apartment, her phone pressed to her ear. "You got a car yet?"

"Yeah, you could call it that. It used to be a compact sometime before the last wreck or two."

"Does it run?"

"Of course. You think I'm throwing my money away on something that isn't reliable?" Maggie demanded. "It's not pretty, but it works."

Crossing her fingers, Anna plopped down on the couch. "I've got a favor to ask, Mags."

"So ask."

"It's my sister, Abby."

"You talked to her?" Maggie asked, suddenly alert.

"No." Anna paused. She was afraid to call. Not

until she remembered why it was so important that she left. "But I remembered her."

Maggie's silence spoke volumes. "Not everything," Anna answered the unspoken question quickly. She wasn't up for an interrogation, not yet. Maybe not ever. But this was something she had to do.

"Abby's all alone, Maggie. I want you to live with her."

"Whoa!" Maggie was probably backing away as far as her telephone would allow. Her New York friend was not used to California's laid-back ways.

"She has a three-bedroom cottage on the beach, Mags," Anna said before Maggie made up her mind once and for all. Once she'd done that, there was no changing it. "And she's only about forty-five minutes from the city, depending on traffic."

"I'm not worried about traffic, Anna. It's your sister. You ask her about this?"

"She won't mind, Maggie," Anna said. "I know she won't." Abby would never turn away a person in need, whether she wanted to or not. And Abby needed Maggie much more than Maggie needed a decent place to stay. "You can have my room."

"Your room?"

"Yeah. The cottage is half-mine."

"You and your sister lived together?"

"Yes, until I came here." Anna took a deep breath. "She's all alone, Maggie, and not, you know, doing all that great. She could use having you around."

"Right."

"You kept me sane, didn't you?"

"You're easy Anna."

"Abby's a lot like me." Well, okay, maybe not in some ways. But she had a feeling Maggie and Abby would hit it off. And couldn't bear the idea of Abby being alone one more day.

"I don't know, Anna."

She was losing her—she could hear it in Maggie's voice. "It's right on the beach, Mags. Think of all the beachboys."

"I'm getting enough pretty boys in the city."

"You can have my room at no charge."

She'd hit a chord there. She could tell by Maggie's silence.

"Please, Maggie, for me?" she asked.

"I'll go meet her," Maggie said grudgingly. "How do I find her?"

Anna rattled off the number at the shop. If Abby wasn't in, someone there would know where to find her.

"And Maggie?"

"Yeah?"

"I don't want you shocked or anything, but when you see her…?"

"What, she looks like Godzilla or something?"

"No." Anna smiled mistily. "She looks exactly like me."

ANNA SPENT the next couple of days making herself crazy. Every waking moment was eaten up with remembering—and searching for the lost pieces of the puzzle that had become her life. More and more frightened by the number of things still unknown to her, she became desperate to discover them, to get the ordeal over with once and for all. To own her life before her baby was born.

And for every memory she had, she conjured up an imaginary one that could explain the gaping holes still left in the picture. The largest hole, the one that mattered most to her, was Jason. Why couldn't she remember him? What was so threatening about an old family friend? She didn't know why it took her so long to come up with the answer—not when it was so obvious. Her only explanation was that she'd simply been too self-absorbed to see.

Sitting with Jason at lunch on Wednesday, she worked up the courage to confront him.

"Tell me about you and Abby."

She watched him put down his sandwich, her stomach a mass of knots. She'd been feeling poorly all morning—ever since she'd figured it all out.

"What do you want to know?"

"Whatever you need to tell me."

"We're friends."

"And?"

He splayed his hands, then dropped them to the table on each side of his plate. "That's all."

She believed differently. And her subconscious agreed—which was why it wouldn't allow her to remember Jason, especially since they'd spent the last three nights together in his bed.

"She was the one you went to see before you left town," Anna said.

"I had something to say to her." His sandwich still lay untouched on the plate in front of him.

"What?"

"That Audrey was gone, you were an adult, and it was time she concentrated on her own life."

Anna frowned. That sounded more like a friend than... "What about that phone call on Thanksgiving?"

"You know about that, Anna." Jason was frowning. "She was alone, it was a holiday, and she wanted to connect with you in the only way she could."

"You're sure that's all it was?" Because there had to have been some reason he'd grown so close to her family, something that kept him coming back. And she already knew it wasn't her. She'd have remembered loving Jason. She was sure of that—especially now that she knew what loving him was like. And besides, if they'd been lovers, he'd have told her. The pain he felt because he wasn't Audrey's father was too real to ignore.

"Of course I'm sure," he said impatiently. "What else could there be?"

"You two could have been in love."

The shock on Jason's face alone drove that suspicion from her mind. "We could have been, but we weren't," he said calmly, staring her down.

Bowing her head, Anna felt herself blush. Okay. She'd missed the boat again. Apparently that was something she was good at.

Light-headed with relief, she actually giggled. At least her beloved and her beloved sister weren't lovers.

ANNA HAD EXPECTED to feel better after her conversation with Jason, but as the evening wore on, she only felt worse. She wanted—needed—to call her sister. She hadn't heard from Maggie, didn't know how Abby was doing, if she was all right. And yet, Abby knew Anna's memory had returned. Anna could only surmise that Abby was respecting Anna's original request, her stipulation for silence between them. She just didn't know why. Her head hurt from trying to make sense of it all.

What was still out there for her to know? What had happened between she and Abby? Why had she extracted the promise in the first place? Why couldn't she remember Jason? And where in hell was the biological? He had to be that Clark guy. But why couldn't she remember him?

Audrey kicked her so hard she doubled over on her couch. She was waiting for Jason's second newscast to come on so she could admire his thick blond hair, the way his mouth curved when he smiled, his eyes. All the while knowing she'd be admiring the rest of him the minute he got home.

The baby kicked again, stealing the breath from Anna's lungs. She lay still.

The third kick scared her a little bit, coming as it did so low in her belly and in her back at the same time. Either the baby had turned miraculously fast, or she had six legs.

Halfway through the news, her water broke. Jason

spoke to her from the television set, his blue eyes warm as they gazed straight at her. She could do this. That was what he was telling her. She was sure of it. She could do this. Never taking her eyes from his face, she reached for the phone.

Twenty minutes later Jason was at the door, a cab holding downstairs. The wait had almost killed her. Especially the last ten minutes when those steady blue eyes had been missing from her television screen.

CHAPTER EIGHTEEN

THERE WAS NO TIME to tell her the truth, in spite of his vow to do so before they had the baby. Jason threw Anna's coat around her shoulders, lifted her off the couch and carried her down the stairs. Six weeks early, Audrey was one determined little girl. *God, please get us there in time. Let them both be okay.*

"We've got plenty of time, Anna. Just relax, honey," he said, helping her into the cab. His heart thundered in his chest.

Please let them have found Dr. Litton. Have her waiting at the door.

"That's it Anna, one, two, three." He breathed with her, holding her in the backseat as the driver swerved in and out of the Wednesday-night traffic.

There was nothing else he could do. Nothing else but worry.

"We have to move my stuff to your place," Anna said after what seemed to Jason a particularly long contraction.

Stuff? Who the hell cared about stuff? How could she think about that at a time like this? They were having a baby here.

"Sure, honey," he said. "We'll do that."

"Right away, Jason." Her voice was stronger. "We'll probably be ready to come home tomorrow or the next day."

Okay. Fine. Whatever. "I'll move everything in the morning." *Now would you just concentrate on what you're doing, please?*

"I can't believe I'm finally going to get to see her," she said, resting her head against Jason's shoulder. She sounded as if she might be going to sleep.

They were having a baby. He was scared to death and she was going to sleep. Nobody had said anything about sleeping during the childbirth classes they'd taken. Sleeping wasn't in the job description. But sure enough she was actually going to sleep.

Right up until the next contraction. That was when Jason went back to work. At least he knew what to do. "One, two, three," he breathed. "Easy now, honey."

"I want to paint her bedroom red," Anna panted through the pain.

Red. Right. "Breathe, Anna."

"And the ceiling blue with a bright yellow sun."

"Uh-huh." And they thought she was actually going to have this baby? Why in hell had they gone to the classes if she wasn't willing to do anything right?

She chattered on about the room as the spasm passed, her voice getting drowsy again. Jason was almost glad this time. If she could just sleep until they got to the hospital, he'd have Dr. Litton to assist him in getting this job done. He didn't think they were going to get much help from Anna.

"I'd love a burger, Jason," she said suddenly. "You think we have time to stop for a burger?"

A burger! She just didn't get it. Giving birth was serious stuff. So much could go wrong...

"With pickles on it, please?" she asked sleepily. "Lots of pickles. Tell the driver to stop."

Jason wasn't sure how much more of this he could take.

But once they got to the hospital, Anna seemed to get more with the program. Dr. Litton was waiting for them in emergency, quickly checked Anna and determined they had time to get her up to a birthing room. Jason was doubtful. However, bowing to Dr. Litton's greater experience, he kept his opinion to himself and pushed Anna's wheelchair silently. And prayed for all he was worth.

THINGS MOVED so quickly Anna didn't have time to be afraid. She smiled at Jason when he appeared, garbed in a green surgical suit, in the door of her birthing room.

"This where the party is?" he asked.

She nodded. "Mm-hmm." They could get on with it now. He was here.

"Anna?" He looked as if he had something important to say.

"Yes?"

He paused. Glanced at the IV in her arm, at the monitor hooked to her stomach. "I love you."

That was all she needed to hear. "I love you, too."

She couldn't believe how excited she was. Soon, very soon, she was going to meet her daughter, see her, hold her.

"I'd expected to be scared," she confessed to Jason. "But with you here I just know everything's going to be fine."

He smiled at her. "Of course it's going to be fine."

It must have been a lot warmer in the room than she thought. Sweat was darkening the cotton surgical garb Jason wore.

Watching the monitor for her, Jason handled labor like a pro. He could tell from the lines on the screen just when her next pain was due and had her already breathing properly by the time it hit. He counted. He cajoled. He offered his arm for her to squeeze and ignored her when she yelled at him to shut up.

A nurse wheeled in what looked like a portable incubator just as Dr. Litton stopped by for one of her periodic visits. Anna looked from the machine to Jason, and then up at the doctor.

"What...?"

"She's close to six weeks early, Anna," Dr. Litton said calmly. "We have to be prepared."

"Jason?" Anna cried, fear choking her as she reached for his hand.

He held her, but looked at the doctor. "Have you any reason to expect trouble?" he asked.

"None at all. We wouldn't be in this room if we did."

"What's the immediate danger?"

"Probably none," the doctor said, smiling at Anna. "The baby's been perfectly active, her heart's strong, everything looks good. But with an early baby I like to be extra careful."

"You worried?" Anna asked Jason as soon as the doctor left the room.

He shook his head, smiling as he smoothed her hair out against her pillow. "Not at all. She knows what she's doing."

That was enough for Anna. If Jason wasn't worried, she had no reason to worry, either.

Jason's scrubs were drenched by the time she'd fully dilated, and by then she was pretty hot herself. And exhausted beyond belief. As the worst pain yet subsided, she wanted nothing more than to go to sleep. They were all going to have to take a break.

"Come on, Anna, it's time to get to work," Dr. Litton said from the end of the makeshift bed.

After she had a little sleep. Then she'd do all the work they needed.

"Now, honey. Push!" Jason instructed, watching the monitor.

She pushed. And wished to God she'd gone to sleep.

"Again!" Jason said.

She pushed again. Jason wasn't watching the monitor anymore. He was keeping company with Dr. Litton, both of them at a party she couldn't get down to attend.

"I see her hair!" Jason said, his eyes glowing

with a light she'd never seen before. It made her want to push again, harder.

Jason's face her cue, Anna did her job, pushing when she was told, holding back as she had to. She watched the birth, not from the mirror they'd mounted for her, but through her lover's eyes.

Then, just as the baby surfaced, as her body found a relief so powerful she cried, she saw an expression on Jason's face she'd seen before. Once. In another life. The intensity of his yearning, the look of pain that resulted from unrequited longing, was completely familiar to her. It was an image she'd been carrying in her heart every day since she'd sent him from her life. She remembered him.

She remembered everything.

"Seven pounds!" a nurse declared, holding the newborn on a scale to one side of Anna's bed.

"Seven?" Dr. Litton was still working on Anna, but glanced over her shoulder at the nurse. "That much? Are you sure? Better check it again."

A pause fell over the suddenly still room.

"Still seven," the nurse said.

Clearly surprised, the doctor checked the scale herself.

Ignoring Jason completely, Anna was vaguely aware of the doctor and nurse, but her gaze was glued firmly on her baby girl. Audrey. A new life for one lost.

A baby born right on time.

Jason stepped back, his ears buzzing, his heart thumping heavily. He had answers to all his questions. As long as Anna and Audrey wanted him in their lives—in any capacity—he would be there. Period. Being someone's first priority was nothing compared to being needed, to being part of a family, to loving. He'd been playing second fiddle all his life. Was good at it. Memories, other loves, be damned. The past, the future. Nothing mattered except being whatever, whoever, his two girls needed him to be for however long they needed him.

SO MANY FEELINGS exploding inside her, so many thoughts clamoring for attention, she wondered if she'd ever see clearly again. Anna lay in her hospital bed the rest of that day, assimilating all that had happened before her accident, all that had happened since and what was yet to happen. And holding Audrey. Almost constantly holding the baby girl who was everything she'd ever hoped her to be and more. So much more.

She'd already made the decision to breast-feed her daughter, and so she'd had Audrey moved right into bed with her, feeding her when necessary, holding her while she slept. Keeping her close. At times throughout that long day, she felt as if Audrey was the only person she'd ever be close to again.

Anger, pain, guilt, all cascaded down on her until she had to send Jason home, telling him to go ahead and go in to work, that she needed to sleep. Unaware she'd remembered, he wanted to talk. She didn't have any idea what to say. Playing for time, she insisted, that she had to rest as much as possible before they released her the next morning.

Except that, of course, she didn't rest after he

kissed her softly goodbye and left. She watched Audrey. Cried over her. Nursed her even though her milk wasn't in yet. Loved her. And thought. She'd bought herself one day. It didn't seem nearly long enough.

BEFORE SHE KNEW IT, before she was ready, she was back in Jason's apartment firmly ensconced on his couch, a blanket tucked snugly around her and the baby she held.

"You're sure you're comfortable?" Jason asked, hovering at the other end of the couch, almost as though he was afraid to touch her—or the baby he'd yet to hold.

Nervous as she was, she couldn't smile at him, but she tried. "Fine."

He nodded, then hovered some more, moving pillows out of her way, the coffee table closer. He was aware that something was wrong. He'd been avoiding her eyes all morning. And now that she'd combined the Jason she'd known before the crash with the Jason she knew now, she could read him like a book. Just as he'd been reading her all these months.

"You should have told me." So many emotions roiling inside her, and anger won out. "I can't believe you didn't tell me."

He stopped dead, just stood frozen beside her.

"All these months and you never said a word."

Pale-faced, he sat down, no longer avoiding her eyes. "When did you remember?" he asked simply.

"Yesterday, the second she was born."

He nodded. "The birth brought it all back."

"No." She shook her head. "You did. I was watching your face." Anna sighed, her anger draining away. He'd done what he'd thought right. Jason always did what he thought right. If only his thinking wasn't skewered by his upbringing. He'd done what he thought right, yet he'd been so wrong, too.

"Dr. Gordon knew," he told her, but not in way of defense. "He said it was possible I was somehow mixed up in whatever you were running from, and so telling you who I was could force you to deal with a relationship you weren't ready to handle."

"After all we'd shared, Jason, you didn't know me better than that?" Her anger was back, but maybe just to camouflage the pain.

His jaw tightened. "We hadn't shared anything in quite a while," he reminded her. "And you were pregnant."

The words hung between them, his unasked question underlined by her silence.

"When are you going to stop being a martyr, Jason?" She couldn't look at him, couldn't bear to hurt him. Yet the words had to be said. Should have been said seven months ago.

"You mind explaining that?" He was angry.

She looked down at her sleeping daughter. *For you, my darling. For all of us.* Then she took a deep breath and spoke.

"You settle, Jason. Always." She glanced at him, saw the stoicism settle on his face as he prepared, once again, to take whatever was handed him. "You make it damn near impossible for people *not* to put everything else first, to think of you last. You're so undemanding one could almost believe you have no needs at all.'' Almost. But not quite. She'd seen the longing on his face.

He remained silent. She wasn't even sure he was listening.

"Think about it, Jason. Did you ever ask your father to be at a game?" She'd had so much time to think those two months she'd been alone in New York. Time to figure it all out, to see where she'd been wrong—and where he'd been wrong. She just hadn't had the faith in herself to know that she could do anything about it.

"He knew when they were."

"But did you *ask* him to be there?"

His silence gave her the answer. "And what about that girl in college? Did you ever try to win her love away from the guy who'd dumped her?"

"You don't win love."

"Yes, you do, Jason." She forced back tears. "Sometimes without doing anything more than being yourself." Which is how he'd won *hers*. He'd certainly never asked for it. "Love isn't easy—it doesn't just fall in your lap and stay there happily ever after. You have to work at it, grasp it with both hands and be determined to keep it, or it's going to just slip away." Her last words were barely more than a whisper, her throat thick with unshed tears. This was a concept he had to understand.

The room fell silent again. Finally Anna couldn't stand it any longer. "And what about your lawyer friend?"

"What about her?" Jason asked, sounding suddenly confident. "I asked her to go to that funeral."

"Yes, but in all the years you'd been with her, had you ever before asked her to put her job second? Or had you given her the impression that you *expected* her job to come first?"

Again his silence spoke volumes. "Don't you see, Jason, not only are you living proof of self-fulfilled prophecies, you actually make people feel that they're pleasing you by doing as they please. That to be lavished with attention would turn you off."

Another glance in his direction. If he couldn't understand this, couldn't see it, their life together was over.

But even if their relationship was going to end, she owed him. Because she'd been wrong, too. The woman she'd been before had never even tried to communicate this to Jason, had never dared voice her doubts, her fears. She'd been too much of a coward to speak up, too afraid of being a problem. Swallowing back her tears, she held Audrey close to her heart and faced Jason head-on.

"I'm just as guilty as you are, Jason," she said. "I did you—us—a terrible wrong, and I don't know if I'll ever be able to forgive myself for that." Once again she pictured that look on his face. She'd seen it twice. The first time, when she'd walked out of his life in California, refusing to leave her sister and go with him. And the second she'd brought a baby into the world, a baby he'd so very much wanted to be his own.

"There's nothing to forgive," he said softly,

gruffly. "I never should have asked. It was unfair, cruel, to expect you to leave Abby so far behind."

"Leaving Abby wasn't the problem, Jason. Or at least, not all of it."

His shocked gaze collided with her sad one. "Moving away wouldn't have made any difference to the bond I share with Abby. What we share isn't dependent on physical closeness.

"And that was the problem, wasn't it?" she asked, still holding his gaze. "Neither of you was willing to share the part of me you each had."

He nodded. "If it means anything to you, we've actually both realized that. We know how wrong we were to expect you to sacrifice one for the other."

"You and Abby have talked about this?"

"In depth."

"And you're friends again?" She could hardly dare hope.

"Closer than ever, I think." He paused, looked down, and then met and held her gaze unwaveringly. "We were wrong, Anna, insisting that we wanted all or nothing. Abby swears—" he stopped, swallowed and continued "—no *I* swear never to do that to you again. To love you is to love all of you, including the part that belongs exclusively to your sister."

That was one hell of an admission coming from Jason. And a prayer come true for Anna. She was free to love both of them. If only...

"Do you know why I chose not to come to New York, Jason?"

He looked away. "You're going to tell me it was

because I led you to believe I expected you to say no."

So he had been listening. Had heard. "You did, but that's not why I said no."

His gaze flew back to her. "Then why?"

"Because I honestly didn't believe you loved me. Not completely. Not as wholeheartedly as I knew I was going to need to be loved if I was going to sever my relationship with my sister."

"After the two years we spent together?" he asked, scowling. "How could you not know I loved you? I told you so all the time."

"Because you didn't need me, Jason. Not really. You always held a part of yourself back, relied only on yourself, protecting yourself for that moment when I'd let you down." She paused, looked down at the child in her arms. "I needed you to need me as much as I needed you."

"And if I'd let you know that I needed you, you'd have come with me?" he asked, even now expecting a negative answer.

"I did come, Jason."

His eyes were pinpoints of steel, boring into her. "You came to sell your book."

"I came to be with you."

JASON WANTED to believe her. More than anything in his life, he wanted to believe her. But his heart couldn't accept what she was telling him. He'd been a selfish jerk. Why would she have come here to be with him?

"You were here for more than two months," he reminded her.

Her eyes filled with tears, and a full minute passed before she managed to get any words out. "After you left California, I hated myself. I hated you and Abby, too, but mostly just myself for not being strong enough to stand up to either of you."

Jason was hating himself pretty thoroughly at the moment, too.

"And I was terrified," she continued, her words making him hate himself more. He'd done this to her. "I was afraid that I couldn't get along on my own. When I reached deep down inside, looking for some imaginary well of strength to draw on, I found that there wasn't one. Not in me alone. Not without Abby. And I knew you were right. As painful, as terrifying as it was, I had to get away from my sister. I had to know I could rely on myself alone."

She stared down at the baby, and Jason looked away. He couldn't look at the child. Sooner or later she was going to tell him about the father. And that she was returning to the man.

"When I broke your heart, I broke mine, too," she said now, crying softly.

Reaching over, Jason brushed the tears from her face, then handed her a tissue. The baby didn't so much as stir.

"I came to New York to be close to you." She wasn't giving up on that one. He still didn't believe her.

"But I didn't contact you, couldn't contact you, until I'd proved to myself that I wasn't just transferring my dependence on Abby to you. I had to come to you whole or not at all.''

After a lifetime of disappointment Jason had no idea how to handle anything else. Stunned, he just sat there, listening as two months of anguish poured out of Anna.

Those first days were harder than she ever would have imagined, but Jason could imagine it. She'd done this for him? She told him about being forced to quit her job when her boss tried to put the moves on her, how she was desperate to work—not because she needed immediate cash, but because she needed to be permanently independent for her own peace of mind. Independent of Abby. Of the shop. She told him how she'd always wanted to write, that working on John Henry Walker's biography was the only thing that had kept her going at times. She told him about finding Rosa and how much she'd liked the older lady.

And Anna saw him on the news. Saw him enjoying Sunny's attentions, saw how easy they were together. She knew she was losing him and that it was her own fault. And his, too, for not fighting for her, for their love. For letting something so wonderful slip away.

She was out walking one night less than a week after she'd left California, afraid, lonely. She walked for hours and still had to hail a cab to take her where she'd been wanting to go for weeks. The television station. That was the first time she'd seen him with Sunny off the air. Seen how close they were. She'd followed them to the Central Deli and Restaurant.

And though she told herself to forget it, she started almost a daily ritual, taking a cab ride down to the deli between newscasts. And each time she saw him with Sunny, she died another death.

"If only you'd come to me." The words were torn from Jason.

She looked at him, her lips trembling. "I couldn't."

Of course she couldn't. He'd moved on—or so she'd thought.

"I met a man, Clark Summerfield, coming out of the deli one night shortly after I first saw you and Sunny there." *Here it comes, the part I've been waiting for.* And suddenly, with the truth at hand, he knew he never wanted to hear it.

"You want something to drink?" he asked.

Startled, Anna looked at him, shook her head and continued. "I was crying, and Clark saw me, came over, insisted on having his driver take me home in his limousine."

"You cold?" Jason asked, standing. "I can turn up the heat."

"I'm fine, Jason."

"What about her? Maybe she's cold." He still didn't look at the baby. Clark's baby. Twenty-four hours ago he'd been willing to settle for that.

"I spent a lot of time with Clark," she said. "He was nice. Mostly he was a much needed balm to a broken heart."

Okay, okay. He got the picture.

"I tried to convince myself I'd be happy without you," she said, her voice thick with tears.

Jason's own throat was uncomfortably tight. They'd made such a mess of things. Both of them. And ruined something beautiful in the process.

"And then came the day I couldn't avoid putting off doing the home pregnancy test I'd bought," Anna said. Her words were like a knife in Jason's heart. "I was getting sick every morning."

Was this the penance he was to pay for not fighting for her in the first place, this cruel blow-by-blow?

"When it was positive, my first instinct was to run home to Abby."

Why not straight to nice, balm-for-the-heart Summerfield?

"But as much as I was hurting, as terrified as I was, I couldn't run anymore. For myself, but also for her." She smiled down at the baby in her arms. "Then, more than ever, I had to know that I was a whole person. How else was I ever going to face raising a baby by myself?"

By herself? Jason stood frozen, every nerve ending tuned to her, listening intently.

"What about Summerfield?"

She frowned. "He'd left for an extended business trip to Europe." She sounded as if she couldn't have cared less.

So he didn't know yet?

There was hope. Not a lot. But enough to speak up.

"Anna?" He sat down, gently taking her free hand in his, his thumb running along her palm. He brushed the hair back from her face with his other hand, his eyes trained on hers.

"You were right," he said. "I do settle." The admission cost him. Far more than he'd expected. Because once made, he couldn't take it back. Couldn't allow himself to settle ever again.

"Growing up as I did, it was just easier."

She nodded, her eyes brimming with tears. "I know."

"I guess it just became habit. I didn't even realize I was doing it."

Anna nodded, waiting.

"Habits are hard to break."

"I know."

Her eyes shadowed with fear, she waited for him to continue.

"But I can't settle for a life without you."

She smiled, her lashes wet with tears.

"I love you, Anna, so very much."

"I love you, too, Jason." Her whispered words drove him on.

"But there are some things I have to have."

She nodded again, still smiling through her tears.

"I have to know that I'm the only man in your life." He couldn't live with the fear that Summerfield may one day return, discover he had a daughter, insist on a place in her mother's life.

"Absolutely." Her reply came swiftly. "You always have been."

"And always will be." This wasn't negotiable.

"As long as we both shall live."

He needed to kiss her, to hold her close to the

heart he'd just bared for her. But there was a seven-pound baby lying between them. He knew she was there. Just couldn't bring himself to look at her.

"I'll gladly raise your daughter, Anna," he said, still holding her gaze, holding it almost desperately. "But only if I have your word that you'll allow me to be a *real* father to her." He stopped. Looked away, then back. "If I'm to love her, I have to do so as though she was my own."

He wouldn't settle for any less.

Tears pouring down her cheeks, Anna said, "I never slept with Clark, Jason."

He stared at her, sure he'd heard wrong.

"I'm not saying he wasn't interested, but he travels so much he knew he couldn't make a commitment—and I couldn't settle for anything less."

She really hadn't slept with him?

"Besides, he knew I was in love with you. He told me before he left for Europe that if, when he got back, I was still single, he was going to set out to steal me away from you."

"You never slept with him?" Jason couldn't quite grasp the gift she was giving him.

Anna snuggled the baby briefly, then held Audrey out to him.

"Take her," she whispered. "*You're* her biological." And then she grinned.

Jason stared at Anna for another full minute, then down at Audrey. His baby. His daughter. His and Anna's.

"She's *mine?*" he asked.

Anna nodded. "Even ultrasounds can be wrong.

She's small, but she's all yours." Jason's heart full to overflowing, he took the sleeping baby from her mother's arms.

"Hello, Daddy's darling," he said, tears in his eyes as he gathered his daughter to his chest.

Audrey stirred, opened her eyes, then fell back to sleep with a little sigh. In that instant Jason knew he was never going to have to settle again.

His gaze left his sleeping daughter only long enough to run lovingly over her mother.

"Will you marry me, Anna?" he asked.

"I'd be honored to marry you, Jason," she answered softly.

After a lifetime of loneliness Jason had a family.

* * * * *

Anna has found love and happiness;
what about Abby?
In THE HEART OF CHRISTMAS, coming
this December, you can read Abby's story.
Share her search for love and fulfillment
this Christmas.

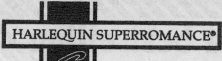

 HARLEQUIN SUPERROMANCE®

proudly presents...

A FATHER'S HEART (#786)
by Karen Young
an award-winning author

Daniel Kendrick has been accused of a horrible crime—a crime so terrible his wife keeps his children from him. Until his daughter runs away to find him in New Orleans.

Tessa Hamilton's testimony helped convict Daniel of that crime. But now, having met him again, she's no longer sure who to believe.

Tessa's daughter, a streetwise teen, knows who to believe—and it isn't Daniel's detractors. If only she could convince her mother, she's sure he'd make a loving husband for Tessa, too.

FAMILY MAN

Available in May 1998,
wherever Harlequin books are sold.

Look us up on-line at: http://www.romance.net

HSFM786

Take 4 bestselling love stories FREE

Plus get a FREE surprise gift!

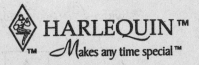

HARLEQUIN SUPERROMANCE®

HOME ON THE RANCH

Welcome back to the Silver Dollar Ranch, near Tombstone, Arizona. Home of the Bodine men—and their wives.

She's the Sheriff (#787)
by Anne Marie Duquette

Virgil Bodine. He's the oldest brother. One-time sheriff of Tombstone and former bodyguard to the stars. He's come home from California with his reluctant ten-year-old son in tow.

Desiree Hartlan. She's a member of the extended Bodine family—his brother Wyatt's sister-in-law. She's also a DA who's talked herself out of a job...and is looking for a new one.

The position of sheriff is open. When Desiree decides to run, Virgil runs against her.

Next thing he knows, he's calling her sheriff. And boss. And...wife?

Available May 1998 at your favorite retail outlet.

Don't miss these Harlequin favorites by some of our bestselling authors!

HT#25721	THE ONLY MAN IN WYOMING by Kristine Rolofson	$3.50 u.s. $3.99 can.	☐ ☐
HP#11869	WICKED CAPRICE by Anne Mather	$3.50 u.s. $3.99 can.	☐ ☐
HR#03438	ACCIDENTAL WIFE by Day Leclaire	$3.25 u.s. $3.75 can.	☐ ☐
HS#70737	STRANGERS WHEN WE MEET by Rebecca Winters	$3.99 u.s. $4.50 can.	☐ ☐
HI#22405	HERO FOR HIRE by Laura Kenner	$3.75 u.s. $4.25 can.	☐ ☐
HAR#16673	ONE HOT COWBOY by Cathy Gillen Thacker	$3.75 u.s. $4.25 can.	☐ ☐
HH#28952	JADE by Ruth Langan	$4.99 u.s. $5.50 can.	☐ ☐
LL#44005	STUCK WITH YOU by Vicki Lewis Thompson	$3.50 u.s. $3.99 can.	☐ ☐

(limited quantities available on certain titles)

AMOUNT	$ _____
POSTAGE & HANDLING	$ _____
($1.00 for one book, 50¢ for each additional)	
APPLICABLE TAXES*	$ _____
TOTAL PAYABLE	$ _____
(check or money order—please do not send cash)	

To order, complete this form and send it, along with a check or money order for the total above, payable to Harlequin Books, to: **In the U.S.:** 3010 Walden Avenue, P.O. Box 9047, Buffalo, NY 14269-9047; **In Canada:** P.O. Box 613, Fort Erie, Ontario, L2A 5X3.

Name: _____

Address: _____ City: _____

State/Prov.: _____ Zip/Postal Code: _____

Account Number (if applicable): _____

*New York residents remit applicable sales taxes.
Canadian residents remit applicable GST and provincial taxes.

Look us up on-line at: http://www.romance.net

COMING NEXT MONTH

#786 A FATHER'S HEART • Karen Young
Family Man

Daniel Kendrick wants the one thing he can never have: his children. Thanks to the testimony of Tessa Hamilton at his custody hearing, he's a marked man. Now his daughter has run away to the uneasy streets of the Big Easy. The only person who can help him find her is...Tessa Hamilton, and Tessa has begun to have second thoughts about Daniel. Could she have been wrong all those years ago?

#787 SHE'S THE SHERIFF • Anne Marie Duquette
Home on the Ranch

Virgil Bodine is the onetime sheriff of Tombstone, Arizona, and a former bodyguard to the stars. Sick of Hollywood life, he's come home, his reluctant ten-year-old son in tow. Desiree Harlan is a former Phoenix D.A.—she talked herself out of one job and is looking for another. Tombstone needs a new sheriff, and Desiree decides to run. So does Virgil. Next thing he knows, he's calling her sheriff. And boss. And... wife?

#788 CUPID'S REVENGE • Ruth Jean Dale
The Camerons of Colorado

Jason Cameron, ex-rodeo champion and all-around ladies' man, is back in Cupid, Colorado. Jason's friends and fellow ranchers consider him too much competition on the romance front; they want him to fall for *one* woman and leave the rest for them. He does. He falls for newcomer Diana Kennedy and he falls hard. There are plenty of sparks flying between them, but Diana's not sure she wants any of them to catch!

#789 THE FAMILY NEXT DOOR • Janice Kay Johnson
Count on a Cop

Judith Kane moves to a small obscure town for one reason— safety. She's afraid of her ex-husband, afraid for her children. So she moves to Mud River, Washington—right next door to a cop. But Chief Ben McKinsey doesn't *want* a family next door. He doesn't want to get involved with an attractive woman like Judith—or her kids. But they seem to need help, and who can you count on if you can't count on a cop?